Somebody did, and—while he managed to solidify his perch by hanging on to the saddle horn like the rankest newbie—Ryan realized that the same someone had also relieved him of the SIG-Sauer, then stuffed it back in his holster.

Then they were riding out through the open gates of the barbed-wire compound, across the starlit prairie.

From behind, he heard the shouted challenge, "Run, little rabbits!" The voice, heard only recently for the first time, was already unmistakable to Ryan. And hated.

"Damn," Mildred swore. "I thought we killed that mother."

"Run far, run fast, little rabbits," Snake Eye called again. "Run and hide! But you'll only die tired!"

**Other titles in the
Deathlands saga:**

Watersleep
Nightmare Passage
Freedom Lost
Way of the Wolf
Dark Emblem
Crucible of Time
Starfall
Encounter:
  Collector's Edition
Gemini Rising
Gaia's Demise
Dark Reckoning
Shadow World
Pandora's Redoubt
Rat King
Zero City
Savage Armada
Judas Strike
Shadow Fortress
Sunchild
Breakthrough
Salvation Road
Amazon Gate
Destiny's Truth
Skydark Spawn
Damnation Road Show
Devil Riders
Bloodfire
Hellbenders
Separation
Death Hunt
Shaking Earth
Black Harvest
Vengeance Trail
Ritual Chill
Atlantis Reprise

Labyrinth
Strontium Swamp
Shatter Zone
Perdition Valley
Cannibal Moon
Sky Raider
Remember Tomorrow
Sunspot
Desert Kings
Apocalypse Unborn
Thunder Road
Plague Lords
  (Empire of Xibalba Book I)
Dark Resurrection
  (Empire of Xibalba Book II)
Eden's Twilight
Desolation Crossing
Alpha Wave
Time Castaways
Prophecy
Blood Harvest
Arcadian's Asylum
Baptism of Rage
Doom Helix
Moonfeast
Downrigger Drift
Playfair's Axiom
Tainted Cascade
Perception Fault
Prodigal's Return
Lost Gates
Haven's Blight
Hell Road Warriors
Palaces of Light
Wretched Earth
Crimson Waters

JAMES AXLER

DEATHLANDS®

No Man's Land

A GOLD EAGLE BOOK FROM

WORLDWIDE®

TORONTO • NEW YORK • LONDON
AMSTERDAM • PARIS • SYDNEY • HAMBURG
STOCKHOLM • ATHENS • TOKYO • MILAN
MADRID • WARSAW • BUDAPEST • AUCKLAND

Recycling programs
for this product may
not exist in your area.

First edition November 2012

ISBN-13: 978-0-373-62617-5

NO MAN'S LAND

Printed in U.S.A.

War may sometimes be a necessary evil. But no matter how necessary, it is always an evil, never a good. We will not learn how to live together in peace by killing each other's children.

—Jimmy Carter
Nobel Lecture,
Dec. 10, 2002

THE DEATHLANDS SAGA

This world is their legacy, a world born in the violent nuclear spasm of 2001 that was the bitter outcome of a struggle for global dominance.

There is no real escape from this shockscape where life always hangs in the balance, vulnerable to newly demonic nature, barbarism, lawlessness.

But they are the warrior survivalists, and they endure—in the way of the lion, the hawk and the tiger, true to nature's heart despite its ruination.

Ryan Cawdor: The privileged son of an East Coast baron. Acquainted with betrayal from a tender age, he is a master of the hard realities.

Krysty Wroth: Harmony ville's own Titian-haired beauty, a woman with the strength of tempered steel. Her premonitions and Gaia powers have been fostered by her Mother Sonja.

J. B. Dix, the Armorer: Weapons master and Ryan's close ally, he, too, honed his skills traversing the Deathlands with the legendary Trader.

Doctor Theophilus Tanner: Torn from his family and a gentler life in 1896, Doc has been thrown into a future he couldn't have imagined.

Dr. Mildred Wyeth: Her father was killed by the Ku Klux Klan, but her fate is not much lighter. Restored from pre-dark cryogenic suspension, she brings twentieth-century healing skills to a nightmare.

Jak Lauren: A true child of the wastelands, reared on adversity, loss and danger, the albino teenager is a fierce fighter and loyal friend.

Dean Cawdor: Ryan's young son by Sharona accepts the only world he knows, and yet he is the seedling bearing the promise of tomorrow.

In a world where all was lost, they are humanity's last hope....

Prologue

With a whistling scream the cannonball arced across the clear blue sky.

Snake Eye could probably have seen it had he looked. The things were often visible in flight, and his human eye was very keen.

So was the other eye, hidden behind a black enameled-leather patch.

He didn't bother, any more than he bothered to duck when the explosive charge went off a street over in the small, deserted ville called Taint. It was well named. Not much to look at, much less visit, even by modern-day standards, Taint was a cluster of a few dozen ramshackle structures of sun-warped, rotting planks, scabbied brick-and-concrete chunks, and even sod, piled together without much thought, much less upkeep, on a stream that ran through a wide, flat valley on its way to the Des Moines River. At the moment, it happened to lie right between the armies of the Uplands Alliance and the Des Moines River Valley Cattlemen's Protective Association, who were coming together in the latest installment of their generations-long war.

Snake Eye was the perfect mercie. He was good at his job, faster than any normal human, and his heart was cold beyond stone. He always fulfilled a contract and took pride in the fact.

As he did in every aspect of his job. A happy mutie was Snake Eye.

If a person despised him because he was a mutie—and never troubled to hide it—that wasn't his problem. He couldn't be bothered to care. If a person tried to give him trouble for being a mutie, that wasn't his problem, either.

He stood in the mouth of a narrow alleyway that stank of piss and rot, where he could have some cover as he glanced up and down the street with his one exposed eye. Because he was confident in his abilities didn't mean he was cocky; it was his heart that was stone, not his narrow, hairless head. He knew that a random piece of shrapnel or a slug could chill him as readily as any dirt-grubber or sheep farmer caught up in events beyond his control and forced to play soldier.

Snake Eye adjusted his slouch hat and moved off with purpose down the narrow rutted street. He had a pretty fair idea where he would find his subject this fine April morning. A ville currently being contested via black powder cannon being fired from outside by two full-on warring baronial armies seemed a pretty unlikely hiding place for a man who was never known for being long on courage.

But the merchant Ragged Earnie was also a noted homebody, and he had more than one reason for sticking tight to the little store where he lived, aside from a desire not to leave his precious goods untended where stragglers might get an urge to loot them—not that he'd confront an armed sec man if one did, of course. Taint prospered, to the extent it did, from lying in essentially neutral ground in the conflict between cattle barons of the river valley and the sheepmen of the higher country above the bluffs to the north. Earnie had prospered, too, if much better than the ville at large, speaking proportionally. Now he might hope to cut a deal with the winner, provided he survived the barrage.

And that was no blue-sky prospect, either: these were the Deathlands, where not even the prospect that the sky would turn a weird venomous yellow and send tornadoes to smash you with debris or suck you up to your doom was as terrifying as when the sky turned orange and tortured and rained down Hell. Naturally his subject had a storm cellar, and shells and solid iron balls raining down from the sky were a pretty fair excuse for taking shelter there, too.

Or just staying out of the way of random bullets and other trouble. A few sec men from both sides had had the poor luck, or worse judgment, to wander into Taint. Now, as Snake Eye left his brief shelter and turned onto the block where his subject had his store, a pair of them were carrying on their own miniature war right in the damn street where Snake Eye needed to go.

Actually, the kid in the hayseed canvas shirt and trousers, with a green Uplander armband tied around an arm, was an obvious conscript who might as well still have sheep feces on the heels of his boots. He was lying prostrate in the street, and the man standing above him getting ready to shove a bayonet into his belly was obviously a veteran. The guy's status as a sergeant was made obvious by the fact that he wore an actual uniform, if of blue-dyed homespun rather than pricier scabbie.

The long, narrow blade made a wet sound going in. Walking calmly down the street toward the little drama, Snake Eye heard the bayonet grate on the hapless kid's spine. The Uplander let loose a gagging, strangling, squealing scream and thrashed wildly.

The Protector leaned on the rifle, driving the bayonet deep. Even without currently being able to see the bearded face, Snake Eye knew he wore a big old grin beneath that blue kepi-style cap. The bluecoat's posture made it clear how much he was getting off on his victim's unbearable agony, as a red stain spread across the kid's shirt.

Smiling, Snake Eye reached up and flicked his eyepatch onto his forehead with a thumb.

The sergeant heard the crunch of boots in the mostly dry mud behind him and looked over his shoulder. Blue eyes went white in a face that showed hard years and harder mileage, even through the wiry black beard and the grime and soot caked onto it.

He looked Snake Eye in his hidden eye and screamed.

Frantically the soldier began to tug on his weapon. He assumed anyone who looked like that, much less a man who would so boldly approach a sadistic murder being carried out under the guise of warfare on an open street in the middle of the day, could mean no good.

And rightly so. But in his sadistic glee he'd plunged his bayonet all the way through the howling boy's skinny body and deep into the mud below. It was hard enough getting a blade out of flesh; that was a big reason Snake Eye preferred a blaster. Now the sergeant's main weapon was well and truly stuck.

Snake Eye was always fast on the draw, but he never rushed. That was part of what made him the deadliest blaster in the Deathlands.

The faster-than-human speed and reflexes didn't hurt, either.

He pulled his right-hand Sphinx autoblaster from below the black duster he always wore, brought the weapon to eye level and shot the sergeant through the face. He smiled, slightly, as he saw the man's eyes go wide and then start from their sockets to either side of a black hole that appeared between them. A divot of skull, like sod with black grass, flew out behind in a spray of blood and brain matter.

The Protector fell right down across the body of his victim, who continued to struggle and screech.

Snake Eye slipped the patch back into place over his right eye.

That kind of moaning scream came from deep down in a man's bones. It hit other humans the same way. It was designed to be heard and responded to, even above other noise—even the sound of a cannonade and the boom of shells.

And as such the horrific scream would draw other humans like flies, that inhuman, keening wail that barely seemed to pause for breath.

As Snake Eye swung by, his long legs never breaking stride, he drew his left-hand blaster and without even glancing around put a .40-caliber Smith & Wesson bullet into the kid's right eye. The mercie didn't need anybody else horning in. He had a job to do, and the dust of a ville that'd been snakebit in the dick even before two armies started to bash the hell out of it to shake off his boot heels.

He was a successful chiller. The best. And as such he had a schedule to keep.

A CANNONBALL HAD created an impromptu skylight in a corner of Ragged Earnie's cramped and crowded little general store. It was either an iron round or another shell that never went off, as was none too uncommon for the state of modern artillery a couple centuries after the skydark. When it existed at all. It had smashed the glass of a display counter to glittering snow on the plank floor, bounced through a shelf of sundries, leaving cloth bales, hammers and broken-open bags of meal from some baron's mill strewed everywhere.

Snake Eye trod on a baby doll from the counter that lay on its back staring toward the sky with blank blue eyes. It was predark itself, high-class scabbie and hence expensive. The plastic body was brittle and readily cracked, but the little voice box still managed to croak "Ma-ma" before he crushed it.

He proceeded through a door behind the wooden counter and into the narrow confines of a storeroom even closer packed with canned goods and unique items than the shelves outside. Snake Eye found what he expected: a wooden hatch in the floor. Squatting well to the side, he grabbed the brass ring and yanked it open.

A flash and a boom erupted from the hole. A charge of buckshot shattered a Mason jar full of prenuke glass eyeballs on a shelf six feet away from where Snake Eye sat on his haunches. Allowing himself the briefest of smiles—he liked being right, even if he almost always was—he jumped right through the hole.

The storm cellar beneath was full of stacked burlap bags, eye-watering gunpowder smoke and one terrified fat man huddled by a cot in one corner pointing a long double-barreled shotgun in Snake Eye's general direction.

"Don't come a step closer," he said in a quavering

voice. "I'll blast you soon as look at you. Sooner, you damned mutie chiller!"

Suddenly Snake Eye had skipped the several paces across the hard-packed dirt floor, grabbed the double barrels and twitched the blaster out of Ragged Earnie's grip.

"So you recognize me, do you?" Snake Eye asked.

"Everybody knows you!" the shopkeeper said. "The coldest-hearted blaster that ever blasted his own mother for pay!"

"I'll take that as an endorsement of my marketing techniques," Snake Eye said, grinning. "Even though I barely got more than a crust of dry bread for wasting the bitch who pupped me. Still, it's the principle of the thing. And speaking of principles, since you know me, you must know I haven't come to pay a purely social call, any more than I have come to make a purchase at this fine, fine emporium."

He drew one of his matte-black Swiss-made blasters and aimed it at Earnie's face.

The old man promptly averted his gaze, closing both eyes tight and throwing up both hands in a ridiculous gesture at self-protection. Snake Eye's human eye, the left one, which missed damned little, noted a darkness that spread across the brown dirt floor around the seat of Earnie's baggy coveralls, glistening slightly in the low light of the hurricane lantern on the floor nearby.

After a moment Earnie pried open his nearer eye. It was a startling blue. It reminded Snake Eye of the eye of the sergeant he had just chilled down the street outside: bright, sharp and as clear as a midwinter morning sky.

He liked to remember such details and cherish them

in his memories as trophies of his chills. Even the ones he didn't get paid for.

"Well," the merchant demanded.

"Well, what?"

"Why aren't you getting on with it? Why ain't you blasted me yet and had done with it? You trying to torture me, you triple-rad-blasted taint?"

Under the circumstances Snake Eye found the slur amusing, the more so for its apparently unconscious resonance.

"Are you in a hurry, old man?" he asked.

"Well, why didn't you shoot me yet?"

Snake Eye shrugged. "Professional courtesy. It's so important in my business. More so, since it's so rare in the world today. I find subjects often like to say a few words before I finish the assignment. Unburden their souls, if you will. It seems only decent of me to allow them their final say. So long as they don't take too long."

The old man dropped his hands and turned his face back toward Snake Eye. His other eye opened. Into both came a calculating look.

Somehow, that didn't surprise Snake Eye.

"What's Big Erl paying?" Earnie asked. "I'll double it."

"You know better," Snake Eye said, "if you know who I am. I always carry out a contract. Integrity is my hallmark. Another rarity in these degraded times."

"I'll pay what I owe!"

"Sorry," Snake Eye said. "It's too late for that. I made a deal. Besides, you must realize you've got more than jack or treasure against your account with Mr. Kendry, now."

Earnie blew out his gristly gray-pink lips in a sigh. His drooping liver-spotted cheeks were fuzzed with patchy gray stubble.

"It was a mistake setting up Big Erl for the Uplander to ambush," he said. "I admit it. But it seemed like the best idea at the time. I owed him money. Times turned hard, with the war back on. I couldn't pay. He was fixing to bring the full entire wrath of his buddy Baron Jed of Hugoville and the Protective Association Army down on my poor chapped old ass. What else could I do?"

"First off, do a better job," Snake Eye said. "Setting up a rich and powerful landowner like Erl Kendry is one thing. Doing it so shoddily enough that he didn't die is another. And getting his son and heir Fank iced in the process?" He shook his head. "That, my friend, qualifies as a mistake."

His finger tightened on the trigger. Earnie flung up his hands again.

"Wait!"

Snake Eye considered the request a moment, then lowered the piece.

"I'm waiting."

He reached into the watch pocket of the lean-cut black jeans he always wore and flipped open the face of an antique fob watch.

"Fifteen seconds, to be precise," he said.

To his credit the merchant didn't piss away any time protesting. "I know something," he said. "There's a great, big fortress hidden nearby—somewhere. The kinda place the whitecoats built back in the old days, back before the Big Nuke and the long winter, so they'd have a place to ride the shitstorm out. It's packed to the rafters with primest scabbie—weps, ammo, commo equipment, meds that would make your eyes pop. Sorry—eye."

"I have two," Snake Eye said equably. "The patch notwithstanding. It's not a sensitive subject."

The allotted time had ticked past on his watch. Ragged Earnie had engaged his interest, though. Still, he ticked a black-taloned thumb against the scratched crystal face to indicate the merchant shouldn't dawdle.

"Some even say it has this magic room, makes you fly from one place to another," Earnie said. "I don't put no stock in that nonsense, of course. But I know it's true. I talked to a man saw it with his own eyes. It's within twenty mile of where we sit now, I can tell you that much."

"So tell me where exactly."

"Nope," Earnie said. "Then I wouldn't be no more use to you, now, would I? What do you got to say to that, Mr. Triple-Smart Mercie? But somebody else who knows the secret—that'd be Big Erl. We were partnered-up about it, but sadly matters took a turn southward between us.

"So now, all that's standing in the way of you and me joining up and getting rich as barons ourselves is Erl his own blubber-ass self! So let's just say we nego-tiate a deal, you and me? You chill Erl and I'll let you in on half!"

"Done," Snake Eye said. And he brought up the blaster and shot Earnie right out from behind his own triumphant grin.

He stood a moment, the handblaster held down by his side, shaking his head at his slumped victim.

"The poor fools," he said, "always say too much and

hear what they want to hear. And now I'll take it all, thank you kindly."

He slid the piece back in its tooled-leather holster.

"See, old man," he said, "it's as I told you. I *always* keep a contract."

Chapter One

"Well," Mildred Wyeth said, staring into the low, pallid blue and yellow flames of their campfire, "this sucks."

They had pitched camp in a low patch of the rolling countryside that, according to the sighting J. B. Dix had taken on his minisextant before the sun went down, had to be part of what in her day they called southeastern Iowa. They liked low ground because it kept them from being silhouetted to prying eyes. Even sometimes allowed them to build a small fire without much concern the light would betray them.

The fuel didn't produce much light nor heat. Nor did the dried cow flop impart a flavor Mildred found pleasing to the brace of prairie dogs Jak Lauren had roasted over the fire while his new best friend Ricky Morales kept watch.

Her companions scarfed them down, of course, as if they were slices of predark chocolate cake slathered with thick icing. Mildred had to admit that she had eaten worse, so she helped herself to the stringy, shit-smoked rat meat.

"Why, my dear Dr. Wyeth," Doc said, "we have found ourselves in much more pressing straits, as surely you recall."

Doc Tanner had an excuse for talking like a professor out of the history books: he *was one*. He was

even older than she was, chronologically, although in
years actually lived through, awake and aware, not so
much, though she looked to be in her late thirties and he
seemed to be crowding seventy. She had been put into
experimental cryogenic sleep when something went
wrong during exploratory abdominal surgery—right
before the U.S. and the Soviet Union had at last gone to
war. Doc had been trolled from his happy family in the
1890s by a cadre of scientists from Mildred's own day,
and cynically dumped into the future when he proved
to be a difficult subject.

"More urgent, yeah," she said. "But it's the irony
that's pissing me off."

"What irony's that, Mildred?" Krysty Wroth asked.
The redhead had her long, strong, shapely legs bent beneath her in what Mildred could clearly see was far too
graceful to go by the name of a squat. Her green eyes
took in the dingy light of the flames and cast them back
as glints of emerald radiance. Her long red hair stirred
about her shoulders in a way that bore no relationship
to the restlessness of the spring night air.

The night was cool to the crisp edge of chilly. The
breeze that stirred the low dim flames like a ladle stir-
ring flavorless gruel would bite deep and hard if it came
any fresher. The night insects hadn't found their voices
yet. Some cows lowed off in the distance.

"This broken world can hardly muster a ville bigger
than a hundred people," she said, "much less a good,
solid war. And here we've gone and landed ourselves
right smack-dab in the middle of the real deal."

"Shit happens," Ryan Cawdor said.

The tall, rangy man stood with his back to the fire,
the breeze flapping his shaggy black hair, and his coat-

tails around his calves. His lone eye, she knew, was gazing off across the rolling countryside. He wasn't comfortable with their setting and circumstances, either. Not that anyplace in the here and now could be called reassuring for a man or woman born into the times, any more than relative newcomers like Mildred and Doc.

She did reflect, bitterly, on how it was just her luck that one of the lamer catchphrases from her own day would survive the intervening century.

"Sometimes it happens to us."

They had jumped into a redoubt that afternoon from Puerto Rico, courtesy of the mysterious mat-trans network. They and only a few others knew of the device's existence. Mildred had long since decided not to cling to those memories. They were nothing she cared to cherish. And there were so many of them...

The redoubt had been thoroughly gutted. Like some, it didn't seem to have successfully weathered the storm that had blown away the world Mildred had known. What had left it with its door jammed open she couldn't guess; the only nuke hot spot she knew of in the vicinity was near what had been Des Moines, miles in the northwest. There didn't seem to have been a lot of other nukes going off in the immediate vicinity. The colossal earthquakes that accompanied the missiles' fall might have done the trick.

Some animals had ventured inside. Small skeletons lay among scattered debris that had long since itself decayed to a sort of compost in the echoing, sterile concrete corridors. Soil and rock slipping from the hillside beneath which the redoubt was buried had covered the entrance long ago. They'd had a hard job working with knives and a folding Swiss-made entrenching tool J.B. carried strapped to his pack before digging their way out into what remained of the day's light.

They'd been rewarded by the sounds of shots and shouts and screams coming their way, fast.

By running flat-out they'd made it to the shelter of a stand of saplings by a small stream that meandered through a valley amid low round hills. Fortunately the spring bloom had leafed out the brush that was clumped around and between the skinny trees enough to offer concealment for the companions.

The two men who were carrying on a running fight on horseback raced over a nearby ridge. From the thick green-gray smoke cloud that traveled along with the skirmish, the companions could tell they were firing black-powder blasters, something prevalent in parts of the Deathlands where stocks of predark ammunition were starting to run dry. About twenty other riders seemed to be trying to kill one another, as well.

The fighters had managed to do little apparent damage to one another before their running fight headed up the far slope of the little valley and away out of sight. Still they left a couple of men lying on the ground behind them. One lay stone-still. The other moved and moaned.

The key thing was, one was dressed all in green, and the other all in blue, as were some of the riders who'd made it past, if not intact, then fit enough to stay in the saddles of their sweat-lathered mounts. The rest, Mildred had seen as they splashed through the stream not forty yards away, all wore cloths of either blue or green tied around their upper arms.

When the last horse's tail vanished over the green

grassy rise, Ryan led his companions from their cover. They sprinted along the stream, at right angles, more or less, to the skirmishers' axis of travel. It was neither the way the combatants had come from, nor where they were going.

None had spared so much as a thought to giving some kind of help to the wounded man. To her shame, even Mildred—a physician born in the twentieth century gave it no more than a flicker of a thought before joining the others in a run. Now was not the time; giving aid might jeopardize her friends.

She'd get used to it all. Someday. She hoped.

THE SUN WAS ALREADY sinking into blood and fire to the west when Ryan selected the campsite. They were as far away from where they'd encountered the cavalry battle as they could take themselves before they had to stop for the night. Whether it was far enough—only time and fate would tell.

Somewhere out in the night a fox barked to his mate. Mildred stiffened; it wasn't a call Jak used with them— they favored bird calls for those undecipherable warnings and signals—but it didn't mean some other party might not. And even if they weren't in a war zone, "outlander" these days was just another word for *danger*.

But the others showed no sign of tension. So Mildred, with a sigh, let go of her own. Sometimes a fox was just a fox, she reassured herself. They'd probably be nursing cubs in their den now, she knew.

"How the hell can they even field a whole army, anyway?" she asked when conversation turned to the battle. "Much less two?"

"This is rich country," Krysty said. "Lush and vibrant."

"But most villes we've visited, even the better-off ones, can barely muster enough sec men for one of those patrols we avoided today," Mildred said. "And something tells me that little set-to was just a sideshow to the main attraction."

"The uniforms," Doc said, "and their arms suggest both are part of far larger organizations."

"Don't get stuck thinking in terms of just one ville, either, Mildred," J.B. said. He took off his wire-rimmed specs and polished them with a clean rag from his shirt pocket. "Could be there's an alliance. Couple alliances, one against the other, by what we saw today."

Ryan nodded. He had hunkered down now to gaze moodily into the dying fire.

"We had allies back in Front Royal," he said. "Not so many as enemies, of course. But yeah, it happens."

"We saw some pretty fair alliances in our travels with the Trader, didn't we, Ryan?" J.B. said, putting his glasses back on. "One or two pretty brisk wars between them, too."

He chuckled. "And being the sorts of natural trouble magnets we all were," he said, "didn't we go and get mixed up in a few of them ourselves?"

"Those were the days," Ryan agreed with a grin.

"So why don't we see alliances springing up among the real hardscrabble villes, places where it's more than a full-time job scraping together the food and water to get by every day?" Mildred asked. "You'd think it'd be more natural for *them* to band together. Pool their resources, you know?"

"Barons like to keep a fist closed tightly on what

they think of as theirs," Krysty said. "The less they have, the harder they want to clutch, it seems like."

"Everyone feels that way, always," Doc said. "The idea that poverty ennobles is a foolish conceit, but a very ancient one, possibly as ancient as civilization itself. Want makes all of us hoard whatever small scraps we may have. Only in times of relative plenty—even if it is still a most mean existence—are we free to think in terms of cooperation and sharing. Barons are people, too, after all."

"For a certain definition of 'people,'" Mildred said.

"It's not as if we haven't seen starving mothers offering their babies for food," Krysty said.

A sort of infinite sadness weighted her words. For all that she seemed actively callous to Mildred's refined twentieth-century feelings sometimes, she in fact had the most *nurturing* nature of anyone Mildred had ever known; only nurses from back in her day came close. It was just that the standard of compassion a person could afford, and still keep their own body and soul together, had changed as harshly as the world.

"So the very lushness of this country may conduce to baronial cooperation," Doc said.

"Got a point there, Doc," J.B. said. "But there's something more. Land this rich offers rich pickings. Like a newly dead buffalo cow draws wolves and coyotes and wild dogs, and rumor of a fresh redoubt being found draws scavengers of the two-legged kind. It'd bring the hungry and the hard."

"I wonder what they're fighting about?" Ricky Morales asked. Jak had replaced him on sentry duty after wolfing his own portion of roast prairie dog.

"What do people ever fight for, boy?" Doc asked.

"Plunder, territory, power. And always, vanity. *Vanitas, vanitas, omnia vanitas.*"

Hunkered down at Mildred's side like a lean brown fox, J.B. chuckled. "Where barons are concerned, I reckon it's usually that last thing," he said. "That and plain cussedness. And, see, once you get barons starting to join up against outlanders, well, what's more natural than they start looking to join up to grab what the other has?"

Ryan slapped palms on his thighs.

"Well," he said, "good to get some idea what we're up against. But going farther without more solid information—such as where the main armies are, and where they're likely to be headed—won't load any magazines for us."

"What do we do now, lover?" Krysty asked.

"Right now," Ryan said, "I'm going to sleep."

From his tone he meant just that. Mildred could sympathize. After their run, and the jump that preceded it, a good night's rest was all she could handle right now herself.

"I mean, after?" Krysty asked.

"We need to get out of here!" Ricky said.

Then his dark eyes got big, as he wondered if he'd screwed up by talking out of turn among the grownups. He was a kid, about sixteen years old, whom they'd picked up during an inadvertent jaunt to his monster-ridden home island of Puerto Rico. Unsurprisingly, he was considerably darker than Jak, and somewhat taller, which wasn't hard for anyone to accomplish, since Jak Lauren was a slight albino with shoulder-length white hair and ruby eyes. Initially thrown together with the band by fate, Ricky had quickly made himself one of them, saving their lives individually and collectively at several turns before they managed to get to a gateway off Monster Island. He still pined for his adored older sister, Yamile, who'd been kidnapped by coldhearts and sold to mainland slavers, and still harbored hopes he'd cross her trail again someday.

He'd fit in quickly and relatively smoothly, or he wouldn't be with the companions now. A natural tinker by nature, weaponsmith by training and cunning trapmaker by inclination, he had almost instantly become doted on by J.B., whom he idolized—almost as much as he obviously did Ryan Cawdor.

Jak had been prickly toward the newcomer at first, the adolescent-male hormones kicking him into reflex rivalry with another male a few years younger. But Ricky had proved his value to the exacting standards of Jak as well, and the natural affinity of a couple of youths roughly the same age amid a gaggle of grownups overcame testosterone poisoning.

But in the small, relatively well-to-do and proper ville where Ricky came from, children were taught to be seen and not heard.

So the thing about this group that made them so strong—made them family, so far as Mildred was concerned, and she knew she was not the only one—was that once you were accepted, your contributions were valued for what they were actually worth, not on any other basis. Each member brought a necessary part to the functioning—surviving—whole. If Ricky, or Jak, or any of them said something foolish, then they could expect the others to slap them down a notch.

But the black-haired youth said only what Mildred suspected all the rest were thinking. She sure was.

"We may be best served scouting tomorrow," Doc said, "in order to locate the main armies."

"Don't we want to go in the opposite direction, Doc?" Mildred asked.

"And how else are we going to know what that is?" he asked blandly.

"Could be tricky getting clear," J.B. said. "If two armies are fighting over this patch of ground, likely means it's in turn right between the places the armies come from. Country where passing strangers are likely to be looked at askance, if you know what I mean."

"I think there's a redoubt around here," Ryan said.

"So close to the other?" Krysty asked.

Ryan shrugged. "Who knows the mind of a white-coat?"

Doc laughed. It was a dry laugh, more than a little cracked. *That* was a wound that sometimes scabbed over, but would never fully heal.

"They serve a multiplicity of functions, these agencies and departments," he said. "Served? Our language does not support the traveling of time well as a concept. One redoubt might be built for one purpose in this place, another not a half day's walk away, performing different abstruse—and need I add sinister?—tasks. Notwithstanding which they might yet be linked by the mat-trans gateways."

"Happened before," J.B. agreed.

Krysty stood up. She encircled Ryan's narrow waist with her arms from behind and nestled her head on his shoulder. Though he was a tall man, she didn't need to stretch up much to do it.

"So why do you think that now, lover?" she asked.

He shook his head. "I don't know. It's just a feeling. Something I heard, saw. Somewhere, sometime. Mebbe."

Detaching himself from Krysty's embrace, he turned and bent to kiss her briefly on the lips.

"Mebbe just wishful thinking," he said. "Tomorrow we'll see what we see. Now I'm getting some shut-eye."

IT SEEMED TO Mildred that she had barely closed her eyes, lying on her side near the banked fire with the warm and comforting solidity of J.B. spooning her from behind, when a sudden commotion shocked her awake.

It was Jak, pounding up on the camp out of the night like a buffalo herd. The youth could move, and usually did, with no more noise than a shadow. The fact he wasn't trying to be quiet was as alarming as anything he could say.

Or so Mildred thought.

"Horses," he said. "Many. Coming upwind. Fast!"

Chapter Two

Ryan had his Steyr Scout Tactical longblaster in his hands when he jumped to his feet, wide awake and ready for action.

It was already too late.

Likely it was just rad-blasted luck, triple-bad, that brought the cavalry patrol right on top of them—up the wind, where Jak's wild-animal keen nose wouldn't catch their scent, nor his ears hear them until he literally felt their hooves' drumming through the ground beneath his feet.

Or perhaps they managed to scout them out first. Jak wasn't the only person in the Deathlands who could move as quietly as a panther. And the locals would know the terrain better than the youth from the bayous of the Gulf Coast possibly could.

Either way, by the time Jak ran in to give his warning they were already had. Ryan saw dark forms looming inhumanly high on three sides of them already. Starlight glinted on eyeballs in human faces and horse heads, and on leveled blaster barrels and long blades.

They still could have bolted northeast, back the way Jak had come. But while a fit man could run a horse into the ground over the long haul—Ryan had done the thing himself, not with notable enjoyment—in the sprint a horse would ride the fastest of them down inside fifty yards. Or bring its rider in range of a cut or thrust with one of their wicked curved sabers.

A man wearing a dark uniform and a slouch hat rode up on a big chestnut with high-stepping white-stockinged feet. The horse's coat glistened in the starlight. The man glowered down at Ryan between bushy brows and a bristling dark beard. He wore a saber on a baldric over one epauletted shoulder.

He leveled a weapon at Ryan's chest. While most of the blasters the one-eyed man could see as the cavalry closed in around his little party were black-powder burners, the one the obvious officer was aiming at him was an unmistakable Mini-14, a combat model in stainless steel with black synthetic stock.

"I'm Captain Stone. Surrender, spies, in the name of the noble Des Moines River Valley Cattlemen's Protective Association and our glorious commander, Baron Jed Kylie of Hugoville!" he declared in a buglelike voice. It was a bit in the high range, but Ryan wasn't inclined to make fun of it.

Ryan stooped to lay the Scout at his feet, then straightened slowly and obediently raised his hands. His companions did likewise. They knew the drill. These pony-troopers had the drop on them and no mistake. They were also clearly wired up with the excitement of their catch, eager to blast—or cut with those giant-ass mutie-stickers they toted. Any show of resistance— anything but instant meek compliance—would get the bunch of them chilled on the spot.

"We surrender," he said. "But we're not spies. We're just travelers, passing through this country. I'm Ryan Cawdor."

"Chill them now, Captain!" a voice said from somewhere behind the front rank. There's always one, Ryan thought glumly.

He just hoped this wouldn't be the time that one got listened to.

The captain shook his head. His hat had some kind of big puffy plume on it, light-colored. Ryan had no idea what it had come from or where it had come from.

"Baron Jed has given strict orders all trespassers should be brought to him immediately for questioning and disposition," he replied. "Sergeant Drake!"

"Sir!"

"See to the securing of the prisoners," he said. "And their belongings."

"All right, you slackers," the sergeant rasped. "Listen up and listen close!"

Ryan wouldn't have needed the captain to say his rank, nor to see the chevrons sewn on the sleeves of his uniform tunic, to know he was a noncom of some sort. When he rode up on his big Roman-nosed black gelding to where Ryan could get a look at him, he could see he was a black guy, probably medium height, double-wide across the shoulders. His face, clean-shaved, looked as if it had been used to hammer railroad iron.

"Ringo, Scalzi, Tayler, Rollin," Drake said. "Shake them down and tie them up. And I better not see anything accidentally fall into one of your sorry drag-tail pockets. Baron's given strict orders all spoils of war go to him for distribution. Do you hear me, maggots?"

"Sergeant!" the four named sec men sang out in a ragged chorus as they dismounted.

They came forward to their tasks. Ryan saw they were dressed in a random assortment of work clothes, but with rags no doubt the same color as Stone's and

Drake's uniforms tied around their biceps. They all had carbines slung across their backs.

"Secure the women with wrists behind their backs," the captain called out in his high, nervous-sounding voice. It seemed to bug his horse. The animal rolled its eyes and sidestepped every time the captain opened his mouth. "They will ride pillion behind two troopers."

"And if I see any sorry sod-buster so much as *try* to feel the merchandise..." the sergeant roared. "I got my eye on *you,* Scalzi, then you best be ready to ride and fight with all the fingers on that hand broke!"

"The men will have hands tied before them," Stone directed. Despite his heftiness and general ferocious appearance Ryan realized he had the voice and manner of some kind of fussy schoolteacher. "They'll run behind the horses."

"We have an old man with us!" Krysty said fearlessly, shaking back her long red hair. It also had the effect, Ryan couldn't help noticing—even now, his single eye missed nuked little—of hiding the nervous motion of the sentient strands. "Surely you can't expect him to run!"

A pair of troopers patted her down gingerly. They seemed to pay a lot more attention to rolling their eyes back around to their sergeant to read the weather report on his face than doing a solid job. So much the better, Ryan thought.

The captain showed her an unpleasant grin. It was made no more appealing by the fact the teeth were discolored and all leaning into each other at crazy angles, like an earthquake or nuke-strike had shaken up a block of concrete buildings in some predark ville, but not quite knocked them down.

"Then he won't pass muster as a conscript in the heroic army of the Association, will he?" Stone said. "Or Baron Jed will be spared the trouble of hanging him as a spy, depending."

"You can't expect us to keep up with running horses on foot," J.B. said calmly, as if he was discussing timing on a wheelgun's cylinder with a fellow armorer. Because while, yeah, in the long term a man could outrun a horse, he'd never make it past the short term alive.

"Quit your bitching," the sergeant said. "It's only three, four miles back to headquarters, and we'll keep to a trot." He smiled grimly. "Unless you fall, that is," he said. "Then we'll drag you at a full gallop until you stop screaming. That should inspire the others to keep up."

IT WAS A BRUTAL JOURNEY, running up and down ridges and splashing through creeks. The buckskin Ryan was tethered to farted incessantly, but at least it wasn't as surly as the roan Jak ran behind. That one kept its ears pinned back what seemed every step of the nightmare run, and tried every time its rider's attention seemed to waver to pause its trot long enough to try to kick the albino youth in the face.

To no particular surprise to Ryan, Doc had little problem keeping up. He had the longest legs of any of them, and despite his feeble appearance he'd hiked all across the Deathlands with the rest of them. After all, he looked decades older than he really was, in terms of his time awake and on his pins; he might be mentally vague on occasion, but he had the endurance of a fairly fit man in his prime.

The person who struggled the most was Ricky. The new kid had traveled around what outlanders called

Monster Island each year with his father's trading caravan. And given how their roads always took them up and down the steep mountains of the Puerto Rican interior, he was strong and not by any means out of shape. But he spent most of his time in his little ville of Nuestra Señora on the island's south coast, working as apprentice in his uncle's armory and mechanic shop. It had been a peaceful, pleasant existence, as well as a mostly sedentary one—until the army of the self-styled leader, El Guapo, trashed the ville, chilled his mother and father before his eyes, gunned down his uncle and kidnapped his sister Yamile. That turned out to be the same day Ryan Cawdor and his companions made landfall at the ville in a stolen pirate yacht, hotly pursued by the pirates they'd stolen it from....

But Ricky Morales had the resilience of youth, and he had a core as tough as boot leather. If he hadn't shown that, along with an acute resourcefulness, courage and loyalty to his friends—more than they showed him, to start with—they would have left him behind to his fate when they jumped out of the redoubt in the monster-swarming mountains.

So he sucked it up and ran.

When they hit the road Ryan's tongue was all but hanging out, and coated with the dust the horse's hooves kicked up. It was a constant struggle to blink the grit out of his eye, although that had the helpful side effect of distracting him, however briefly, from the fire in his calves, the exhaustion he carried on his shoulders like a backpack stuffed with lead and the ache in his shoulders from when he went a little too slow or the buckskin's rider went a little too fast, and his arms got wrenched cruelly halfway from their sockets.

His first reaction when they hit the road was that now the troop would pick up the pace and they were all screwed. But the cavalrymen were well trained and kept good order. They didn't speed up or slow down a flicker, Ryan could tell, and he was tuned in to little details like that pretty tight by now.

The road was actually decent. Mostly it was what remained of a predark road that Ryan reckoned had once upon a time been two lanes wide. Though cracked here and heaved there, the asphalt surface was mostly flat. It had eroded around the edges, bringing it down to a single lane at best much of the way, so that their actual course tended to meander slightly to follow the surviving pavement, where it had washed out it had been filled in with some kind of fine, hard-packed gravel.

After they'd been on the road awhile, Krysty, riding a couple places ahead of him in the single file, shook her hair back again. She used that as an excuse to glance over her shoulder. Her eyes caught Ryan's and she gave him just a flash of a smile.

It warmed him like the sunlight. That was conspicuously absent out there in the wind, where it had gotten noticeably chilly. He wasn't a mind reader, but he still knew Krysty's thoughts as plain as if she'd yelled them through a loudspeaker: hold on, lover. We'll get out of this one free and clear. Just the way we always had before.

He sucked in a deep breath, squared his shoulders and carried on.

Chapter Three

The size of the Protectors' camp took Ryan by surprise. About a hundred tents of various sizes and shapes were laid out with mathematical precision in a square grid of "streets."

In the center was a cleared space with a big tent at one end of it. Actually it was a cluster of bigger-than-average tents, clumped around one with a large room and what seemed like several lesser wings to it. The troop stopped in front of this one and dismounted.

Though it was very early in the morning, Captain Stone sent a rider galloping ahead to bring word to the baron that they were bringing in some captives. Which in turn was evidently an event of some note, since not only did the commander haul his butt out of a warm bedroll, but when the captives were prodded into the biggest tent at bayonet-point he also had a cluster of what had to be his senior officers gathered around him.

Lanterns filled the big canvas-walled room with yellow glow and the tang of kerosene. One man was seated, while the others stood around him, their eyes baggy and bleary from getting roused from their own bunks.

"Kneel before Baron Jed Kylie of Hugoville," a sergeant barked. This was a new one, blond and fresh-faced, who seemed to have charge of a small bodyguard detail. Their uniforms, which in the light Ryan could make out now were blue, looked fancier than the ones on the patrol that captured them, somehow. "Glorious general and commander in chief of the ever-victorious Grand Army of the Cattlemen's Protective Association!"

Good thing they cut short the title some, Ryan thought. Otherwise we'd be here all night before they stopped walking all around the muzzle of the blaster and got to the damned trigger.

He was tired, and whether he was going to sleep on the ground as a prisoner, or lie cooling in the open air staring up at the stars, he and his friends were going to rest soon. He wanted to get right to that, whichever way it came.

The one-eyed man knelt right away. It didn't even jog his pride. They'd done worse to survive.

They *had* survived. And the smile he'd gotten from Krysty had reminded him that they would this time, too.

Jak, of course, had to make trouble about it. The bodyguards looked outraged by his refusal to bend his knee. But the trooper from Stone's patrol who herded him in gave him a quick disinterested jab of his carbine-butt in the kidney, and down Jak went, gasping and glaring, with his hair hanging in his furious face like bleached seaweed.

"So," Baron Jed said, leaning forward in his folding camp chair and squinting. Or Ryan thought he was squinting, anyway. His face was such a mass of seams and wrinkles it was hard enough to see his brown eyes to begin with. "What have we here."

"Trespassers, Baron General," announced the familiar brass notes of Stone's voice. "We caught them in the hills by where Dirty Leg Creek crosses the Corn Mill Road."

"Ah." Baron Jed sat upright again. He was a skinny little specimen, although the way his blue tunic was tailored couldn't hide the fact he had more than a bit of a kettle belly hanging off the front of his wiry frame. His head started wide with a shock of sandy-colored hair and tapered steadily to a long chin that looked like you could use it as the thin end of a wedge to split rails with. His nose was long and thin, the mouth a bloodless slash.

"They got women, Dad," a big blocky redheaded kid who stood behind the baron's right shoulder said. "I like them."

"At ease, Buddy," Jed said, irritation briefly twisting his face even tighter. "We got business to attend to."

The youth looked eighteen, with a broad freckled face and mean brown eyes. He had a saber with a bucket hilt buckled to one hip and some kind of handblaster in a flapped holster on the other. Whether he could use either one was a question Ryan reckoned remained open. He had yellow metal bars on his collar; if the Protectors' army followed the conventions of the long-dead U.S. Army—and from what Ryan had seen so far, they did—that made him a captain.

He let the corners of his mouth twitch in a smile that would almost be perceptible from the other side of it. He had to be stupe, mebbe even a simp, Ryan thought. Otherwise Buddy would be a full colonel, at least.

"So," Jed said, "One-Eye. You're the leader. You talk. Explain your presence on the holy soil of the Protectors' Association."

The lie was so well practiced Ryan could have recited it in his sleep. Most of it wasn't even a lie; that made it all easier, of course.

"We're just travelers, Baron," he said. "We come down the 'Sippi to Nubuque and are headed west looking for work."

"You lie," said the officer who stood to the baron's left. He was a dried-up specimen even smaller than Jed himself. His skin seemed to have shrunk right down onto the skull protruding above his high uniform collar. All the color seemed to have been bleached out of him as well, except for the vivid blue of the scar that ran down the right side of his face, and the blue eyes that stared like inmates from some kind of crazy-hatch windows. He slapped a pair of gloves from one white hand into the other as he spoke in clipped, vicious words.

"Relax, Colonel Toth," Jed said. Ryan knew the man for what he was: a sec boss, and a triple-nasty specimen. "Let's let them have their say."

He frowned at Ryan.

"But west lie hard-core Deathlands," he said. "The worst hot spots and thorium swamps in the whole Midwest. If not the continent. Why would you be going that way? Hey?"

"Reckon there'll be less competition for gigs, anyway," J.B. said.

The blond sergeant—or guard—stepped forward and slapped the Armorer across the face.

"Speak when you're spoken to, outlander," he said.

J.B. gave his head a couple of upward nods to settle his glasses back on his nose. He blinked mildly through the circular lenses at the sergeant as the man stepped back to his place and said nothing.

The sergeant didn't know he was a marked man. If

anything, J. B. Dix had less bluster in him than Ryan did, and he was slowest to anger of any of the party. But if you did anger him, you were in trouble.

"It's true, Baron," Ryan said. "It may seem triple-stupe to you, but we have no choice in the matter. Especially since we had to relocate in something of a hurry."

Which, of course, was true enough.

"So," Toth hissed, "you admit you are fugitives from justice."

Yep, Ryan thought. Sec boss.

Jed waved him off. "They're not fugitives from my justice," he pointed out. "Not yet, anyway. So, you're not spies for that treacherous dog Baron Al, are you?"

"We never even heard of the man until you spoke the name, Baron," Ryan said truthfully.

The baron sat forward and stared at him intently. His map of wrinkles got a marked furrow down the middle of the forehead region, suggesting careful thought or scrutiny.

"You don't know, do you?" he said at last, leaning back in his chair again. "Al Siebert, baron of Siebert, so-called, is the vile, claim-jumping bastard in command of that band of land-stealing ruffians who call themselves the Uplands Alliance. And who are nothing but a bunch of dirty, low-down, mangy sheep herders."

He said that as if it was the worst insult in the whole world. Ryan found that interesting, although he had no clue on Earth what use it could be.

I know a lot of people take stock in the notion that the enemy of my enemy is my rad-blasted friend, he thought. But the enemy my enemy hates that much might be eager for a little help in making himself a worse enemy. He thought he knew some people who might like to sign on for just that job, once they cleared up a certain current misunderstanding.

"They're lying," Toth said, though rather blandly this time. "You should let me torture them, Baron. I'd have the truth out of them in a flash!"

"You just like to torture people, Bismuth," Jed said. "Which is fine. I like a man who enjoys his work. Keeps his mind serious. But would you say, Sergeant Drake, that these men are fit?"

"All ran all the way from where we caught them, General," said the black sergeant from behind Ryan. He sounded...not awed of the baron or his officers, by any means, and that much less fearful, but as if he'd rather be almost anyplace else, right now.

"Even the white-hair?"

"Even him, sir. Ran like a damn deer, for all he looks like he couldn't cross the room without going flat on his wrinkly old face."

Ryan actually heard the sergeant brace even tighter behind him. "Sorry, sir!"

"Why?" the baron asked. "Very well. I need soldiers more than you need torture victims, Colonel. And these five men are obviously fit to fight, and have all their part, minus the eye from the crusty bastard here. Which I reckon he doesn't miss the use of much. He's a stoneheart if ever I saw one."

He stood up. "Gentlemen—and I use the term loosely—I welcome you to the Grand Army of the Cattlemen's Protective Association of blah-blah and so on. No, I can't stand all those nuking titles, either, but they impress the troops and the citizenry. So, off you go to your new duties."

"And our weapons, Baron?" Ryan asked. The latest twist of events hadn't surprised him even a little. If Jed's army had another serious army to fight, it needed fodder for the brass muzzle-loading cannon he'd seen lined neatly along one side of the parade ground.

Ryan could tell he smiled by the way he showed his teeth.

"Like your sorry asses, young man," he said, "they now belong to me. You'll be issued with whatever happens to be available, like any new recruits. Now, off with you! Sergeant Stone?"

"On your feet, ladies," Stone rasped. Krysty and Mildred stood up, promptly if not looking too happy about it. "You others, on your feet, too!"

"Speaking of the womenfolk, Dad—" Captain Buddy began, licking his fat lips.

"They belong to me, too, son," Jed said. And then to his guards, "Put them in the special annex. I'll see to them later."

Chapter Four

Like most of the companions, Krysty was capable of falling asleep given the slightest opportunity. Sleep was a commodity as precious as food or water, to anyone who wanted to stay breathing. Like everybody else, except Mildred, Krysty also slept lightly, and came awake at the slightest change in her surroundings.

She smelled him before she even heard the rustle of the tent flap, and the graceless heavy clump of his boots: Buddy, the baron's redheaded son. He had an unclean scent to him that seemed to come from something more than the fact he didn't bathe often. The fact he had drenched himself with some kind of awful predark perfume that smelled as if a skunk had been drowned in sugar-water only made it nastier.

She cast a quick look at Mildred, who lay near her in the small tent near the baron's. Both women had been stripped with ruthless and probably fear-based impersonality by Baron Jed's bodyguards, before being stuffed willy-nilly into frilly dresses over several layers of underclothing, which apparently their captors found far more suitable to females—even prisoners—than the masculine dress both women wore.

Krysty found it itchy and uncomfortable as well as impractical. Plus she was fairly sure the pink dress clashed with her hair, although the yellow really sort of flattered Mildred.

The unappealing smell of Buddy was followed at once by the apparition of the far less appealing Buddy himself. From up close Krysty could see that the tunic of his blue uniform was carefully tailored to hide more than a substantial start on a paunch.

She knew better than to let that lead her to underestimate the redheaded kid. He still had a chest and broad shoulders that owed precious little to his flab. Plus his square, loose-lipped face, juvenile and freckled though it was, seemed to just radiate malice.

"So," he said, straightening to his full height as he stepped into the small tent where Krysty and Mildred had been thrown after they were tied up. "What do we have here?"

"Prisoners," Mildred said sharply, sitting up. "And your daddy told you to keep your grubby hands off us!"

For a moment Buddy's face fisted and ugly light glinted in his eyes, then he relaxed and laughed. He might not be the brightest candle in the box, but he knew he had the whip hand here, and Krysty could just tell he knew how to use it. Or better, abuse it.

He emitted a halfhearted chuckle. "Well, now, he surely didn't mean me, his son and heir and all."

He made a big show of peering left and right, as if the little tent, even with its crates, could hide anything bigger than a healthy rat.

"Anyways, I don't see my daddy hiding nowheres around here. Do you, girls?"

"You're about to make a terrible mistake, Buddy," Mildred said.

He backhanded her, and she fell back on the ground.

Krysty gave him a flat gaze. "Don't touch me."

He brayed another laugh, much louder this time.

"What, bitch? Are you so stupe you don't know your sweet round ass belongs to me right this very minute? In fact mebbe I'll just give you a good old fuck in it right now and let you know how things stand around here, you red-haired gaudy slut!"

Leaning down, he enfolded the back of her head with a huge, clumsy paw and crushed his mouth to hers. His tongue pushed against her tight-sealed lips like an urgent worm. His breath smelled as if a mouse had crawled in his mouth and died there. Last week.

His other hand groped her crotch, though what he might actually feel down there through all the layers of heavy fabric his father's goons had wrapped her lower reaches in she couldn't even guess.

By way of response Krysty abruptly head-butted him. It squashed his nose. Blood squirted out his nostrils and down over his mouth as he stumbled backward into Mildred. She caught the still-stunned youth around the neck from behind with both legs. She squeezed her powerful thighs together until his face turned red.

Krysty writhed to her feet. The companions' gear was stored at one side of the tent. The clothes she and Mildred had been wearing had been discarded beside them. She turned her back and knelt, while Buddy struggled futilely to escape Mildred's grip.

Her fingers found what they were looking for. Deftly she manipulated the little hideout knife from her clothing to sever the cotton cord that held her wrists crossed behind her back.

She stood up, knife in hand. Buddy lay on his back, trying alternately to pry Mildred's legs loose or hit her with his wildly flailing hands. She had a look of not altogether holy relish on her face as she fended off his efforts.

Krysty cut her friend's hands free, then she stood up and began to slice her long skirt methodically into strips. It would do for tying and gagging the youth, she reckoned.

"You seem like someone who's already got some experience at rape," Krysty said, "along with the taste for it."

"Bitches asked for—" Buddy began, then his eyes bugged out wider as he realized his admission. "No! Wait! I mean—I wouldn't do that! I never—"

She frowned and shook her head.

Buddy wrenched free from Mildred's leg hold and tried to retrieve the bowie knife sticking out the top of his boot.

"Sorry, Buddy," Krysty said as she slashed his neck with her knife. "This is goodbye."

Buddy didn't make a sound as he collapsed to the floor and started to bleed out.

"Baron Jed's service is easy, maggots!" shouted the man in the black hat with the emblem pinned to the front. He had sergeant's chevrons on the sleeves of his blue tunic. "All you got to do is what you're told, when you're told, and you'll be fine!"

Having been stripped of their weapons and thoroughly searched, as well as being relieved of all their belongings, Ryan, J.B., Doc, Jak and Ricky had been marched off to a little bonfire on the outskirts of the camp. Doc still had his ebony swordstick, which meant he had the sword concealed inside. Whether that would give Ryan and company the edge they needed to get clear somehow and get to the thorny problem of rescuing Krysty and Mildred was another thing entirely.

The sergeant, whose name was Bolton, had been told off to see to the formalities of inducting them officially into the Grand Army of the Des Moines River Valley Cattlemen's Protective Association, which, so far, consisted of yelling at them in a remarkably loud voice.

"Tell them the penalties, Sergeant," said one of the two guards keeping the captives under control at the point of a musket. He wore pants as loose as his lower lip, held up by suspenders over an unbleached muslin shirt. The only signs of uniform to his person were the armband on his sleeve, closer to black than blue in the light of the cow-chip fire, and the kepi-style cap from which hair almost as white as Jak's hung to his shoulders.

The other trooper had black skin and a more soldierly manner, which was to say, he looked bored to Ryan's eye, but there was something about him that suggested he wouldn't mind livening up his evening by using the butt of his longblaster on an unruly recruit. Or the other end either.

"Penalties are simple," the sergeant bellowed. As far as Ryan could tell that was his sole level of volume: loud enough to wake the dead in the middle of a cloud-busting prairie thunderstorm. "First infraction—flogging! Second infraction—death by hanging! And none of this pussy neck-breaking shit, either. You swing and choke and kick until you just hang there and don't move anymore. Baron Jed is a real man who wants his punishments to punish! Am I clear?"

His eyes grew wide, then they popped right out of

their sockets to dangle like obscene white grapes by their optic nerves. The middle of Bolton's forehead bulged outward. He dropped like an empty sack.

Already pretty sure he knew what fate had so quietly overtaken the noncom, and not wasting a blink thinking about it, Ryan was already in motion. He sprang from his crouch by the campfire, grabbing the musket behind the bayonet socket and thrusting it high in case it went off.

The kid opened his mouth to shout a warning. Ryan caught the longblaster with his other hand as well and used both, plus a powerful hip rotation, to piston the steel-shod musket butt right back at its former owner. Teeth exploded outward as if a gren had gone off in the soldier's face. He fell down as limp and final-seeming as his sergeant had.

Quickly reversing his grip on the musket, Ryan looked to the burlier black guard. The soldier was trying to raise his own musket, but he was also dealing with the little problem of Jak not only having a hold of his arms, but also having the albino's sharp white teeth latched on to his throat. Jak was hanging on like a weasel clamped to the neck of an eagle.

But even as Ryan looked, strength and sheer self-preservation and fury got the better of tenacity. The soldier managed to shove Jak off. Skin and a fair amount of blood from his neck followed the albino, but Ryan could clearly see there was nowhere near enough to show Jak had bitten through a jugular vein.

Apparently the albino had done the soldier enough hurt that he couldn't yell; he made a weird rasping sound as he prepared to drive his bayonet into the slim body of the kid he'd just knocked to the ground.

Ryan realized the reason the soldier didn't just shoot Jak was that the two soldiers probably weren't being trusted with loaded weapons off the line of battle, which was also why Ryan couldn't shoot down the soldier to save his young friend. He prepared to try throwing the musket like a spear. It was a shitty idea, but all he had.

Then he heard a wet punching-sliding sound. The soldier's eyes bugged out. Dropping his musket, he threw both hands to his throat as, with a fruity sucking sound, the slim blade of Doc's sword was withdrawn from the man's neck. He went down gargling his own blood—flowing freely this time—and kicking the cool sod with his heels.

Mildred stepped out of the night. She carried two backpacks, giving her a silhouette like some kind of giant awful one-off mutie. She was looking very pleased with herself and working the bolt on a funny-looking longblaster with a short, wide barrel.

"You know," she said, "I could get used to this De-Lisle of Ricky's."

"Weren't you used to it enough to shoot that other bastard sec man before he chilled Jak?" Ryan asked.

Looking sheepish, Mildred handed the carbine with its built-in silencer to its rightful owner, Ricky Morales, who was dancing as if he had to take a pee with the effort of holding in his desire to snatch his beloved weapon away from her.

"Sorry, Ryan," she said. "I'm a handgun girl. I sort of forgot about working the bolt in the heat of the moment."

"Don't you mean to say, 'Thank you for shooting the bad man, Mildred?" Krysty asked sweetly. She likewise had two backpacks.

Ryan exhaled between pursed lips. "Yeah," he said. "Reckon I do. Thanks for shooting the bad man, Mildred. Thanks for rescuing our triple-stupe asses, both of you."

"It would appear the pair of you have released yourselves on your own recognizance?" Doc asked.

"I'm the only other one here got the slightest clue what you're talking about, you old coot," Mildred said. "But, yeah. That happened."

Krysty knelt, carefully depositing the pack she held in her right hand in front of Ryan. He saw that it was his own, with his Steyr Scout strapped to the back of it.

"You managed to liberate our weapons and gear, too?"

Krysty grinned. "And managed to drag them along. They thought it was an ace idea to stash them in the same tent where they stashed us. I guess they thought of us as just more sundry valuables, lover."

"Seems like they also thought of us as the gentler sex," Mildred said, gratefully unburdening herself of the weight of J.B.'s pack with Uzi and M-4000 shotgun strapped to it. "Wrong."

"We should probably get out of here as fast as we can," Krysty said.

Ryan searched the dead sergeant for anything useful and came up dry. "Don't want to stay too long," he said. "But seeing as how they stuck us out here away from the rest of the camp, probably to keep us from being a bad influence on the other grunts, we ought have a little breathing space. Especially seeing as Mildred used that whisper-quiet longblaster and—"

"No," Mildred said, looking strained. "You don't understand. Ah, we took care of Buddy before we left."

From the center of camp they heard a marrow-chilling scream. It went on and on, rising higher and higher until Ryan actually saw sweat bead on Krysty's taut pale face in the firelight.

The scream broke off.

"That wasn't pain," J.B. observed, picking up his fedora and dusting it off. "Leastwise, not the physical kind."

"It was the cry of a man who just found his son dead," Krysty said grimly. "Buddy attacked me, but I made sure he wouldn't be raping any more women."

"So which way do we go now, gentle friends?" Doc asked. "I perceive these environs are due to grow uncomfortably warm in the very near future."

"West," Jak said with certainty.

Everybody looked at the albino teen.

"Horse corrals that way," he said. He didn't have to explain the smell had told him. "Figure, better we ride, they don't."

"Two pronouns," Mildred said in wonder, "in the same sentence? Jak, you've gone and used up your whole year's allotment!"

"I do admire the way he thinks, though," J.B. said.

"Yeah," Ryan said, as lights flared up in the middle of camp and commotion began to grow. "So why are we still standing here jawing about it?"

Chapter Five

As silent as a panther, Jak crept through the night.

Since he approached with the wind in his front—to keep the horses from detecting him and showing nervousness—the equine smell was almost overpowering. He didn't need it to track the sentry, whom he'd spotted standing bolt-upright in the open, a shadow-form in starlight.

Then Jak heard a snap, smelled sulfur, saw an orange firefly ember arcing tightly upward. Unbelievably, the sentry was lighting a smoke. Tobacco, by the acrid smell.

Apparently the Protectors had no fear that their enemies would try to raid this particular herd. It wasn't an entirely stupe notion, Jak thought. They had cavalry pickets riding circuits of the camp pretty close in, as well as random-sweep patrols like the one that bagged Jak and his friends earlier that evening.

They were about to learn that they had just made a whole new set of enemies. As far as Jak was concerned, his bunch was a bigger threat than the whole army of sheepmen coming any day of the week.

The breeze had freshened, bending the spring-green grass. It also covered the sound of Jak's passage over it...had he made any.

Puffing on his stinking smoke, the guard swung

around toward Jak just as the youth gathered himself to spring. The glow of his cigarette underlit an expression of utter shock.

The man wasn't shocked enough not to try to swing up his bayonet-tipped musket, which he had leaned against his side as he'd rolled and lit his cigarette.

Rattlesnake-fast, Jak grabbed the rising barrel with his left hand. His right slashed his big bowie knife across the man's throat.

Then he pivoted briskly to the side to avoid the gusher of blood, black in the starlight, from the man's severed throat.

The sentry tried to scream, but all that came out was gagging and gargling as blood filled his throat and fouled his windpipe. Clutching his neck futilely with both hands, he fell into the grass to thrash away the miserable, brief remainder of his life.

"Frank?" a voice called tentatively from behind Jak's new position. "Frank, what's goin' on?"

Jak whirled. His left hand was already grabbing for the grip of his Colt Python handblaster.

A man was emerging from a brushy little draw, pulling the strings that held the fly of his baggy canvas trousers. He had a bayoneted musket tucked under one arm. His eyes widened as he saw Jak standing above the still-flailing, still-spurting form of his partner, Frank.

He began a mad effort to get a grip on his longblaster so he could shoot the pale intruder. At the same time he opened his mouth to cry a warning.

Jak already knew he could blast the man before the man could blast him. But what he could *not* do was prevent the alarm from being given. Whether the man shouted out loud or Jak shot him—and Jak's .357 Magnum revolver was probably as loud as that smoke-pole the guy was juggling, with a sharper report that carried farther in the night air—the whole damned army would be alerted. *Including* the mounted pickets that still lay between Ryan's companions and the open prairie.

Standing off a good distance, Ryan, who was never one to waste ammo on something like mercy for strangers, had finished both off with head shots from the sniper longblaster he carried before he got his new, handier Steyr.

Thanks to Krysty's killing Baron Jed's son and heir, the camp was already pretty much on full-alert. Alerting the vengeful baron and his hundreds of uniformed sec men to exactly where they *were* wouldn't end well.

Even as he turned and grabbed for his own blaster, Jak cocked back his right arm to throw the bowie. He knew his chances of doing enough damage fast enough to the sentry to keep him from raising the alarm were about the same as the chances of riding a motorcycle naked through an acid-rain cloudburst. But even the skinniest-ass chance was better than the stone certainty they were all triple-fucked.

Suddenly the lower half of the sentry's face erupted in a black cloud. He staggered. The musket fell to the turf as he clutched at his face. His head jerking to the side, he dropped straight down in that boneless way that told Jak he was an instant chill.

From the darkness stepped Ricky Morales, jacking the bolt of his funny, short longblaster with the sausage-fat barrel. Jak grinned and nodded his thanks.

When the kid first joined up, more or less by accident, Jak didn't see the point of him. He sure did now. Also, it was kind of nice having somebody pretty much his own age...younger, even. Ryan, Krysty and the others were family, but they were still a great deal older.

Actually, until just about exactly now, Jak hadn't really seen the point of having the Puerto Rican kid back his play, either. He'd basically humored Ricky, on condition the newbie hang back and not spook the game.

Jak made a *peet-peet-peet* sound, like a killdeer flying in the night. An owl hoot answered. The rest of the group was hustling up to secure their four-footed transport pool, which hadn't even been spooked by the commotion, since Ricky's funny blaster made so little noise, and the smell of blood was also carried away from the herd by the stiff breeze.

"How so quiet, blaster?" Jak nodded to the carbine as his friend drew near.

"Bolt action's tight, so no gas gets out of the breech. Also no sound of the weapon cycling like with a semi-auto. And the bullet goes slower than sound, so no little sonic boom. That's why my uncle was always so obsessed with making a DeLisle like this one in his shop."

Jak looked away so as not to embarrass his new friend by noticing the glimmer of moisture in his eyes. His uncle, his parents and the rest of the seaside ville of Nuestra Señora—where he'd grown up—had been chilled by another army of coldhearts, on the same day Jak and his companions had arrived in the little harbor on a stolen yacht, closely pursued by the pissed-off pirates who were its rightful owners. Or anyway its most recent ones. The loss still smarted like a fresh wound— as did the fact his adored older sister Yamile had not only been kidnapped by the coldhearts, but also sold to slavers, who took her to the mainland where Ricky had no hope of finding her trail. He still liked to imagine he'd get wind of her someday.

"Don't just stand there beating your gums," Ryan said gruffly, loping past them. "We need to move with a rad-blasted purpose."

"WHOA," RYAN SAID, tugging the dark mane of the chestnut gelding he rode. The animal bounced its head, eager to follow the rest of its fellows thundering on ahead along the sandy soil of the dry creek. But the Protectors trained their cavalry mounts well; it obeyed.

Looking around, Ryan saw his companions weren't all enjoying the same easy success he had. But they got it sorted out fine, once J.B. ran down Mildred's recalcitrant mare on his stubby little paint pony and got her turned back where she was supposed to be.

Ryan had seen the party mounted, not all of them comfortably, especially since they had neither saddles nor bridles, but had to ride bareback and do their best to steer by tugging on the horses' manes and sheer force of personality.

Their task wasn't made easier by Ryan's insistence that they not only stampede the enemy's mounts, as a reflex precaution, but also actually drive the herd before them, west, and almost at right angles to the direction to the main body of the Uplander Army, which from conversation they had overheard lay camped a dozen miles north.

"Why stop?" Jak called. He was up ahead with Ryan and J.B. chasing the stolen herd, about sixty head, before them.

"Reckon we still got a lead, J.B.?" Ryan asked.

"Yeah," J.B. replied. "Even as riled up as they were,

it would take them time to organize pursuit. Not that they had much trouble finding our tracks once they did, of course. We probably have half an hour. I'd give it fifteen, if I was a cautious man."

Ryan grinned. "Okay. Ricky, you still got that rope you liberated from that redoubt in Rico?"

"Yeah," the kid called back. He was having almost as much trouble as Mildred in controlling his mount. While he had told his new companions he was used to dealing with donkeys, traveling with his father on his annual trading trips around south and central Puerto Rico, Ricky Morales had little experience with horses. And none riding them.

"J.B., grab the rope and start divvying it up for leads. I want everybody to lead a remount when we shake the dust of this gully off the horses' hooves. Jak and I'll cut them for you before we chase the rest of this bunch off north along the arroyo here."

J.B. nodded. "Ground's hard here," he said, "with lots of thick grass. Pursuers'll likely follow the easy trail of the rest of the herd up the soft sandy bottom."

"That's what I'm thinking," Ryan said. "If you can rig some kind of makeshift bridles so we're not clutching mane and hollering to get the beasts to do what we want, do it."

"You looking at riding a long ways, lover?" Krysty asked.

Ryan shook his head. "Reckon the best way to approach a new baron is to bring the man presents. Especially seeing how we got off on the wrong foot with that last one, and all."

"You speak of Baron Al Siebert?" Doc asked. "But

why, Ryan? Why not simply ride west until we lose them?"

Ryan glanced toward Mildred, who had gotten her mare stopped and was tentatively patting the beast's neck in a placatory way. The horse had her facedown in a green clump of bush and was chomping away at it, paying its rider no mind.

"Speaking of *presents,* given the kind of farewell gift Mildred and Krysty left for that sawed-off little bastard Jed," he said, "I kind of reckon he'll be liberal about spending his sec men's time, effort and horses running us down wherever we go. Not even those stupes are going to take forever catching up with their stolen herd. Plus we're a long shot from out of the woods right here. There's always a chance of running smack-dab into some random Protector patrol anyplace inside mebbe a hundred miles of here. And I'll remind everybody we're running more than a bit light on the supplies."

"Thinking big, Ryan?" J.B. asked.

"Yeah."

The Armorer rode his horse up alongside Ricky's. The beasts were used to being in each other's company, though Ryan knew full well horses had their own likes and dislikes.

"I'll get right on those leads," J.B. said.

"Okay," Ryan said. "And get them done in ten!"

"HALT, IN THE NAME of the Uplands Alliance!"

As if rising straight up out of the Earth, a party of eight or ten mounted men appeared before the companions. Ryan reckoned that was just about the way of it, too. He gathered they'd come out of a draw hidden at the foot of the long, slow decline the fugitives had ridden down. There was a stand of brush growing there, a shroud of leaves black in the starlight, that might have masked it.

The new set of riders held remade carbines and short double-barreled scatterguns leveled on Ryan and his friends. Still holding the rope by which he led his chestnut gelding, Ryan raised his hands. His companions did likewise.

"State your names and your business," the man who'd first challenged them said. Like most of his men he wore a wide-brimmed hat with the front pinned up by a badge of some sort, presumably the insignia of the Uplands Alliance. He had on what looked like a uniform shirt, with a double row of buttons at the front, that was probably part of the Uplands Alliance uniform, although he wore baggy pale canvas pants. He toted a pair of revolvers in flap-cover holsters, and a saber hung in its scabbard from his saddle. His gloved hands were empty.

"I'm Ryan Cawdor," Ryan called out. "These are my friends. Our current business is running away from the Protectors. Though we're looking to sign on to do some contract sec work for your baron."

"Baron Al?" the young lieutenant asked.

"He's not our baron," snapped a rider with a lever-action carbine aimed at J.B. "He's commander of the army, yeah. But he's just baron over Siebertville, not the rest of us."

"Yeah, yeah, Starbuck," the lieutenant said, waving a hand. "Whatever."

"We still thought he might appreciate these horses we brought him as a present," Ryan said. "Sort of sweeten the deal."

"Don't trust 'em, Lieutenant Owens," said another rider, a middle-height man in his forties. Ryan didn't need to see the chevrons on the sleeve of his shirt to know he'd answer to "sergeant." "Could be a trap. Remember about Greeks bearing gifts and that."

"Those are just old stories, Koslowski," Owens said. "Doesn't mean they're all true. Anyway this dude isn't speaking Greek, and these horses aren't wood. Fact is, they do look pretty handsome, though this isn't the sort of lighting conditions I'd care to pay for horseflesh in."

The fact was they were some pretty prime rides Ryan and friends had trolled along. As a baron's son, Ryan had grown up knowing not just how to ride, but how to judge horseflesh with the eye of someone who might have to buy riding stock for himself, his family and their sec men. Rolling for years with the Trader had taught him a different appreciation for the beasts—Trader being a man who preferred wags with engines to those drawn by livestock, and better yet armed to the eyeballs, but overall he preferred turning a handsome profit where one could be secured. Which sometimes meant leaving the gas-burners behind for locations only grass-burners could reach.

Jak had helped. His brief stint as a rancher in the Southwest had given him both an eye for horses and better skills at cutting them out of the herd and driving them where he needed to go than Ryan had. Between them they'd secured seven nice-looking animals. Although the fact was none of them were broken-down plugs; from their cursory acquaintance he didn't judge too many Protector heads were in danger of exploding from an overload of brains, but to give the bastards their due credit, they did know how to lay their hands on some mighty fine horses, and care for them properly.

Even on short notice J.B. had parceled out rope leads and even rigged some nooselike bridles that'd fit over a horse's snout and provide steerage pressure without pinching off their ability to breathe. He'd had a good deal of help from young Ricky, which should have surprised Ryan less than it did. The kid was scarcely less handy than the Armorer himself; and while, of course, his actual knowledge wasn't a patch on the ass of what J.B. knew, he had a good grounding and learned like lightning. No wonder J.B. had taken such a strong and early shine to the kid.

As it turned out, they'd only needed makeshift bridles for Mildred and Ricky himself. The rest of the crew felt comfortable as they were, steering the animals with knee pressure and tugs on their manes. Ryan was grateful the Protector pony soldiers didn't roach off their mounts' manes triple-short the way some outfits did.

Despite his qualified approval the fresh-faced young officer frowned. "I think we do need a little bit more by way of bona fides before we completely trust you people," he said. "Baron Jed's a cagey bastard. He might be willing to give up a few ponies—"

"Trojan horses," said Sergeant Koslowski, who was clearly not a man who let go of much of anything readily.

"Take us back under guard if you care to," Ryan said. "Be the smart thing to do, in your boots—"

Before he could say he'd likely do as much himself, something moaned past his ear like the world's biggest bumblebee with a rocket up its butt. A horse shied and bucked away from a solid thump in the ground right ahead of it.

A couple heartbeats later the crack of a black-powder weapon going off rolled down from the south.

"Shit!" Lieutenant Owens exclaimed.

"Troop, spread out!" the sergeant barked. "Dismount. Form firing line."

He didn't yell, but he sure talked emphatically, like a man who knew his business, Ryan thought—briefly, since his own business right now was trying to calculate how to get out of line of their pursuers' fire without their new acquaintances chilling them on general principles.

As the patrol began to fan out in obedience of J.B.'s voice, calm yet as authoritative as the sergeant's knuckles-on-oak rap had been, spoke up.

"Might not wanna do that, boys," he said. "You'll empty a fair number of saddles, sure. Then the rest'll ride you into orange mush."

The pony soldiers were moving to obey their sergeant. The lieutenant gave the Armorer a hard look.

"Why do you say that, outlander?"

More blastershots banged out from the night behind, a couple hundred yards off yet, to Ryan's seasoned ear. The Protectors had to be panic-firing in hopes of preventing their quarry from getting away.

"Because likely as not, Baron Jed has every ass that can keep a saddle riding right on our tails," J.B. said, as cool as if he were discussing whether to have cold beans or reheated for dinner. "Seeing as we sort of left his son and heir to bleed out when we left."

The lieutenant's eyes flew wide, but he recovered quickly. "Ace," he said. "Protectors shooting at you

bona fides enough for me. Troop, get ready to ride fast
back to camp!"

"What about the prisoners?" Koslowski asked.

"Detail men to keep an eye on them. Now move!"

Chapter Six

Big Erl Kendry sat back against the cushions piled on his chair in his tent, luxuriating in the feel of the hot cloth in his face. He was waiting for his servants to give him his morning shave.

He always enjoyed these peaceful times. Never more so than today. Baron Jed was raging like a jolt-walker about his son Buddy's unfortunate demise. He was going to be a mighty handful.

Not that the baron was a patient man at the best of times. Still, Big Erl could understand the frustrations of the born leader of men if anybody could. He experienced the ingratitude of his own tenants on a daily basis.

Except when he was out here in the field protecting them, of course. Then at least he got respite from their ceaseless bitching.

He began to shift his considerable bulk in the chair. He wondered just where his shiftless servant had wandered off to. As precious as this break was, he was mindful that if he dragged his ass into the HQ tent too late, Baron Jed would give it a thorough chewing. His teeth were sharp this day, and he hungered for blood.

Not that Erl feared Jed's shedding of his own blood would be anything but metaphorical. Aside from being a member of the baron's staff, Big Erl was an important man in his own right—a landowner with substantial holdings...and substantial influence.

Still, Jed had a way of making things mighty uncomfortable on a body, whether he got to chill you in the process or not. And the towel on Erl's big face softening his beard for the razor was getting lukewarm.

"Watkuns!" he bellowed. "Watkuns, get your lazy ass in here now! Or I'll have the hide whipped right off it, you hear?"

It worked. Of course, the lower orders were lazy by nature. But they understood two things: threats and volume. Erl heard the canvas tent flap rustle and his servant scurry in to get about his damned business.

"That's more like it," he grumped, as he heard his servant's shuffling step. The man had a bad hip; broke it years back when a horse kicked him. His fault for not getting his lazy ass out of the way, of course. Erl Kendry was no man to let that give him license to slack off.

He heard the familiar scritch of the straight razor being trued up on the leather strop and settled deeper into the cushions with a satisfied sigh. He kept his eyes closed. He had a hard road of a day ahead, and Erl intended to take it easy while he could.

"Not that I'm all that all-fired eager to come into the presence of our esteemed commander," he admitted. "That sawed-off little bastrich is gonna be hopping around like a toad frog on a hot griddle all day."

He spoke frankly to his manservant of many years. He needed somebody he could unburden himself of his many cares and concerns that as a man of power and influence—not as much as he deserved, mind you, nor yet as much as he intended to have—he naturally accrued. He certainly didn't dare to speak frankly to any of his peers on the Protective Association army's general staff. Nor needless to say any of his lessers. They were nothing but a pack of ravening mutie coyotes, eager to tear him down to build themselves up. So he let it all hang loose where his servant was concerned.

The gimpy old fuck knew what'd happen to him if he dared run his face, anyway, Erl thoughts.

"Not that I blame poor Jed," he admitted, as the towel was lifted from his face. Erl kept his eyes closed as Watkuns brushed warm lather on his cheeks and chin.

It was his usual habit. Why did he have to watch? And he was going to trust the man with a razor-sharp blade—being as it was a razor and all—right up against his throat. Of course, Watkuns had a family—a couple daughters, some grand-brats; who had time to keep track? He also knew what would happen to *them,* while he watched, should his hand chance to slip.

"I mean, what's a man supposed to feel in his position? His own son and heir left to bleed out like a strung-up hog by those bitches from that gang of coldhearts the patrol trolled in last night. Be enough to break the heart of a cee-ment statue."

Erl started to shake his head. Then he chuckled—as the keen straight edge began to scrape at the dark-and-light bristles that sprouted overnight on his considerable jowls. Triple-stupe move I almost made there, he thought.

"Before he let us all finally go the hell to bed last night—this morning, more like—he was offering the sun, the moon and the stars to anybody who ran them coldheart fuckers down and dragged them back. Dead or alive. Not gonna happen. They've hightailed it all the way to the Red River by now. Along with thirty head of prize cavalry mounts."

"Interesting," a voice said by his ear.

Erl felt his brows crease in a scowl. It wasn't like Watkuns to comment on things his master said. It wasn't his place.

Then it hit him: the soft, sibilant hiss wasn't anything like his long-time servant's half-simp drawl, either.

Erl's eyes flew open. The face close to his was as narrow and hard as a bowie blade and had a yellow cast to it. There was a shiny black patch over one eye, and a hint of fine scales at the edges of the lean jaw and around the eyes, and colorless, almost invisibly thin lips. It was as unlike Watkuns's saggy old face as night from day.

The big man went rigid with terror. His hands gripped the arms of his comfy chair fit to pop the tendons. For a moment his mind went white in sheer panic. A stranger with a razor to his neck!

Then he relaxed. He recognized the stoneheart he himself had hired a week or two back to transact certain…business for him.

"What the fuck do you think you're playing at, you mutie bastard!" Erl yelled, then thought better of it. He didn't want to startle the man, to call him that, as a body probably oughtn't, taint that he was.

The thin lips smiled. "Ease your mind, Mr. Kendry," he said. "I just wanted to report the successful completion of my mission. And receive my payment due, of course."

He continued to shave Big Erl's cheek with a steadier

hand and smoother motion than his servant managed after almost two decades' practice.

"But—Watkuns—my servant…"

"Don't worry," Snake Eye said.

That was the chiller's name. Erl remembered it now. A notorious man. A man who always fulfilled a contract.

That was why Erl hired him. That old sag-bellied bastard Earnie had a way of slipping out of the tightest places. For various reasons connected to his important position in the community Erl couldn't act against his former partner directly. And none of the men he'd paid to chill Earnie before had come through. Erl reckoned the bastard had bought them off.

"I persuaded your servant to let me take his place this morning," the assassin went on, as easily as if he was discussing a fair day's weather.

Erl scowled deeper. He was going to need to have words with Watkuns over this. More than just words, mebbe.

"Tell me about it," he said, anger and residual fear making his voice husky.

Snake Eye briefly tipped his head in what Erl took for a form of shrug. The chiller had on a black hat and a white shirt with a black velvet vest over it. He and the clothes smelled clean, not of days, if not weeks, of accumulated sweat. That was an unusual thing in itself, and Erl chastised himself for not noticing the man who shaved him smelled differently than his servant before now.

"He was in the shop he ran," Snake Eye said. "Cowering in the basement. Not that I blamed him overmuch. Both your army and your opponents were busy shelling the stuffing out of the place. I found him there. He tried to buy me off. I reminded him of my invariant policy and dealt with him accordingly."

Erl had to restrain himself forcibly from nodding in eager satisfaction. "Ace!" he exclaimed.

"And now," the mercie said, "there's the issue of my compensation. Don't get up—just direct me to where I may find my payment for successful completion of my contract."

"In the lockbox by the foot of my cot," Erl said, rolling his eyes toward the objects in question. "There's a velvet pouch. Royal blue."

"Tasteful," Snake Eye said with a nod.

"It's right on top, now," Erl said. "Don't go grubbing around in there."

"Tut tut, Mr. Kendry. Surely you don't mean to impugn my professionalism."

The yellowish, dry-backed hand paused briefly with the razor edge close to Erl's mostly shaved right cheek. Erl's blood cooled down many degrees in a hurry.

"No," he admitted, "I surely don't."

Inwardly he seethed. I don't care what it costs me, he thought. I'll make this mutie bastard pay for this! I'll have his scaly yellow hide stripped off and have him kept alive to watch it made into a pair of boots!

"I thought not." Snake Eye resumed his expert shaving. "I charge premium prices for my services. And as you know, I am most exact in delivering them. As indeed I have."

"Yeah" was all Erl could manage to say to that.

"There is one thing, Mr. Kendry."

The coldheart finished shaving Erl's right side and moved with silky smoothness to the left. Now that he wasn't mimicking Watkuns's lame-legged gait he made no more noise than the thoughts in his servant's narrow hairless skull.

"Before his demise, Earnie told a most diverting story," Snake Eye said. "A tale of a hidden underground bunker filled with marvelous treasure. Old-days tech, abundant and beyond compare. A trove he and a certain erstwhile partner stumbled across in their younger, more…congenial days."

Erl's mind was still stumbling around the word *erstwhile* when the import of the rest of the mutie's statement hit him. He went dead still. If his blood had gone cold before, it was a wonder it didn't freeze solid enough to break.

"Now, circumstances prevented him—and you—from exploiting your discovery, he said," Snake Eye continued. "Then or later. But he attempted to use its location to buy his life."

"Well," Erl said weakly, "isn't just that cowardly, greasy old weasel all over?"

The blade had moved down to Erl's neck. "He failed, of course. When he wouldn't divulge the actual location, I went ahead and finished the job.

"But he'd said too much. They always do."

"He was weak," Erl said, none too strongly himself. "He was always weak. That's why he tried to get me chilled, in the bushwhacking that cost me my son! My boy. Poor Fank."

He felt his eyes fill with tears. His vision blurred. Not solely out of grief.

The edge of the razor tapped against his Adam's apple. "But you know the whereabouts of the entrance to this wondrous store of scabbie," Snake Eye said. "Don't you, Mr. Kendry?"

Erl's main reaction to that was actually outrage; he felt momentary pride in the fact.

"You—you're trying to put the arm on me!" he sputtered. "After all this fine talk about professionalism! It was all a bushel of bullshit."

"Not at all, Mr. Kendry," the chiller said calmly. "You see, before he died, Earnie also offered me a contract."

Tap-tap against Erl's throat. He felt his eyes go wide. "Against me?"

"Who else? I told him who sent me, after all. It was the courteous thing to do. Not to mention the fact that you specified he would know why he was being chilled, and who was responsible."

"But...but—that's ridiculous!"

"How so? I place my services on the market for anyone to purchase, so long as they have the wherewithal to pay. As Earnie did have."

Erl's thoughts flew like bats caught in a Deathlands twister. He tried to will them into some kind of plan. Some kind of way out.

"I can pay you to cancel the contract!" he blurted. "Pay double! Triple."

Snake Eye reached up and twitched the patch onto his forehead. Erl froze in shock.

The eye that was revealed was fully intact. And fully inhuman. Perfectly circular, staring and lidless, it was a blazing yellow with a black slit pupil.

A rattlesnake's eye.

Snake Eye smiled regretfully and continued to tap

the cold, thin steel edge against Erl's quavering, helpless throat.

The last of Erl's resistance evaporated.

"Listen, I can take you to the place! The hidden treasure! It's not twenty miles from here."

"Is that so?" The blade was withdrawn.

Erl almost melted in relief. His thoughts, contrarily, suddenly came together.

"You'll never find it without me," he said in firmer tones.

He felt a sudden sting across the front of his neck. It wasn't until a red mist of his own blood sprayed out before his horrified eyes that he realized Snake Eye had slashed his throat with a single rattlesnake slash.

"Why?" his lips said. All that came out was air gurgling from a cut windpipe, bubbling through blood.

"I beg to differ, Mr. Kendry," said the chiller, who had stepped neatly aside, out of the way of the pulsing blood. It was already dwindling before Erl's eyes as he gagged and fought for breath. "If two idiots such as you could find the treasure once, I can find it now. And I'm sure I can track down other rumors about it to narrow the location further."

Erl's vision was fading. He saw the hateful face of his killer smile.

"As I said, Mr. Kendry—" the stoneheart's words came as if shouted down a well that was somehow growing deeper as he spoke "—they always say too much.

"And last of all—you should take with you, wherever you're bound, the fact that I always, always keep my contracts."

Chapter Seven

Baron Al Siebert of Siebertville, commander in chief of the Uplands Alliance Army, was a man as big as his blood-foe Baron Jed was small, Ryan saw as the companions were ushered into the command tent under guard. Baron Al was also as unkempt as the rival general was fussily neat. He wore canvas trousers with the fly unbuttoned, held up—if barely—by suspenders stretched over a big gut. They looked as if the Baron had slept in them, and his wiry black beard and the hair around his gleaming sunburned skull were wild.

The troopers with the companions were casual. They kept their carbines slung. Though their longblasters were stashed with their packs in the tent where they'd spent the night after Lieutenant Tillman Owens's patrol had brought the companions inside the lines, they still openly wore such sidearms. And accordingly they hadn't been frisked at all, to say nothing of the half-assed job Jed's sec men had done earlier in the evening. Both the fresh-faced young lieutenant and whatever superiors he reported to had accepted the newcomers as what they purported—truthfully enough—to be: mercies seeking gainful employment with the Uplander Army.

Now the sun stood high over a surprisingly clear sky. A good breakfast, hot and plentiful and with lots of chicory in lieu of the hard-to-come-by coffee, still warmed Ryan's gut. And by the looks of it, the Uplander general had only just recently hauled his mass up off his cot.

Baron Al was bent frowning over a map spread on a low table. Old and faded though it was, Ryan recognized a U.S.G.S. contour map, no doubt of the terrain he and the Protectors were currently facing each other across. He didn't look up as they entered.

Several men were clustered around the map table. In the daylight Ryan had noticed that the Uplanders seemed more casual in their approach to uniforms than their opposite numbers. Most of the troops he'd seen obviously wore whatever they left home in, with a green armband, often nothing more than a random handkerchief or scrap of cloth, tied around one biceps to denote affiliation. At most, some of the officers and the odd noncom wore a green uniform blouse or tunic, although these were of a sufficient variety of patterns that "uniform-like" would probably hit closer to the bull's-eye. The baron himself wore not a scrap of green, evidently trusting his substantial height and distinctive appearance to identify his own allegiance.

Unlike their boss, the obvious junior officers—aides and subcommanders, or so Ryan reckoned—who studied the table with Al did wear uniform uppers, tailored-looking and even reasonably clean. Only the man who hovered at the baron's right elbow wore a complete set: spotless green tunic with a double row of double-shiny brass buttons, crisp green trousers with yellow stripes down the sides, brown boots polished like mirrors.

"You overslept again, General," the fashion plate was saying in a prissy tone of voice. He was good-looking enough, if a person went for that type: fine features, long nose, keen brown eyes, black hair. The only thing that spoiled his handsomeness was the fact that, though clearly Al's junior by a decade or two, the man had a bald spot on his narrow head almost as big as the one the baron sported. "Are you sure that's the example you want to set your men?"

"Who gives a rat's ass what kind of example I set, Cody?" Al rumbled, running a stubby forefinger along a terrain contour. "The men know why we fight. Better for them if I get enough sleep so I can think straight. It's not as if our pickets wouldn't warn us if Jed tried a sneak attack. Not that he'd take the ramrod out of his skinny ass long enough to try any such unorthodox maneuver."

He raised his head, lacking only a set of short horns to look like an old, if admittedly pattern-balding, bison bull. "Dammit, where's my chicory?"

A young man in a gray shirt and baggy pants rushed into the tent bearing a big mug of white-speckled blue steel with steam coming off the top.

"Sorry, General!" the youngster said as he bustled up to Al. "Cookie wanted to make sure you got first mug from a fresh pot of coffee!"

"Chicory, son," Al corrected without heat. "Call a thing what it is."

He offered thanks as he accepted the mug, though. He took a sip and grimaced as the youngster retreated from the tent with evident relief.

"Brr," Al said, shaking his big head, this time like a dog trying to dry his ears. "Tastes like cat piss, and I'm sure it's got no more go-juice to it. But I can't think straight in the morning until I got a gulp or two in this big old belly of mine."

The fussy-looking specimen called Cody pinched his mouth like an asshole and squeezed his fine brows together. It looked like a well-practiced expression to Ryan.

"You really could drink real coffee, General," he said. "You *are* the commander in chief, after all."

Al took another hearty slug with more urgency than enjoyment. Then he wiped his bearded lips with the back of his hand.

"If it's good enough for the men, it's good enough for their commander," he growled. "You nag me as bad as Jessie Rae does, Colonel Turnbull. And about the same rad-blasted things, too—commonly my late rising habits and my refusal to act according to my pree-rog-uh-tives—" he drew the word out to contemptuous length "—of rank. And my slovenly habits of dress, as I'm sure you won't omit to get to shortly."

Turnbull's narrow cheeks flushed pink. "Appearances are important, General!"

"Obviously you think so." He looked for the first time at the newcomers, then turned to Lieutenant Owens. "So what have you brought me today, Tillman Norbert?"

"These are the folks we brought in last night," the young officer said. If he saw anything unusual at so superior an officer—the boss of the whole nuking army—addressing him with such familiarity, he showed no sign of it. Not even the prissy Cody showed visible offense, meaning it was either the custom among the Uplanders, or their general's custom, so ingrained he'd given up getting his skivvies in a wad over it. "The ones who brought in the fine cavalry mounts from the Association herd. They say they want to join up."

Al ran his gaze across them appraisingly. His eyes were a startling blue beneath beetling black brows.

"Ladies," he said at length. "Gentlemen. I trust you'll forgive my manners, which are execrable. That being stated and taken for granted, I will be moved to say that you are a mighty unlikely-looking assortment of blasters-for-hire. And that you have among you a fine-looking pair of fillies, blessed with abundant and indeed overflowing racks."

Had Ryan been the sort to take offense at another man overtly appreciating his mate Krysty—as he was not, no more than he was about a man giving the eye to Mildred—the gleam in Al's eye would still have drawn some of the sting. And the way the baron's words made Cody turn bright purple and sputter in wordless indignation would've excused a wide variety of behaviors.

Anyway, Krysty caught Al's eye and grinned back. "Thank you kindly, Baron," she said.

Ryan glanced aside at J.B., who shrugged. Krysty was her own women and all, but Ryan was tempted to remind her of the risks entailed in liking a baron. Except he found himself more inclined that way than harsh experience would dictate, as well.

"I'm Ryan Cawdor," he said. "These are my friends." He introduced them in turn.

"We may not look like much, General," Doc said when the intros were performed. "But our very unprepossessing appearances can lead foes to underestimate us. As I believe your opposite number discovered to his sorrow last night."

A cloud seemed to cross Al's big rugged features at

that. "Speaking of which," he said, with his beard sunk to his breastbone, "it seems I heard tell this morning that you killed Jed's boy Buddy."

"If we might say a word in our defense, General?" Krysty said.

He looked at her. "If you ladies want to sign on to shoot Protectors," he said, "I'll gladly pay you do to it. But if your men are the sort to hide behind your skirts—metaphorically speaking, of course—"

"What Krysty means, General," Mildred said, "is *our* defense. Hers and mine. We were the ones who killed Buddy Kylie. We were tied-up captives in a storage tent. Buddy came in and tried to rape us. It was a bad misjudgment on his part all the way around. We managed to get free and it ended up that Buddy wouldn't ever get a chance to repeat the kind of acts he was bragging about on another woman."

Al's brows went up, giving a washboard appearance to his tall forehead. "That surely does put an entirely different complexion on the matter," he said. "My apologies, ladies. I had heard rumors to that effect—about that boisterous young man's behavior—but never entirely gave them credence. What he attempted to do to you was unconscionable. Your response was altogether justified, and leaves this dirty old world a slightly cleaner place. So—" he swept them all with that penetrating gaze once more "—it appears I may have indeed underestimated the lot of you. Now, I understand that along with those fine smokeless-powder handblasters you carry, you brought some impressive longer arms with you, as well."

"Which we should allocate to the appropriate individuals, General," the colonel said. By which Ryan just knew he meant the well-born ones. "This ragged lot can enlist as common troops along with the rest. The females can serve as healers, perhaps, if they have the talent. Otherwise we can use cooks and washerwomen."

"That very notion led to our disagreements with Baron Jed," J.B. said softly. He always spoke mildly, seldom if ever raising his voice. From the look Al gave him the general wasn't stupe enough to think that made the little man soft.

"They got advanced blasters," Al said, "and on the evidence they know how to use them. If they got their own ammo to burn, I don't see the sense in handing them charcoal-burners and wasting them on the line with the regular troops."

"I believe you're heading down the same path we are, Baron," Ryan said. "We can serve you best acting as a unit ourselves, which we're accustomed to doing. Small-unit stuff. Hit and run. Carrying out raids and reconnaissance, targeted to do the enemy the most damage."

Al smiled. It was a big wide smile that overtook his whole vast and homely face. Still and all, it wasn't an altogether pleasant expression, as Ryan suspected his own smile wasn't.

"Come over here and look at this confounded map, my friends," Al said, beckoning with a vast paw, "and tell me what you can do for the Uplands Alliance. I got a feeling I'm gonna enjoy this."

"Reckon you will at that, general," J.B. said. "I reckon you will."

THE LITTLE WIRY MAN with the face like a wrung-out gaudy-bar rag and a shock of hair like sandy ash was ranting to a half dozen or so acolytes in spiffy blue uniforms when one of them finally noticed someone new had slipped into the Protector army headquarters tent unannounced.

It was a young dude in a hat with a pheasant-tail feather stuck in the band, of all the ridiculous things. He spun around, fumbling at the holster flap that protected his six-shooter—mostly from himself, apparently—with a hand encased in a buckskin gauntlet.

Snake Eye showed him his nice, even, white teeth. "I wouldn't do that if I were you, son," he said.

The kid's fever-bright green eyes never left Snake Eye's lone orb. Sweat broke out on his forehead. The yellow gauntlet moved away from the heavy leather holster flap. He took a step back into a group of other obviously young aides and tried visibly to become invisible.

"How the name of a buffalo-fucking whore did you get in here?" the baron demanded, leaning forward and clutching the arms of what was a bit too grand to be called a camp chair. More like a throne, Snake Eye thought, amused.

"Skill," he said.

The man who stood at Jed's left elbow snapped, "How dare you come into the baron's presence uninvited, bearing arms?"

He was a sawed-off little stick himself, as pale as a day-old chill and as dry and shrunken-looking as if he were halfway to mummification. The only hint of color to his face was the scar that ran down the length of its right side, which was a blue a couple shades lighter than his spotless uniform blouse. It was obvious what he was; and his eyes were as black as his sec-boss soul.

"If I wanted to chill the baron," Snake Eye said amiably, "he'd be staring up at the tent roof this moment, wouldn't he?"

"What do you want, barging in here like this?" Jed demanded. Curiosity seemed to have overwhelmed outraged fury. For the moment at least.

Time to pour some gas on the embers, Snake Eye thought with frank amusement.

"First off, I no doubt should mention that I just chilled your Colonel Erl Kendry. Not that his loss should be keenly felt."

The obvious sec boss stared at him. His face, which had purpled with fury when the mercie announced himself, went white, as if a mask had fallen away. That meant he had gone from being nuke-red mad to fixing to do something about it.

Keeping his gaze locked on Jed, Snake Eye nonetheless kept his eye at soft focus. If his peripheral vision, which was triple-fine, caught any sign the sec boss was preparing to order his men to kill the intruder Snake Eye would drop him instantly.

He would count on the confusion that would produce among the stupe's blue-coated bully boys to buy him the time he needed to do whatever needed done. As he would count still further upon the proved principle that it is indeed easier to get forgiveness than permission.

The sec boss's mouth, which had no more lip than Snake Eye knew his own to have, compressed. He read the mercie's intent loud and clear.

He turned. "You should order this impertinent piece of filth torn apart between horses, General."

Snake Eye smiled. "Feel free to try, gentlemen."

Jed waved his sec boss off as he would a mosquito whose whine had begun to irritate him.

"That's enough, Colonel Toth." He fixed his eyes on Snake Eye, and his forehead rumpled even further into a frown.

"I admit you got me curious. What the fuck *do* you want, outlander? And what in the name of *glowing night shit* possessed you to barge in here to announce the murder of a member of my general staff?"

"Who happens to be a highly important man in the Association," added Colonel Toth, who was obviously not easy to squelch.

"Happened," Snake Eye corrected. He decided the scar-faced man had to be better at his job than he appeared to be, for his baron and general to put up with him. Or perhaps just that much better than whomever Jed could find to replace him. Thinking on it, he considered the latter the far more likely possibility.

"Allow me to introduce myself," he continued. "I'm Snake Eye."

"That's the name your mother gave you?" Jed asked.

"That's irrelevant. It is the name by which I am known as the premier assassin in the Deathlands. I understand you have chilling work you want done— targeted retribution against those who have done you and your flesh-and-blood wrong."

He smiled.

"Consider my little announcement presentation of my bona fides."

"Ridiculous!" Toth exclaimed. "Intolerable!" Or so Snake Eye guessed that's what the man had said, anyway; the man was sputtering like an engine with water in the fuel line, so he was hard to make out.

Jed made a chopping gesture with the edge of his hand. "Oh, bullshit, Bismuth," he said. "It's not as if that fat nitwit Big Erl is any big loss. He mostly was a device for turning huge amounts of food into flab and gas."

He leaned forward on his throne. His eyes glittered like polished shards of glass from a predark beer bottle.

"This job could use a man with skill and balls," he said. "Since nobody's shown a hint of having enough of either to track down the cowardly coldhearts who killed Buddy and bring them back here to face my righteous wrath."

Snake Eye reckoned he ought give the man his props for having the presence of mind to speechify for the benefit of his hangers-on even in the grip of such apparent passion.

"I'm your man, Baron," Snake Eye said.

"Fair enough," Jed said. "Get the fuckers who killed my boy!"

"Do you know the miscreants' names, Baron?"

Jed settled back in his chair with a look of something like wild glee on his narrow rumpled features.

"Like they were tattooed on the inside of my eyelids," he said. "A man named Ryan Cawdor, his whores and cohorts."

"Ryan Cawdor?" Snake Eye said. "Long drink of water, lean as an old gray wolf, shaggy black hair and a lone eye as blue as mine is yellow? Travels with five friends?"

Jed frowned. "You know him?"

"Let's say I know of him," Snake Eye said. "He enjoys a certain...reputation in the circles I run in, Your Excellency. My professional fraternity, if you catch my drift."

Toth utter a crow-caw laugh. "Well, you're wrong about one thing, mercie," he said. "This coldheart has six worthless bastards trailing the tails of that long coat of his, not five."

Snake Eye raised a brow. "He must've added a new member to his pack," he said. "Interesting. So, he had with him a big strapping redhead with tits to here, a somewhat shorter black woman, a gangly white-hair, a sawed-off runt in a hat and spectacles, and a young albino of slight stature?"

"A what?"

"Albino," Snake Eye repeated. "Someone born without pigment in skin, hair and eyes. People commonly mistake them for mutants."

"Anyway," the baron said, "the fucker had one more coldheart running with him. Just a kid, not much bigger than the...albino. Looked like a Mex."

"Interesting," Snake Eye said. "His son used to run with him, then up and disappeared. Cawdor's particular about those he lets tag along with him. Well, so that's seven targets, rather than six. Sweetens the pot, I should say. Wouldn't you, Baron?"

"I'll pay whatever price you ask," Jed rasped, his face now suggesting an open wound, "if you get them and bring them back. But the one-eyed bastard and his two bitches—they have to be alive."

Snake Eye nodded. "And so they shall be, Baron," he said. "But understand—you don't bring down a man like Cawdor cheaply. To say nothing of his pack. A formidable bunch, all told."

"If he's so nuke hot," Toth said with a sneer, "what makes *you* think you can bring him and his mongrels down, mutie?"

"Because while Cawdor's good," Snake Eye said, "I'm the best. I'm the fastest blaster in the Deathlands, far faster than any man. And I always carry out a contract."

From an inside pocket of his long black duster he drew a black cheroot, flicked a match alive on the talon of his thumb and lit up.

"Now," he said, puffing blue smoke, "if you'll kindly order up one of your lackeys to bring your new partner in righteous retribution a chair and something fit to drink, Baron, let's talk us some turkey, shall we?"

Chapter Eight

A pair of big dust-colored oxen nodded long-horned heads as they strained into the padded yokes that pulled the covered wag. Riding just out in front was a serious-looking trooper in a blue tunic and a black hat, holding a Winchester-style lever-action carbine in a gloved hand. Ricky had no way to tell whether it was loaded with black powder—the preferred propellant for both these Protectors and their Uplander rivals—or smokeless, like the blaster he and his friends carried. It was rare enough to see a longblaster in either camp that wasn't single-shot, and indicated better than the young soldier's fierce and self-important expression that the cargo the five wags carried was worth protecting.

Ricky, lying on his belly on the cool earth, watched the convoy's slow progress through the open sights of his fat-barreled carbine. The nearer pair of outriders came so close he could have made a good shot of hitting one with a thrown rock…no more than twenty yards away.

But the blue-bloused riders never glanced his way.

The day was bright, the sky blue, brushed with a few purple chem clouds. Their new pals in the Uplander Army told them real Deathlands orange skies and acid rainstorms were rare in these parts, this time of year; they tended to hit more in late summer and autumn. It was a cool day despite the bright light of the sun shining down from halfway to zenith.

The wag convoy rolled along a rutted dirt road that ran down the middle of a wide flat-looking expanse set among stretches of rolling country, a few miles west of the Des Moines River. The river was fairly wide here but not deep enough to be navigable by boats carrying much cargo, which was why both sides depended largely on land resupply.

But the "flat-looking" part was a cruel deception. It seemed to offer no more cover to Ricky's eye than his poor mother's dinner table did. But he'd spent his whole sixteen years of life on the island of Puerto Rico, which was mostly mountainous.

The landscape, already showing many signs of greenery despite the fact this morning's breeze bit through Ricky's light scabbied windbreaker with winter's teeth, in fact broken by many hummocks, folds and clumps of vegetation. No matter how unimpressive the area looked, it offered an impressive quantity of what Ryan called "dead ground," spots too low to be covered in the field of vision even of a person on horseback.

Jak, at first his bitter rival and now his increasingly inseparable friend, had installed him in his current hiding spot behind a bush of some sort that was beginning to bud out, its base, as well as him and his carbine, concealed by long windblown tan grass.

Watching over his open sights, waiting, Ricky felt a twinge. It wasn't as if he owed a duty to the bluecoats. They had treated them badly, stolen their stuff and tried to make them soldier slaves in the ranks, fresh meat for the Uplanders' black-powder cannon. And, of course, there was still what their commanding general's son, Buddy, tried to do to Krysty and Mildred.

But he didn't have anything personal against this young soldier, nor the trooper in the grimy-looking long-john shirt with the blue rag tied around the arm and the pair of baggy blue canvas pants, who sat on the board beside the driver of the lead-covered wag cradling a short double-barreled scattergun. Nor the other gun-riders in the five-wag convoy.

He *did* owe a duty to his friends, and to his lost sister, Yamile. He needed to stay alive long enough— somehow, against all odds—to cross her trail and free her from the unknown mainlander to whom El Guapo had sold her.

The trail rider came abreast. Ricky tried hard not to see the details of the gray-stubbled jowly face of the Protector cavalryman as he lined the top post of his front sight up on the right ear, just below the black slouch hat. He had already gulped a deep breath, trying not to make a gasping sound that would give away his position.

Then he let out half the breath, steadied himself and squeezed the trigger.

The steel butt-plate of the replica DeLisle carbine kicked his right shoulder with authority. He worked the bolt quickly as he brought the weapon back down.

The only sound that came to his ears above the sighing breeze, the creak of harness and wag wheels, the groan of bearings and the *plop-plop* of slow hoof beats, was the thump of the bullet striking on target, just behind the trooper's right ear. The man slumped down and out of the saddle, chilled instantly by a 230-grain .45-caliber ball to the brainpan.

Forgive me, Ricky thought. But he believed even more strongly in duty than he did in mercy. As he mentally whispered the prayer to the dead man's spirit, he was already lining up his next victim.

The rear rider of the pair of mounted escorts on the far side of the wag convoy was a much younger man, not so very much older than Ricky and his new *hermano* Jak, perhaps. He had long blond hair, which was a very pronounced yellow in the sunlight although fairly stringy, almost obscuring his right ear and neck. He was also a much longer shot, closer to fifty yards away than forty and moving, if slowly, over not so even ground.

But Ricky was a good shot. His fear was forgotten now and he acted without hesitation. It was what he had always been like, turned into a skill by his uncle's teaching and stern supervision: a craftsman who poured his whole being into anything he did with his hands.

Even taking the lives of other men.

His second shot hit nearer the exact aim-point than the first and shorter one had. Ricky actually saw blood squirt from the young rider's suddenly violated earhole as the bullet bored through his head. The kid didn't even lose his hat until he tumbled off the far side of his shiny, dark brown mount.

But the rear right flank rider, much nearer to Ricky now, happened by triple-bad luck to be looking right over at his opposite number. Whatever words he'd been about to call to the other young trooper turned into a cry of alarm.

"Herb! What the nuke?"

The other far-side outrider, ten or fifteen yards ahead of the late and now lamented Herb, called out, "Attack! Bandits!"

Well trained by his uncle, Ricky was automatically jacking the bolt action again. The riders still had no way of knowing where he was hidden, and he could thin their ranks by at least one more before they could find him and close in for the kill.

And that was the exact moment when a fire ant bit him smack on the head of his dick.

THE LEAD ESCORT had just ridden past J.B.'s hideout when the Armorer saw the trail guy fall out of his saddle. He allowed himself to feel satisfaction in what the youth he had taken under his wing was accomplishing for his friends. Kid comes through for us again, he thought.

His face and body remained immobile as he kneeled behind a low, humped mound that was almost certainly some predark car, stranded by an EMP trashing its electrical or just running out of fuel. Most likely it had been drifted over by blown dirt, then overgrown with grass and weeds.

His location was a calculated risk. The buried long-derelict automobile was a fairly obvious hideout spot, a bushwhacker, of course. But even if it was just dirt under there, it would give cover as well as concealment—maybe better than the old wag body, if it was of cheap late-1990s construction, as was most likely. But J.B., like Ryan, had reckoned that for all their firepower and display neither escorts nor wag-drivers would actually expect trouble, back here well behind their own lines.

The Des Moines River flowed past the Association's capital of Hugoville as well as, further upstream, the leading Uplander settlement of Siebertville. Though wide, it also ran shallow, too shallow to allow passage by much more than canoes and flatboats, which could not be heavily weighted-down. So most of the resupply for both armies happened overland.

The small size of the wag convoy and the relatively large size of its escort indicated relatively high-value cargo, which was why after a couple of days scouting, the companions had targeted this convoy.

A handful of heartbeats later, the rear-left member of the pair of flankers went down. Most of the ambush group was sited on that flank—in order to minimize the risk of crossfiring one another.

Obscured by one of the wags, a right-side flanker shouted a warning. For some unknown reason, Ricky jumped to his feet and started yelling.

The lead escort was turning his horse when J.B. loosed his first buckshot blast from his M-4000 scattergun. The shot missed, but the guy stiffened as a handblaster cracked off a round.

It was Mildred. The Armorer knew the way the thud of a .38 round differed from the big boom of Doc's LeMat replica and its .44 cartridges.

The fight was on. The shotgun guard on the lead wag raised his double-barrel, looking around for targets. Then he jerked back against the backboard as two shatteringly loud reports exploded.

Jak, J.B. thought, swinging his scattergun to track the front-left flanker, who was spurring back toward where Ricky was hollering and dancing like a mad thing. That chromed Python made an almighty racket lighting off those .357 Magnum rounds. The weapon had a nastier report and worse side-blast than any handblasters the Armorer knew, and he knew most.

The driver of the lead covered wag had two clear

choices. Well, three—freezing in panic when the shit-hammer fell unexpectedly was always an option, and a not uncommon one, even though it was almost always the worst. But the wag driver picked the one that wasn't jumping off the buckboard he shared with the dying trooper and bounding off over the weeds like a jackrabbit. He started fumbling over the back of the box in the canvas-covered wag box behind, obviously seeking some weapon of his own.

J.B. felt mild surprise. Their new employers had told them that, unlike most of the Uplander transport, Protector wags and teams weren't owned by the same folks who drove them. Instead of contractors, they were just more people from the landowners' estates; their rides and draft animals belonged to their barons and bosses. So they didn't feel as driven to defend their wags as if their livelihoods depended on them.

But perhaps the thought of the flogging his master would give him for giving up the goods without a fight inspired the man. Perhaps the driver, a burly middle-aged guy with a paunch and a salt-and-pepper bush of beard, was the hero type. Or maybe it was just the first member of the fight-flight-freeze trinity of hardwired reactions to sudden danger kicking in.

Whatever it was, it brought Jak onto the buckboard with him in a wild panther leap, white hair flying like a cavalry pennon and a bowie-bladed combat knife in his alabaster grip. The albino teen scrambled right over the guard, who was wheezing his last breaths as much through the holes in his chest as his bearded mouth, to grapple the driver.

J.B. took all this in as he lined up and loosed another blast at the lead outrider. But at just that instant the man ducked his horse between the lead and second wags. J.B.'s shot blew holes in the front of the wag's canopy, right over the head of that vehicle's guard, who ducked so hard he almost dropped his long-barreled single-shot scattergun.

Before he could recover, Doc's LeMat boomed out and he jerked. J.B. swung his blaster, looking for more targets to take down.

So far it was a picture-perfect ambush.

Except for poor Ricky's unexplained dancing act.

Ah, well. The kid had potential, to J.B.'s way of thinking.

Too bad he was clearly about to die.

Chapter Nine

The pain was like nothing Ricky had ever experienced. It was like nothing he ever imagined. He had always been afraid of being burned alive, and tried to imagine how awful that would feel.

Now he couldn't imagine it could be worse than this.

The sensation was on the whole probably not that different than being on fire, but he felt the special strange throb of a poison sting. Plus the awful knowledge that he had foreign toxins running through his blood.

For a moment all he could do was jump around and yell. There was just no controlling the reaction. That it happened to one of the most sensitive spots on his entire body—one very special and dear to him, as an adolescent boy—didn't help.

The flash of a longblaster going off right at him, the bang of the shot and the crack of the ball going past his ear faster than sound snapped his self-control back in place in a hell of a hurry.

Two riders were bearing down on him, one winging out to his left, one to his right. Rather than doing the smart thing—dismounting and taking a shot from a steady platform—they had chosen to blaze away at the gallop.

The man to Ricky's right had fired a carbine that looked like some kind of Civil War replica—his uncle had taught him history along with weaponsmithing; the two just went hand in hand, he explained. The rider approaching from the left fired a lever-action longblaster, one-handed. The shot went so high the blast noise didn't hit Ricky nearly as bad as the first shot's had.

Unable to manage recocking their weapons single-handed, both riders stuck them back in saddle scabbards by their legs. The man on Ricky's left drew some kind of steel-head hatchet or tomahawk. The one to the right produced a full-cavalry saber. Whooping like sailors on a three-day bender, they spurred right at the boy.

His wits back, and his blaster as well, Ricky had a cold choice to make. He could shoot one. The other—well, if he missed his cut, his scary-huge horse would simply smash the life out of him with those pounding iron-shod hooves.

The man with the swinging sword scared Ricky more. He got a flash sight picture on the rider's center of mass, between the rows of shiny brass buttons, and squeezed the trigger.

As he did, the man's black horse took a little bit of a bound to clear some irregularity in the rapidly diminishing stretch of ground between it and Ricky. The bullet smacked into the man's lower left side. He reeled. The saber fell from his hand, and the horse veered aside.

His partner loomed over Ricky, blotting the sun with a monstrous shadow. The tomahawk swung high. Seeing the flash of grinning teeth in the shadowed face, Ricky threw his blaster upward in what he knew was a futile attempt to ward off the deathblow.

The man stiffened. A black plume burst from his shadowed chest, turning red when it hit the sunlight. It splashed hot across Ricky's face.

This horse shied away too as the distinctive sound of Ryan's Tactical longblaster reached the ears of the boy whose life he'd just saved.

KRYSTY HELD her Smith & Wesson 640 on the trio of drivers her friends had captured alive. One had gotten away. Another had pulled out a single-shot flintlock handblaster and tried to shoot Doc. A bullet from Ryan's rifle had ended that plan.

At least one of the outriders had escaped wounded but alive. Possibly he'd stay that way, if Ricky's shot hadn't pierced his stomach wall—or if his higher-ups had antibiotics they were willing to share with a common trooper, and one who, moreover, had failed to safeguard their precious wag train.

Krysty hadn't taken part in the ambush. She'd been tending and guarding their horses, as well as the mules they'd led to carry away any particularly valuable, and portable, scabbie from the convoy. She was the logical choice. Though she was a good shot, her snub-barreled handblaster was the least useful of all in a full-on firefight.

Of course, she was used to pitching in and fighting side by side with the others, bravely, skillfully and to excellent effect. She would have been more outraged than anyone at the very idea that Ryan was trying to shield her from danger.

Not that he would dare dream up any such a stupe notion. Their was little on the ravaged Earth, burrowing beneath its soil, or flying in the sky above it, that Ryan Cawdor feared. But he would like to avoid the righteous wrath of his flame-haired life mate.

Anyway, it hadn't been such a big risk—this time.

It had gone incredibly smoothly for such things. She knew well they'd gotten lucky in that, and their targets were arrogant and thus sloppy. They wouldn't get such an easy crack at their foes again.

The only thing resembling a real wound any of them had gotten had been incurred by their newest member, Ricky Morales. And as painful as that was, she suspected the most lasting blow he'd taken was to his pride.

He stood to one side now, his trousers pooled around his shins. Mildred squatted before him, scowling professionally at him. His face, which he kept carefully averted from the rest of the party, was as bright red as she guessed his wounded penis had to be.

"No permanent damage," Mildred said. "You aren't allergic to fire-ant bites. Or you'd be dead by now. Other than washing your penis, and giving you some aspirin for the pain and inflammation, there's not a lot to be done for you."

"Wondered why the boy jumped up and started yowling like a panther with its tail stepped on like that," Ryan said. "Got to say I kind of understand it now."

"Too bad the villain young Ricky shot managed to get away," Doc said. He had stuffed his LeMat back in the shoulder rig he wore under his coat, and was now brandishing the slim sword he'd drawn from his ebony swordstick, for no particular reason Krysty could discern. Since he wasn't brandishing it at them—Theophilus Tanner was a peaceful soul by nature; that was part of his problem—even the captives ignored him.

"Don't hurt us," the wounded driver was saying, over and over. He was cradling his arms against his chest. That was mostly where he'd been cut by Jak's big knife

in their brief scuffle before he'd given up trying to grab
a weapon and surrendered.

Krysty was rather surprised Jak had let him live.
While few of the group had any compunction about
finishing off anybody who might later come back and
threaten them again, even Krysty, or Mildred with her
antique predark qualms, the wag drivers were unlikely
to pose the least danger to her and her friends. In the
unlikely event they ever crossed paths again.

"I know something," he said. "I got a secret. Don't
chill us, and I'll tell you."

Since no one was actually threatening them—Krysty
was more holding the handblasters and looking pur-
posefully at them than covering them, herself—she
wondered if he might be going a little shocky from pain
and blood loss. Mildred had promised to patch him up
after she'd tended to Ricky.

The other drivers looked at him in disgust. "That
crazy yarn again, Norvell," said the older one, a stumpy
brown-haired guy of about thirty. "Give it up."

"It's true, I tell ya," Norvell said. "There's a place
buried not far from here. Some kinda secret. All filled
with cement metal walls and old-days stuff!"

"Where might that be, friend?" asked Doc, looking
at him with sudden interest.

He wasn't the only one whose ears had perked up.
Ryan had mentioned thinking there was a redoubt in
the vicinity. If it had a working mat-trans, it might en-
able them to leave the Des Moines River Valley and its
bizarre war far behind.

"Nowhere," said the other driver. This one was a
young woman with greasy black hair sticking out from
under a black hat. "Just in his addled head."

"I tell you it's true!" he insisted. "My Aunt Goosy saw it when she was just a kid. She found it poking around, back when the Uplanders still paid tribute to the Association. She even brought out a souvenir, a wondrous thing, she said, gleaming black plastic with colored lights that still came on and everything!"

"And where might that have gotten to, Norvell?" Krysty asked in her most soothing voice.

Norvell shook his head sadly. "Away. She was on her way back to the farm when some coldheart took a potshot at her. Hit her in the head. Din't kill her, but knocked her stone out for a night and a day. When she come to, her fabulous thingamajig was gone. Her clothes, too—the story gets pretty fuzzy, at that point."

"So I take it your Aunt Goosy never recollected exactly where she found this underground treasure house," Ryan said.

He stood on the buckboard of the third in line while Jak rummaged around inside. The oxen had been unharnessed and driven off with swats to their broad rumps. They had gone about thirty yards and begun to crop the grass in a small, contented herd.

Norvell shook his head. "Her wits was always somewhat scrambled after the event," he admitted. "But it was somewheres north, that I know. Out right around where the Uplander Army is right now, I reckon. Say, could somebody give me hand, patch me up here? Or mebbe at least let me make a bandage to cut down the bleeding? Getting a little light in the head here."

"You was always light in the head, Norvell," one of his comrades said. "Your crazy Aunt Goosy, too."

"Pull your pants up, young man," Mildred said to Ricky, as she stood. "You're as patched as modern medicine can make you. And by modern I naturally mean over a century after the end of actual civilization."

She turned to Norvell. "Okay, buddy, your turn. And stop whining. I've been cut like that, and I've been bitten by fire ants, too. Given where this poor kid got his, it hurts way worse. And I am not in the mood."

"Yes, ma'am."

Obeying Mildred's command, Ricky turned and buttoned his fly. His smooth, young olive-skinned face creased into worried lines as he looked at the captive drivers.

"We gonna chill them?" he asked.

Norvell, already wilting under Mildred's professional scrutiny, emitted a whimper. The others just looked bored. Or resigned. They were used to having their fates decided by others, Krysty knew. Armed others, who thereby held the power of life and death over the common folk.

"Dark night!" J.B. said. "Why in the name of glowing night shit would we go and do a thing like that, boy?"

Ricky looked even more miserable. He idolized J.B.

"They, uh, they can identify us!"

Ryan laughed. "What's wrong with that, kid? I want that treacherous bastard Jed to know who stung his dick the way that ant did you."

Ricky turned beet-red. Nonetheless Krysty saw his worry smooth into relief.

"I'm not usually willing to cross the road for vengeance," Ryan said, "for less than bloodshed. Bad business and it doesn't load me any blasters. But after what Jed did to us, I'm pleased to take such vengeance as opportunity offers."

"Anything of interest in that wag, Jak?" J.B. called out. He had replaced his shotgun with his Uzi machine pistol and was standing on top of the odd humped hummock he'd hidden behind prior to the ambush. The highest spot in the immediate vicinity, it gave the best lookout against approaching strangers. Such as a Protector cavalry patrol.

Jak came out holding his arms up to the sides. One fist held a yellow dress. The other held something black and lacy.

"More lady things," he called out. "Don't understand. Why bother?" His expression was about the same as if he were toting week-dead prairie-dog carcasses.

Ryan shook his head. "We did get some good stuff," he said. "Some meds. Some black powder and caps, which will make a nice boom when we burn what we can't carry off. But mostly it seems like booze and this stuff. Why would they bother shipping all that to an army camp."

Krysty and Mildred exchanged looks. Then they both burst out laughing.

"They have women at the Protector camp," Doc said. "As well as at that of our new employers."

"So?"

"Don't know why they wouldn't send that stuff by boat, anyhow," J.B. added.

"Boat's slow," Norvell said. "Upstream and all. Got to pole, or get pulled by ox teams, same as the wag."

"Everybody likes booze," Ryan said. "But the dresses and dreck?"

"Clearly," Krysty said, "you men have a lot to learn about women yet."

Chapter Ten

The strains of sweet music filtered out through the open windows of the big house where Al had shifted his headquarters as Doc and friends approached. Doc's heart filled with bittersweet emotion. Ah, he thought. Yes. *Eine kleine Nachtmusik*. A favorite.

Emily's favorite.

It was in almost a dreamlike state that he followed their cavalry-officer escort, Ryan, and his friends inside the baron's big house. After the outdoor morning, cloudy though it was, the house was dim. Doc blinked several times before his eyes adjusted fully.

Baron Al sat in the parlor with his bearded face propped on a fist and a scowl beetling his brows. Flanking him stood a man Doc recognized as Colonel Turnbull and a strikingly beautiful blonde woman in a low-cut green silk gown. Various lesser officers stood by chatting. By the wall to Doc's left, the string ensemble played. Incredibly, the instruments were in good condition. More incredible was the fact that people could read music.

The young officer who had escorted them approached the Uplander commander to announce his mercie raiding party had returned. Though the beautiful blonde looked a combination of bored and pained, the baron sat up and visibly brightened.

It came to Doc that, in his admittedly most limited experience of their new employer, he had never seen the baron simply sitting. He had always been doing something.

He called for Ryan and his friends to step up. At Al's request Ryan gave a concise account of their doings and the outcome, in that admirably professional way of his, with amplifications provided by the Armorer or the others as needed. For his part Doc was called on to contribute little, and he found his eye straying often to the blonde who stood at Al's elbow looking progressively more mutinous.

It was only natural. In terms of years actually lived through, experienced, Theophilus Tanner was a man in his mid to late thirties—even he had lost track by now. And chronologically he should have been dust long before skydark ever occurred, now a century and more past. His experiences after being time-trawled from his home and the bosom of his family had prematurely aged him in many ways, but hadn't taken a toll on his fine intellect, honed as it had been at Harvard and Oxford.

But he still had a fairly young man's eye for feminine pulchritude. Or maybe that was something that never really went away.

Certainly the woman, whom he took for Baron Al's current wife, Jessie Rae, was highly magnetic to the masculine eye. Her sunshine-yellow hair was piled on her head in intricate and expensive curls. Her face was perfection suited to a statue, with a slightly snubbed nose and blue eyes, even if the alabaster smoothness of her brow was somewhat spoiled by a little frown, and her red lips pressed into a pout.

But somehow, as admirable as her outline and the

details within were, she seemed to keep blurring into features less showily gorgeous and yet infinitely more beautiful and dear, beneath a prim bun of brown hair. But, ah, when Emily let down her long, lustrous hair, behind properly closed doors, that primness was set aside so thoroughly as to take a man's breath away....

"So you let the drivers go?" the woman said in a petulant tone. "Just like that?"

"What would you've had them do, Jessie Rae?" the baron asked, confirming Doc's none-too-difficult guess as to her identity.

"Why, tortured them for information," she said. "Or killed them. They're the enemy, aren't they?"

"They're just drivers," Ryan said. A man who knew him as well as Doc did could hear an edge of distaste to his voice. The lean and wolflike one-eyed man had been the recipient of sufficient feminine attention in his time to have gained a certain immunity to it. And he was well armored in the scarcely less extravagant but far less...brittle beauty of Krysty Wroth. "They don't know much. Their bosses just tell them where to go and tell them to git. And it wasn't as if they weren't eager enough to talk as it was."

"Then why didn't you chill them?" she asked challengingly.

"Jessie Rae," the baron said, and Doc thought to hear something he'd never have expected from this man: the slightest hint of hesitant quaver in his bluff, gruff voice. "It's not like they're soldiers. Or even volunteers, for that matter. They're just workers. Ain't like they got much choice in what they do."

Her pretty features pinched in an unpretty moue of distaste and even hatred. "Then shouldn't they be destroyed to damage their baron, the way your men would burn their crops?"

"Lady," Cody Turnbull said, "calm yourself. We all know your enmity toward our common foe is unmatched. But the general's right. We maintain certain civilized standards of behavior, even if our enemies don't. And for all their roughhewn appearance, clearly our new employees are men and women of principle."

Doc thought he heard Jak half suppress a snigger at that. He was certain Ryan himself would scoff at the notion. But as for himself, Doc was more than half inclined to agree. Harsh principles, perhaps; and certainly principles shaped to fit the unyielding dictates of survival in an uncompromisingly brutal world. But indeed they all had principles, strong ones. None stronger than Ryan himself.

Jessie Rae tossed her head. The spit-curls dangling before each dainty ear flew in fine contempt.

"Men." She turned and marched out, accompanied by a pair of serving women who had been standing so unobtrusively behind her that Doc hadn't noticed them.

"Enough." Al's growl interrupted the music. Apparently the quartet understood it was directed at them.

"Go on," he said. "Git. I've heard enough, thank you kindly."

"Baron," the colonel said, "think what your wife will say? You know she wants you to have more culture."

"Well, she ain't here anymore, now is she, Cody? What she don't know won't do her a lick of harm."

As the musicians hastily broke off and began to gather up their instruments, Al turned to Doc.

"Sorry to interrupt your listening, Doc," he said.

"Fact is, my ears were all full of fine music. But you seem to have an appreciation for it, sir."

"Indeed, Baron," Doc said. "I've always considered the Serenade No. 13 for Strings in G major to be Mozart at his finest."

The baron's big flushed face—sweating, as usual, though it wasn't all that warm even inside—rumpled in a grimace.

"If you say so."

Al graced his visitors with a smile. "You've done good, my friends," he said. "And I did good to hire you. Now, let me have the rest."

With his customary admirable succinctness, Ryan completed his report.

But Doc was no longer aware of his surroundings. He was going away, into the almost diabolically beautiful strains of Mozart, and the even more beautiful world of his dreams…his memories…where Emily and Jolyon and Rachel always lived.

And where he always lived with them.

SNAKE EYE RODE down the dirt road from the Protector camp to the site where the ill-fated supply wag convoy had met its ill fate.

As he came upon where he reckoned the spot to be, he saw a draw, currently not running water although the bottom was damp, and showed the hoofprints of about a dozen horses. The cut bank would provide nicely complete concealment from the road and the convoy.

He didn't dismount yet, just brought his black mare to a halt and leaned out of the saddle to peer down at the imprinted earth. There were some prints of boots interspersed among the hoof marks. Cowboy boots. By

the length of stride and their depth they were worn by
a woman, tall and more heavily built than average. But
muscular, he reckoned. Not fat.

Nodding, he rode on.

The ashes in the bed of the charcoal wag had gone
cold. Standing next to the burnout, Snake Eye judged
that had happened before the light, chill rain began to
drizzle from bullet-colored overcast onto his black hat
and duster.

The canvas canopy had burned completely away,
leaving not even charred scraps hanging from the blackened and heat-sagged metal hoops that had held it up.
Inside lay bundles of burned cloth.

He shrugged and turned away, concluding they were
clothing for the higher officers and their ladies. Uniforms, to call them by the most complimentary name,
for the lesser ranks would've come by flatboat up the
Des Moines. If the Protectors bothered to send such
at all. This had been a relatively small convoy, with
a relatively stiff guard complement. That suggested
high-value cargo.

Snake Eye surveyed the other wags. One had burned
out so completely it wasn't much more than a scatter
of ashes with charred wheels lying in it, and even the
canopy supports melted to stubs and slag. High-quality
drink for the baron and his buddies, Snake Eye judged.
That would account for the added heat: better fuel.

There had clearly been a fifth wag. He could tell by
the shallow blackened crater with the axles and random
chunks of debris buried in it, and the general pattern of
wreckage thrown out by one or more powerful blasts.
Apparently that wag had carried barrels of gunpowder,

which the marauders had quite professionally used to blow everything to hell.

He had identified where most of the ambushers had hidden on his ride in. It wasn't hard to spot where they'd gone to ground. They'd picked obvious hiding places. Why wouldn't they? It wasn't as if the convoy or even its army escorts were expecting trouble so far behind their own lines. They hadn't been wary of driving into good ambush ground here, any more than they had been going into equally good spots to lay traps on the way from Hugoville. No reason to.

Not before this. He chuckled slightly to himself. He was used to being his own best company anyway.

Cawdor and his friends—if his suspicions were correct, and that's who the perpetrators were—were living up to their reputations.

Leaving his horse to graze, with reins trailing to the ground, he walked back to examine the ambushers' location more clearly. What he found significant was precisely what he didn't find: empties. The ambushers had obviously done a thorough job picking up their spent casings.

He found where four had hidden to the left of the track—west—and one to the east. That left one unaccounted-for by accounts he'd gleaned of the group over the past few years—reports he'd followed up with interest that only increased as he learned more tantalizing hints and scraps. Or two, if what Jed and his retinue had said about an extra member was correct.

And in this case Snake Eye saw no reason to doubt even a baron's word.

He recalled the survivor's feverish half-conscious account. A search along the convoy's back trail showed

Snake Eye's trained vision flattened grass behind a hummock west of the line of march. A sixth ambusher had taken position there. On the small side, a woman or boy. Boy, he decided from the tracks.

Moving back to the ambush site proper, Snake Eye ran his gaze over the corpses. The chillers had left them for the wolves. They hadn't omitted to strip them of their boots and search them for any valuables, as Snake Eye confirmed quickly.

He noted that three of them had been shot from the direction of the grassy hummock south, one in the back of the head, one in the side and one in the front. Snake Eye found it interesting that apparently that shooter had seemingly sniped at least one of the convoy guards without alerting the rest.

The survivor had said he heard no sound from the blaster that wounded him. Jed's sec men were inclined to chalk that up to the heat of battle, where sometimes men heard little but the roaring of their pulse in their own ears. Or just didn't notice what they heard.

Now he wasn't so sure. The slug the healer had dug out of the wounded trooper was a copper-jacketed .45—"modern" ammo in the sense that it hailed from the twentieth century and the era of smokeless powder. A handblaster bullet. Could the shooter from the rear of the wag train have made such expert shots with a silenced handblaster?

The survivor said he didn't think it was possible any of the drivers survived. But Snake Eye found only one body that was clearly a civilian. Apparently Cawdor had let the others escape.

Snake Eye smiled thinly. It just went to confirm what he'd learned about the man: that he didn't enjoy chilling for its own sake, took no joy in the simple act of chilling. As Snake Eye most definitely did.

But Snake Eye didn't chill without necessity any more than Cawdor and his people did. In his case, well, he liked drinking alcohol, too. But he indulged in it sparingly. He indulged sparingly in killing for much the same reasons: to keep his edge; and to avoid becoming intoxicated.

Also professionalism, of course. Chilling was what he was paid to do; it made no more sense to go around the country putting the freeze on people at random than it did a carpenter to run around building cabinets out in the back of beyond. And finally, because Snake Eye understood the distinction, generally lost even among the baronial classes, between *gourmet* and *gourmand*.

Smiling with the satisfaction of a job well done, he headed back to his horse. The missing convoy riders had left a trail easy to follow as a predark superhighway. And why shouldn't they? They had no motive for stealth, just speed—to get clear away before the coldhearts who'd wiped out their convoy changed their minds. Anyway, they weren't professional evaders.

He put his boot to the stirrup and swung into the saddle. He didn't know what information he might glean from accounts from actual survivors. But then, that was why a man sought information in the first place, wasn't it?

Snake Eyes clucked and booted his mare's black flanks and set out at a trot, following the slogging, obvious tracks. West.

Chapter Eleven

"So here's where we are," said the officer, bending over and pointing to an ancient contour map.

He was Lieutenant Tillman Owens, the fresh-faced blond kid who'd brought the companions into the Uplander camp in the first place. Ryan gathered that Baron Al liked to rotate his junior officers into staff duty and then back out into the field on a pretty much daily basis. It was an unorthodox system, even by the standards of the day. But Ryan saw the point to it, clear enough. And he reckoned the Trader, his old boss and mentor, would approve.

"And here," he said, moving his finger south, "are the Protector lines. And back here's where you struck the wag convoy."

Ryan nodded. He and his people knew all this, of course. But the baron had told the lieutenant to get them up-to-date on the military situation, something that could be important to their continued survival. So it was important to Ryan. The kid was simply making sure they started on the same page; he had no quarrel with that.

"Now you'll notice, as you no doubt did when you rode across the country both ways, there's not much terrain of any kind of strategic importance we're battling over here. Some high points, some low points, some streams draining into the Des Moines. But we're both fighting on this side of the river, which is the only significant barrier to way deep in the Association territory."

"Did make a bit of an impression, son," J.B. said, polishing his glasses with his handkerchief.

"Well, the land you rode over, which our two armies are battling over, happens to be prime growing land, which was originally settled, years and years back, by what are now called Uplanders—us. But the cattle barons downstream, the ones who eventually formed the Association, grew bigger and stronger than we were. First they pushed us back into the Uplands. Then they actually conquered us."

Ryan sat frowning in a folding chair. "Don't see how all this history stuff loads a single magazine for us," he said.

"Mebbe it doesn't, Ryan," J.B. said. "But then again, how will we know until we hear it?"

Ryan looked at his old friend in surprise. The Armorer seldom said much, never without a point to make, and the points he made were invariably good. That wasn't the same as right, but Ryan wasn't triple-stupe enough to imagine anybody was right all the time.

With his left thumbnail he scratched his neck beneath the turn of his right jawbone. "So how does knowing any of this help us?"

"Seeing as how we're fighting alongside these people," J.B. said, "just seems to make good sense to have some idea what their stake in the whole fandango is. All respect to you, Lieutenant, it's good to know what kind of skin your people got in this game. Is it serious blood business, or just some baron's ego-puffing party, and the people who got our flanks and backs are liable to vanish like an old white dandelion head in the first puff of wind?"

Owens shrugged.

"Fair enough, Mr. Dix," Ryan said.

"Dark night! Don't call me that, boy. Just getting my bones in motion each and every morning makes me feel old enough for any given day."

Ryan felt his frown deepening. "All right," he growled at last. "You're right, J.B. I was blind not so see that."

"Baron Al's ancestor," the young officer went on after a brief uncomfortable pause, "mebbe fifty, sixty years back, led the rebellion that drove out the Association overlords. His newly formed Uplands Alliance reclaimed the territory we sit in now, and a ways beyond it south. Two sides have been swapping off control of it ever since."

"So it's a pretty long-standing grudge," Mildred said. "That's like an underground fire, like in a root system or cool seam. You might not always see it, but know it's there. Might not even smell the smoke. But one of those can burn forever, and there's no telling when it might suddenly burst out in a full-on blaze."

The lieutenant looked at her a moment with blue eyes wide, then he laughed.

"Never thought of it that way before, Miz Wyeth," he said. "That explains a lot, though, now that you mention it. Especially considering how peace was concluded just last autumn after six months of stalemate."

"How was that evidence of a long-simmering grudge, young man?" Doc wanted to know. He was focused and attentive. He saw the possible merit of this history lesson as clearly as J.B. did. Not too surprising, given his own training and history. It meant he was staying sharp and in the moment.

"Well, when talks began, both sides agreed to pull back and leave a no-man's-land. Snow was coming on, and that always makes campaigning hard. An agreement was reached.

"But then at a midwinter gathering to celebrate the final signing of the treaty, Jessie Rae got in a screaming fight with Jed's wife, and it was back on like donkey pong. Are you feeling distressed, Miz Wyeth? Should I call for an orderly to bring you water or something?"

Mildred waved him off. Her expression suggested to Ryan she was trying to choke back laughter. "I'm fine," she said. "I just don't know which hurts worse—the way you mangle a phrase from my own time, or the realization it somehow survived."

He frowned his incomprehension. "Your time?"

"Her childhood," Krysty said brightly. "Mildred has a nostalgic streak, you see."

Mildred shot her friend a narrow-eyed look under lowered brows, then her face began to smooth as she realized she'd screwed up. The fact she was a freezie, born way back before the Big Nuke, wasn't common knowledge, nor was it the sort of knowledge that would do her—or her friends—a bit of good. People feared and hated that which they didn't understand.

"Uh, yeah," Mildred said. "I grew up…someplace pretty far from here. Remote, too. So it always kind of surprises me when I, you know, hear or see something that reminds me of my…homeland."

"Oh." From his expression the lieutenant didn't really catch what she was talking about. But he also pretty clearly decided it was his fault for not getting hold, and he'd rather plow on than look like more of a stupe, which suited Ryan down to the ground.

"So...uh...one thing that sorta helps things along—and please don't let on as to how I told you—the baron's wife, Miz Jessie Rae, happens to be the younger sister of Joyleen Kylie."

Ryan sat back. He felt his eyebrows crawling up his forehead.

"Wait," Ricky said. "Isn't that a security risk?"

J.B. looked a bit stern at that—the kid was his protégé, after all, and his habit of blurting ran directly counter to the Armorer's taciturn nature and instincts. For his point, Ryan thought it was a double-good question.

But to his increased surprise the lieutenant burst out laughing.

"Sorry, no way you'd know," he said, reining himself back into businesslike-briefing mode, though not without a smile tugging mischievously at the corners of his mouth. "Two women hate each other like owls and crows. They can't spend longer than mebbe ten minutes in a room without one flying right up into the other's face, screeching and clawing. And so it proved to be the end of the peace celebration."

He sighed. "Also the peace."

"You are a likely young buck," Doc said, "to say nothing of a cavalry officer, one whom we've seen display the customary élan of the breed. Yet you seem distressed at the resumption of that very war that brings you the prospect of glory."

Owens looked uncomfortable. "Well, glory has its place, I give you that, Professor," he said. "But I've seen what war costs us. My family—all of the Uplanders. Nuke, I've seen what it does to the common folk in the Association, too. Most of them are just victims, got no more say in what their masters do than their dogs do. Less than some of the landowners' favored hunting dogs, I'd say.

"Plus, I've seen what it costs my men. Glory doesn't look so glorious when some kid who you grew up friends with your whole life is rolling around in the grass kicking and clutching at a ball through the belly. Nor sound nor smell so triple-fine, either."

"Good for you, kid," Ryan said. "Lots of people never notice that fact even when the blood and shit's spattering the toes of their boots, which in the present case translates to you're less likely to do something triple-ass stupe because it'll make you feel like a big hero, and get us all chilled.

"You gave us the background, and I admit I can see that might be of some use somewhere down the line. But now, how about we get to counting blasters? What do they have? What do we have?"

Owens nodded. His smile quit trying to grab control of his face. He had no trouble going all-business now.

"Fact is, Mr. Cawdor—" he began.

"Rad-blast!" Ryan exclaimed. "J.B.'s right. That 'mister' shit just makes me feel old. Chill that, boy. Call me Ryan, if you feel moved to use a name."

"As you will, Mist— Uh, Ryan. The fact is, the Protectors got the edge on us in pretty near every way you might care to put a name to. They got more land, and are richer. Hence, more men, more blasters. More horses and cannon, and more fodder for the lot of them."

"But your people have managed to keep the war

going since you won your independence from the lowland barons," Krysty said.

The lieutenant nodded. He scratched a pink cheek that Ryan doubted would muster anything rougher than peach fuzz for another few years yet. Should the youth live and all.

"I guess that gets back to, uh, J.B.'s concern about how motivated we Uplanders are," he said. "The fact is it's only that we're willing to fight like badgers for every inch of soil that keeps them from rolling us right down like a buffalo stampede. Sure, we have pretty fair defensive terrain. Fairly broken country, good cover readily available. As the Association found out when we booted their asses back to the lowlands.

"But down here it's just nothing but guts and mebbe being too triple-stupe to know when we're beat that allows us to hang on to anything. We need this growing land to feed our people. But the open country that's so fertile and all also allows their advantages in numbers to come into play."

He looked from one of their faces to the next. "Mebbe I'm about to speak out of turn, here," he said, "seeing as you're hired mercies and all, but Baron Al trusts a man with the job he gives him, even us junior officers. He told me to brief you straight, so straight is how I'll give it to you.

"It seems like only a matter of time until they bring us down, this go-round. Baron Al's a shrewd old bast—baron. Oh, he may not look it or sound like it, and Jessie Rae and some of the better-polished officers like Colonel Turnbull are always on him to quit acting like such a hayseed. But he likes it that way, and not just 'cause it fits him like an old pair of shoes. It inclines people to underestimate him. He likes that."

"But even his cunning has its limits, am I correct?" Doc asked.

"Baron Kylie doesn't have triple-many flies on him, either," Owens said. "I know he likely didn't make the best impression on you-all, there at the outset. He's got a short temper and isn't a particularly kind man at the best of times. But he's triple-smart, too. Got to be, to hang on to power in the lowlands like he does.

"Association isn't like us in the Alliance. Political power's a big prize to them. They play the game for blood—win or die."

Ryan pressed his lips together. He wondered if in fact the Alliance was as immune to power games as young Owens so fondly believed. A baron's son himself, he found himself inclined to doubt it. But seeing to that part of the youth's education wasn't part of his mission. Seeing to the welfare of his own was. Owens was a good kid, but he wasn't an insider.

"So you told us your commanding general will trust a man to do his assigned job," he said, "no matter how low in rank. Question is whether Al will listen to a kid like you."

Owens frowned, considering. "Baron Al listens to anybody he thinks talks sense," he said, "no matter how high or low. But he'll help you if he thinks you *aren't* talking sense. High or low."

Ryan nodded. That squared with his assessment of the man. But he hadn't brought himself and his people this far taking anything for granted.

"Here's the deal," he said. "What if we had an idea of how to speed things up, win the war for your Alliance? Mebbe not all time—wars don't usually end for all time, unless everybody on one side's chilled—but for the time being? I reckon that's the sort of thing he'd best hear first from one of his own, instead of what you so rightly term mercies."

"Why would mercies want to speed up the end of a war?" Owens said. His face flushed beet-red. "Sorry, no disrespect. But I mean—"

J.B. chuckled. "At ease, kid," he said. "Natural you'd think we'd want to spin the gig out, as long as we could."

He paused to take off his glasses and wipe the lenses with his hankie.

"Natural but wrong. In our case, anyway. We're not too fond of the whole fighting thing ourselves. As far as mercie work's concerned, getting paid to guard stuff or keep the peace is miles more comfortable. Also survivable."

"I calculate," Ryan said, "if we can play a big enough role in bringing events to a satisfactory conclusion, a man like Baron Al might feel moved to generosity."

"You bet he would!" Owens exclaimed, visibly nonplussed. "The baron might even be able to find land for them to settle in. Give you-all status among us Uplanders. A permanent place and stake."

Not looking at Krysty, whose green eyes were on him big and as bright as beacons, Ryan slid past that comment by agreeing.

"I think I see a way to get the Alliance an advantage," he said, "and how we can help you do that thing. And as I say, I reckon it's best if somebody on the inside broaches that notion to Al on our behalf."

"I'm listening," Owens said, trying not to sound too

eager—failing, but he was smart enough to try. Ryan reckoned he was a pretty good kid. Smart, committed to his cause. He might even live to a ripe old age. Not that the odds ever favored that outcome, in this here and now.

"Then listen close," Ryan said, not failing to note the way all his companions leaned in tight, if anything more eager to hear what he was about to say than the cavalry officer was. "I got a plan...."

Chapter Twelve

"We never had us a chance," the man with the bandaged side was saying over his cracked mug of beer. "Not one fucking chance at all."

The beer looked like piss and no doubt tasted much like it. The gaudy around them was the sort of gaudy to serve beer like that.

Which was to say, the Deathlands' standard gaudy: dark, dank, low-ceilinged, reeking of spilled booze and vomit. It was the sort of place where one or two dozen lost souls gathered by the light of stinking lanterns fueled by river-fish oil or turpentine, and tossed back booze in hopes of getting drunk as quickly as possible.

There was a reason why Snake Eye always paid the premium for booze from the bottle. He might not know where it really came from, but at least he could see what he was pouring in his shot glass.

"You talking about life as a citizen in the Association," Snake Eye said, sidling down the bar to where the man sat a little apart from what may have been companions, but were unlikely to be friends, "or did you have a specific incident in mind?"

He was pretty sure he knew the answer to that question before he asked it. That was his favorite kind of question, of course. He had tracked several of the survivors of the ambushed convoy's wag drivers here to this nameless dive, in an equally nameless settlement of rasty shacks tacked together from scabbie planks and sheet metal a dozen miles or so west of the ambush site.

He doubted it would be far enough if the Association, or their individual masters, got it in their heads to hunt them down and punish them for desertion. Or for their carelessness in losing a whole convoy worth of luxury goods for the baron at Protector HQ. Their fear of punishment was likely why they'd simply deserted in the first place.

Barons were all alike. They never took the blame for their own losses or failures. That's what underlings were for.

But Jed Kylie had some bigger fish to fry just now, not least being the almost-certain perpetrators of the raid. And if the baron in command of the Protector Army had more important things to do than hunt runaway wag drivers and outriders, his lesser barons did, too.

"Ease up, there, Norvell," said one of the men standing by the bar next to him. "It's not good to talk to outlanders."

Snake Eye chuckled indulgently. "Ah, but I'm no outlander," he said, sidling right up to the wounded man, who was visibly the most inebriated.

His drunkenness suggested a pair of things to the mercie. One, that he might well prove easiest to get answers out of, although admittedly *sense* was a different thing altogether. And second, that he might well feel extra motivation besides the pain in his side for wanting to get more hammered than his buddies.

"I'm a benefactor," Snake Eye said. He pushed over a

tumbler and poured a couple of fingers of murky brown liquid into it. "House's best. Drink up."

Norvell grabbed the greasy tumbler with both hands, threw back his head and shot the drink straight back down his throat. As Norvell shuddered, Snake Eye reflected that he might have been offended at the treatment of the whiskey, but for the fact he had sampled it himself. He reckoned the less risk that any of it might splash on one's taste buds, the better for all concerned.

"Ah," Norvell said, slamming the glass back down on the uneven bar with unnecessary force. Then he turned a bloodshot but cagey look on Snake Eye.

"Look, mister, I don't know what you want in return, but I got to tell you, I don't swing that way."

Snake Eye laughed indulgently. Of course his life made normal men blanch, as Norvell's reluctant companions did, which was fine with Snake Eye. He reckoned he had his mark.

Norvell, of course, wasn't a normal man. Norvell was a very drunk man.

"Just answers to a few questions, my friend," Snake Eye said. "That's all I want from you. Such as how did you wind up here in the ass end of nowhere in the first place?"

Norvell's two buddies gave the mercie narrow-eye looks over that query. It wasn't the sort of place you asked a question like that of a man. Not that the Deathlands offered many such places.

The tiny settlement, hard even in today's terms to dignify it with the name *ville,* lay out on the fringes of the no-man's-land between the warring confederations. But not completely out of it, either. It was plain as day to a man with an eye much less keen than Snake Eye's trademark yellow one that its sole reason for existence was to service the illicit trade that inevitably went on despite the generations-long conflict. It was too much trouble for either side to try to close down all such concerns. So they seldom tried at all. The fact was, both sides had reasons of their own for wanting such trade to continue.

All the same, the sort of people you'd encounter in an illicit trading outpost would be even touchier than usual about questions regarding who they were and what they were doing here. For example the three young men glowering at Snake Eye from the darkest corner of the badly lit bar room would probably react poorly at the first syllable of any such question Snake Eye aimed their way. Deserters, he took them for. There was nothing uniform about their assorted duds, aside from general dirt, rumpledness and general raggedy-assedness. Not that they had any exclusive claim on those things. But for most soldiers of either Alliance or Association, shedding the "uniform" took no longer than stripping off the green or blue armband and chucking it in the weeds.

To Snake Eye, they just had that look. Not that he cared. But he routinely sized up everyone he came into a room with. Just as he never entered a place without knowing a good and fast way out. It just made good sense.

"Why do you…wanna know?" Norvell said. It really had taken him the better part of a minute to frame the question. Snake Eye had practically heard the gears grinding in his head.

"Friendly curiosity, partner," Snake Eye said, reckoning the man was drunk enough to take that for the obvious lie it was. "I'm a businessman, independent entrepreneur. Always on the scout for a new opportunity."

Which, at least, was as true as Snake Eye's heart was hard.

"Well, I done fell on hard times," Norvell said, "and that's a fact."

He stopped, clearly waiting. After a moment he looked to his benefactor, wagged his eyebrows like caterpillars dry-humping a leaf. When that action didn't make his meaning clear he rattled his now-empty glass on the bar.

Laughing, Snake Eye poured him another. Given the liquor's quality, it was better in every way that it went into Norvell's gut than his.

"Ambushed," he said. "That's what happened. T'me and my friends here."

"Include us out, Norvell," said the younger and leaner of his companions. "Dammit."

"There we was, driving a convoy of luxury goods for the baron and his pals," Norvell continued obliviously. "And outta nowhere—bang, bang, bang! Coldhearts ever'where, shooting our asses off. Escort troopers droppin' like flies. And then this wild-ass mutie kid with white hair and red eyes—*red fucking eyes*—jumps up on the board next to me and starts stabbing the shit outta me."

He's not a mutie, thought Snake Eye, who knew what an albino was, and also a thing or two about mutants. He said nothing. It wasn't his business to correct Norvell's inconsequential view of the world.

Norvell held up forearms wrapped in bandages. "I fought him off best I could. But he was crazy like a catamount. I thought I was done for until his boss coldheart called him off. There was a scary dude, I tell you, and I never saw him lift a finger against nobody, although he was carrying a longblaster with a scope that looked like it had seen some recent use. Tall dude, lean as a wolf. Just one blue eye and a patch on t'other. Like yours, except ice-blue insteada yellow. Seemed to stab right through a body."

"Did he have black, shaggy hair, the one-eyed man? The other one, I mean."

"Yeah." Norvell nodded convulsively. To encourage him Snake Eye poured him another drink. "That's the man. Friend of yours?"

Snake Eye laughed at that. "Not a friend, no. I do know his reputation. His and the white-haired youth's. What about the others?"

"Others?"

"Focus, now." He moved the bottle away. Norvell's eyes followed as if attached by strings. "Who else did you see among the coldhearts?"

"Coldhearts?"

"Who ambushed you."

"Oh. Them. Well, there was a brown slut with her hair all done in beaded braids and titties out to *here*. And then another woman, hair like fire, built like a brick shithouse, brought up the horses and pack mules."

"Pack mules?"

"Uh-huh. Raiders loaded up some high-value shit, like primer caps, meds, bottles of triple-prime hooch. Weps, including some off the dead guards. And boots off the chills. Everything else they burned. Or blew, in the case of the powder wag."

Snake Eye nodded. "All right. Who else?"

"Who else?"

Snake Eye held up the bottle enticingly. "The one-eyed man and the white-haired man. Surely they had some other dudes with them? Not just the two women."

Speaking of women, in a manner of speaking, a gaudy slut had slouched in and was trying to peddle her wares in a halfhearted way. She wore a patched red dress, which may or may not have been silk and may or may not have been lingerie, but didn't do much to conceal those wares. Not enough, in Snake Eye's opinion.

"Oh," Norvell said again, "yeah. The others. Lessee. There was a tall, gawky oldie with a cane. A little Mex-looking kid, come out of the bushes by our backtrail holding a funny kinda longblaster with a thick barrel. And a sawed-off little runt with a shotgun, wore specs and a fedora."

"Very good." Snake Eye poured another drink.

The gaudy slut approached the three deserters in the corner and was rebuffed without so much as a glance her way. Looking around the bar, she spotted Snake Eye and made right for him.

"Ah," Norvell said, having pounded his drink as if it was the last he'd ever get. He wiped his mouth. "Yeah, we're lucky we made it outta there alive. Them was some stone brigands, I tell ya. If it wasn't for me swapping the tale to them of the secret place my aunt found, don't think they would let us leave on our pins."

"Oh, bullshit, Norvell," the older driver said.

Snake Eye sensed the approach of the gaudy slut on his right side, the side away from Norvell. Felt her warmth. *Smelled* her.

"Hey, honey," she said in a voice like sandpaper.

"Back off," he snapped without looking around. "Keep your stink away from me."

"Aw, honey, that's just the smell of my love juices flowin' at the sight of you. A hard man like you is good to find. Let's me and you—"

She put her hand on his arm.

His reaction was immediate—he whipped around, as fast as a striking rattler, and backhanded her onto her bony ass. She stared at him, her eyes murky green pools amid incongruously black and blue paint, her mouth a scarlet smear, her hair hanging in her face like bleached seaweed.

"I told you to keep away from me!"

"Here, now," the bartender said, bustling up behind his important leather-clad gut.

Snake Eye turned a hard yellow look on him. That was enough. The bartender stopped short, as if bumping his nose on an invisible force field, and found some glasses that needed the grease and muck smeared around on them with a rag as foul as his gaudy slut.

The drivers with Norvell made protesting noises. One made as if to move toward Snake Eye.

Snake Eye turned his left side away from the bar to face the two sitting men. His hand swept back the tail of his coat, revealing the black steel gleam of his left-hand blaster. The driver, his eyes huge, backed off.

"Now," Snake Eye said, still looking at the two, "what was this about your aunt's discovery?"

The older driver moistened his bearded lips. "It's just a crazy story, mister," he said. "We don't want no trouble with you. But no reason to let you think there's anything to it. Folks who hit our train, they didn't buy it for one little second."

Snake Eye nodded brusque acknowledgment, but he turned back to Norvell.

"I want to hear more of this story of yours anyway, Norvell," he said. "I'm a collector of curiosities as well as an independent contractor. So I'd like you to tell me all about it."

He gave a final glare to the slut who was scooting her skinny rump backward across the floorboards away from him, throwing up a sort of bow-wave of sodden sawdust. It was purely for show now.

Though for a fact Snake Eye wasn't interested in any woman degraded enough to be attracted to him. Even for a commercial transaction. When he needed that sort of relief he bought the services of high-class sluts at one or another place he knew here or there—paid handsomely, as he could well afford to, for the privilege not only of using her sexually, but also of letting her know in intimate detail what a worthless bitch she was. Like all women.

As long as he paid—and left no marks—the proprietors and proprietresses of those high-class houses reckoned there was no harm done.

"Somewhere else," Snake Eye said, clapping Norvell on the shoulder, "where we won't be subject to so many rude interruptions."

"IN HERE, MISTER?" Norvell asked at Snake Eye's after-you gesture. "But this is just an old alley. Nowhere particular."

"Nowhere particular is fine with me, Norvell," Snake Eye said amiably. "It will ensure privacy for me to hear the rest of your story in peace." Actually, the alley was no darker than the street, to call it that. But its narrow walls did restrict sight lines, which was the effect Snake Eye was looking for.

The drunk looked back uncertainly over one shoulder.

"One thing you oughta know right out the gate, mister," he said. "I ain't into no funny stuff."

Then a dim light of calculation lit his eyes. "Unless you got the jack, of course."

"Rest easy, my friend," Snake Eye said. "I have jack. But all I want from you is the rest of the story."

"All righty, then," Norvell said, and stumbled into the alley.

Several minutes later Snake Eye stepped out of the alley. He was alone.

The cut-up wag driver had had little more to tell him. Mostly it served to confirm the late Erl Kendry's assertion that the lost redoubt entrance was located in the environs, and a hint that it was underground. Which was hardly surprising, really.

Still, it was a lead. Most important to Snake Eye's mind was that Norvell had mentioned it to Cawdor and his bunch. They also showed a keen interest in the lost old-days facilities. That was something he'd learned tracking down the rumors about them. It seemed to go deeper than a yen for scabbie, although Snake Eye wasn't sure what else they might be seeking.

Norvell's buddies hadn't thought the ambushers were interested in Norvell's wild tale. Snake Eye thought otherwise.

"Hey, you," a voice called quietly from behind. "Turn around. Triple slow. Keep them hands where we can see them."

A hairless eyebrow shot up. Feeling a smile he refused to show on his thin lips, Snake Eye complied.

It was the three deserters from the gaudy. One man held a scattergun with both barrels and butt sawed off

short. It had to hurt like a bitch when it went off; Snake
Eye wondered if the sheer intimidation factor meant the
man didn't have to shoot it often.

His two pals had revolvers leveled from their waists
to Snake Eye's.

"You friends of Norvell's, too?" he asked.

"Huh?" said the central member of the trio, a tall
man with long hair spilling lankly from around a dark
slouch hat.

"I suppose not." It was a far-fetched surmise, of
course. Still, that others might have been concerned
with the driver's fate was pardonably on his mind at
the moment.

Norvell had been so remarkably guileless. Like a
child. And as easy to distract, simply by looking past
his shoulder at the alley mouth and saying, "What's
that?"

Obediently, Norvell had turned and looked. And
hadn't even had time to react when Snake Eye seized
his neck from behind and expertly broke it.

For a further moment Snake Eye wondered if they
might be following some triple-stupe quixotic notion of
avenging the putative honor of the gaudy slut.

Then the swag-bellied man made a prodding motion
of his short-barreled double gun. "Well?"

"Well, what?"

"Your valuables, mister. Hand them over. Start by
undoing that fancy-ass gun belt of yours and handing
it over. Nice and slow."

"Very well," Snake Eye said. "I'm lowering my
hands now."

"See what I did there?" the paunchy scattergunner

said to his friends. "I get him to give us his most valuable traps, and disarm himself. All at once!"

Of course, had he handed over the exquisitely sewn and hand-tooled leather belt with the matched pair of Sphinx blasters in the holsters, Snake Eye wouldn't have been disarmed. Not in any sense, although as he liked to put it, even naked on an ice floe he wouldn't really and truly be *unarmed*.

But of course, all that assumed he really planned to comply. As these three stupes manifestly did.

When the shotgun man turned his beard-stubbled jowls back to bear on Snake Eye, his pig eyes shot wide. It was a half a heartbeat before the orange flash of the blaster that had appeared in Snake Eye's left hand was reflected in them.

Even before the muzzle-flare erupted Snake Eye saw the dark hole appear between the would-be mugger's eyes. Before the man started to fold like an empty grain bag the right-hand gun went off and the tall man in the middle staggered back, his own blaster dropping from suddenly unresponsive fingers.

The third deserter was faster than Snake Eye anticipated. He fired.

But not quicker than Snake Eye was prepared for.

And not faster than Snake Eye. Nobody was.

The mercie pivoted clockwise on the heel of his left boot. The dragon's breath of the charge of black powder exploding out the revolver's barrel passed him by without doing more than giving him a warm air-puff to the face. So did the bullet riding invisibly in front of the rush of rapidly expanding gas and smoke.

Even as he turned, Snake Eye was raising the Sphinx in his left hand. As if he had all the time in the world, he thrust out his arm so that the square muzzle almost touched that deserter between the eyes. They widened rapidly in horrified astonishment before muzzle-flame hid his face, and the 9 mm bullet blew out the back of his head.

He fell, reeking of scorched hair and flash-fried skin and eyeball.

Snake Eye had both blasters holstered before the last coldheart hit the rutty street. Without a backward glance he turned and walked away, not hurrying but neither dawdling, out of the tiny settlement and into the dark, where he'd left his horse hobbled in a dry gulley.

He reckoned he'd used up his welcome in this place. Then again, so far as he was concerned, he'd used up this place, too.

His business—and his pleasure—now lay elsewhere.

Chapter Thirteen

"Yes, Master Thom," the gaunt, white-haired wrinklie in the balding felt vest said. "It shall be as you direct."

He obeyed the landowner's spoiled and cruel son without the least reaction, inside no more than out. Even the resentment had been whipped from his bony frame, decades before. All he had was his servitude to Colonel Ramie Clark and his family. They were more dirt farmers than cattle ranchers, and seemed all the more touchy about their importance and prerogatives over what their peers among the wealthy of the Association considered a severe social defect.

But she's your only granddaughter, a voice inside his narrow, half-hairless skull cried in a degree of anguish the rest of him wouldn't let himself feel. She's so young, so innocent.

The realistic part of Jabez Hawshawe thought without any kind of passion at all that sooner or later, she had to learn the reality of life as a tenant of a Protector baron. Might as well be this night as the next one.

The front door blew open, or so he thought at first. He cringed a little, knowing eighteen-year-old Thom Clark would have him flogged for his carelessness if he hadn't closed it tight enough. Or might just beat him half to death with a silver-knobbed cane from the stand by the door.

Or not even stop at the midpoint. Jabez had seen that happen, too.

But instead of a wind what came in the door was a stranger. And strange he was: tall and rangy in a coat that flapped around the calves of his blue jeans. He had a single blue eye that burned like a beacon in the light of the oil lanterns hung in the hallway, and a patch over the other.

"Everybody out!" he ordered, waving the barrel of his cocked blaster toward the door. "Take everybody with you that you don't hate bad."

"What are you talking about?" Thom demanded. "What do you think you're doing here."

"Burning this house to the ground," the intruder said. "Who're you? Baron's puppy?"

"I am the heir to Baron Ramie Clark!" the young man screamed, his normally sallow face now bone-white. "My father will burn you, when he catches you!"

And he grabbed for the shotgun hung in brackets by the wall.

The flash of the big handblaster was as dazzling as its report was deafening, as the ringing in his ears didn't manage to drown out the panic-hammering of his pulse. Jabez saw the young master take a step back, grease-smeared velvet vest smoldering and stinking. His eyes were wide. Sweat poured down his narrow face.

"You—" He coughed, felt his chest, then looked down at his hand.

Thom looked up in amazement from the blood that stained his palm. More ran out the corner of his mouth.

"How dare you!" he screamed, and threw himself forward.

The stranger's second shot caught him in the throat. He fell, kicking, thrashing, strangling on blood.

"Any other baron spawn here?" the intruder asked Jabez. "Any sec men?"

Wordlessly, Jabez shook his head. At last he managed to reply, "Only myself, my granddaughter and some tenant servants."

A woman with red hair spilling out from beneath her slouch hat stuck her head in the doorway. Despite his years, Jabez's heart actually picked up the beat at the glimpse he caught of her lush-bodied form, out in the darkness of the stoop.

"Perimeter's secured, Ryan," she said. "No resistance, no guards. Just a lot of frightened tenants."

"Anybody liable to show up with blasters in the near future?" the man asked.

"N-no, sir." He hated himself for calling this coldheart *"sir."* But the whipped-in habit of utter obedience to authority kicked in. And this tall stranger exuded authority, even without the big handblaster and his demonstrated willingness to use it.

"Okay," the woman said, and ducked back out.

"Then get your possessions out," the man said to Jabez. "You and the rest of the servants." He grinned. The expression chilled Jabez's blood. "Rad-blast it, take anything you want. Anything that's ever caught your eye! We're not carrying it away with us. And fifteen minutes from now this whole place goes up in a blaze of glory."

Jabez heard scuttling sounds from behind him, then excited whispers. Some rose to moans.

He glanced back. Fat Hattie the cook and Larry the handyman were there, along with a couple Hattie's kids who helped out. They were all staring in wide-eyed fascination from the body of the Clark heir, lying there with his eyes staring at the wall and his blood soaking into the carpet, and the man who put him there.

"Mister," Jabez said, "Baron Ramie ain't what you'd call an understanding man. He'll have us all pulled apart by horses when he gets back and finds what you did."

"Then you all better pack plenty of food and water," the stranger said. "The baron must have some wags here and horses to pull them."

Overcome, Jabez nodded. It felt strangely light, as if it might lift his frail old body up and carry it away like a balloon from this unbelievable scene. Was this a nightmare, or a dream come true.

"Then hitch them up, load them up and head out fast as the horses'll pull," the coldheart said. "Me, I wouldn't so much as slow down until I'd shaken the dust of the Association and this rat-hole little war all the way off my horses' hooves. Take everybody with you with sense enough to go."

He shook his head, looking around the foyer with some emotion Jabez couldn't so much as guess at.

"Can't promise you a better life," he said, "but looking at you and the rest—and based on my own experience with the Cattlemen's Protective Association—I reckon there's a chance of you managing to do better than this. Understand me?"

"Y-yes, sir," he said. Somehow he no longer begrudged the use of the title. "Yes, *sir!*"

"Then move!"

"You seem to have an unfortunate habit of killing sons and heirs of the ruling class, Mr. Cawdor," Colonel

Cody Turnbull said. Mildred thought he looked worried as he poured himself a glass of some dark beverage.

"I didn't see that I had much of a choice," Ryan said. "Come to that, don't really think Mildred and Krysty did with Buddy Kylie, either. The Clark kid wouldn't stop coming at me—I'd give him credit for balls, but what I really think is, he was just too arrogant to believe anyone would dare lift a finger against him."

He shook his head. "Not that I see either him or Buddy as a tragic loss."

"I notice you don't mention they were both enemies of ours, Mr. Cawdor," said Al, sitting slouched on his chair.

Ryan shrugged. "Truth to tell, Baron," he said, "that didn't have a lot to do with either chill. It just seemed a matter of doing what was needed at the time."

"Chilling enemies is one thing," J.B. said from just behind Ryan. "Chilling mad dogs is another."

Cody's handsome, aristocratic face twisted in brief pain. He didn't seem to care to hear members of his class characterized that way. Especially not by a passel of blasters for hire.

The companions were gathered in the parlor of Baron Al's big house. It belonged to a middle-aged pair named the Lenkmans, who apparently had been roughly treated by the Protectors before the Uplanders recaptured their estate. Now they stayed on, insisting on acting as servants to the baron and his army staff.

No matter how genteel, the room smelled mostly of unwashed bodies and clothes stiff with dried, stale sweat. It still managed a Victorian stuffiness that reminded Mildred of old ladies who were too fond of tea, lavender and cats. The baron's chair even had a lacy

antimacassar, mostly white, thrown over the back of it.
If Mildred remembered the word right.

Also the house smelled of cinnamon, for some unknown reason.

Though Ryan, who was of a generally restless nature, preferred to stand, most of the group was seated,
either on the sofa, chairs, or in Ricky's and Jak's case,
perched on an ottoman.

Cody and a small and ever-shifting swarm of staff
officers and aides came in and out of the sitting room.
Fortunately it was spacious, what Mildred thought was
called a great room, open for two stories up to a pitched
roof, with a gallery for the second floor over one end.

"Tell me again," Cody said, "what exactly was the
purpose of burning the Clark house in the first place."

Mrs. Lenkman ghosted in, wearing an apron and
carrying a plate of cookies. "Here," she said listlessly,
"I made these for you."

"Thanks, Maisie," Al said. "Put 'em anyplace. The
boys—and, uh, girls—will help themselves."

She smiled wanly at him and went out again. From
her funereal silence and the fact her worn long black
skirt hid the motions of her feet she appeared to travel
by levitating and gliding above the polished wood
floors and threadbare throw rugs.

"Sad case," Al said, shaking his head when the lady
of the house went out.

Cody nodded. "That it is."

He looked sharply at Ryan. "You were saying?"

"Wasn't," Ryan said, "but I will. The Protectors got
it all over you in manpower, firepower, pretty much
any kind of numbers you want to put a name to. You've
managed to hold them off, somehow, which is to your

credit. But they've got to know that if they only play a waiting game, they can just wear you down."

Al rumbled deep in his chest, a sound like distant thunder. "They can't afford this damned war to go on perpetually, no more than we can. And we're just up against flat busted."

He shook his head. "Ah, if only those damned fool women…"

He let his voice trail off without, so far as Mildred could tell, seeing the way Cody Turnbull's face stiffened and went pale.

"What we're saying, Baron," said J.B., perched on a wooden chair, "is that the Protectors have been just too nuke-blasted comfortable. They've got the edge, and their brass in particular haven't faced any consequences. If anybody eats in their army, it's them. Anybody goes hungry, it isn't."

Cody looked puzzled. "Isn't that the normal order of things?"

"Yeah," Ryan said. "That's why we want to sting the barons—the landowning higher-ups—where it hurts. After what happened to their pal Clark they're all going to have half a mind on their homes and the holdings they left behind, which up until now've been safe."

"What purpose does this serve, Mr. Cawdor?" Cody asked.

The way Mildred had the man sized up, he was far from stupid. He seemed to be pretty knowledgeable about military business, and cared for his men, even if he was pretty uptight about maintaining the distinction between the grunts and their betters. But he wasn't the most mentally agile monkey in the troop, either. He had habits of thinking and found it hard to shift outside them.

"Well, anything they're thinking about that isn't a way to screw us over helps, Cody."

This time the baron, who was looking at his officer, did see his face turn red. He waved a big hand. "Relax, Cody. I'm not busting your chops. The fact is, if we make Kylie's commanders nervous, looking over their shoulders, they'll be distracted. If nothing else, that'll distract Jed. Cloud his thinking."

Cody shook his head. "And I'm not trying to be stubborn, General. But I don't see any substantial way in which this helps us."

"Call it stage one," J.B. said, sitting back down after helping himself to a cookie. "Early days yet. We got a few tricks to pull before you start seeing benefits."

Cody frowned. "I thought it was a primary principle of strategy never to engage in any action that doesn't potentially lead to winning the war."

"Not so easy for a group as small as we are to pull off, Colonel," Krysty said. "Unless we assassinate Baron Jed directly, and since that would be a suicide mission, it would be hard for you to pay us enough to do that."

Al and some of his aides laughed. Cody looked pained.

"So what—"

"Like J.B. said, Colonel," Ryan said, "it's a process. We get them off balance, get them angry. Get them stupe. Then they're prime for you to hit them."

"So you have a graduated plan of action mapped out," Cody said, with just a hint of sarcasm. "I presume you plan to involve us at some point."

"That'd be the general idea, yes," Ryan said, refusing to be baited.

"Very well," he said. "What's your next move? Captain Muller, why don't you set out a map and our friends can show us where they mean to sting our enemies next."

A slightly plump officer with curly blond hair, who always seemed to hang around on Al's staff but never spoke up much, moved to unroll a map on the gate-leg table by one side of the room. Mildred wondered at that; the baron tended to rotate his staff officers in and out of the field. Maybe Captain Muller wasn't any great shakes as a field commander, and his baron felt safer with him on-staff all the time. Or maybe he was just a wizard at paperwork.

"Now," Cody said, smiling at the companions over the U.S.G.S. contour map, "if you'll point us to your next target so we can have some idea what to expect—"

"Isn't that a bad idea?"

Everybody turned to stare at Ricky Morales. His olive-skinned face went dark with embarrassment.

"I mean, isn't that a security breach or something?"

"Ricky," J.B. said, "pipe down."

"He's got a point, J.B.," Ryan stated.

"Oh, come now," Cody said. "We want to have some idea whether the Uplands Alliance is getting its jack's worth from you. We're your employers. It isn't so much to ask."

"To tell the truth," Baron Al said, rubbing his big powerful hands together, "I just plain want to know. I feel like a schoolboy at my birthday all over again."

Though Ryan's face never changed expression, Mildred could tell he wasn't happy. But as a baron's son

himself, he knew that barons—even a baron as sharp
and basically decent as Al had shown himself to be—
had a will of iron.

"All right," he said, sauntering over to the map.

As it happened, they'd already discussed the plan—
the whole thing, not just the next stage. Ryan and J.B.,
who were the strategists of the bunch, had dreamed
up the broad outlines, then the rest of them had helped
flesh it out and mold it into shape.

It was a crazy plan. What else was new? Mildred
decided to give in and have herself a cookie.

But when she looked at the occasional table the
dainty china plate with daintier flowers painted on it
was bare except for a few crumbs.

Dammit.

Chapter Fourteen

"Stay frosty, people," Lieutenant Card said. "Word come down from the top that those mercie coldhearts the sheepfuckers hired are gonna be mounting a play at this depot tonight. Baron Jed would take it as a personal favor if we all gave them a triple-warm welcome."

Asshole, Private Reiser thought.

Unseen overhead a killdeer flicked past, trailing its distinctive *whit-whit-whit* call as it wove between the powder warehouses. From behind the small waterfront sec detail came the sound and smell of the Des Moines River slogging against the wood pilings of the dock.

The lieutenant strutted importantly in front of the four-man crew on duty. "Us here in the organic security detail aren't expected to have to do much. Baron's sent down a full troop of his best cavalry to get ready the surprise party."

"Why, gee, Lieutenant," said Haldeman from behind Reiser. "We were plumb unaware of the fact that sixty-some horsemen crowded into this happy little base of ours just before the sun went down. Not like we *keep tabs* on what goes down around here or anything."

As usual, Reiser didn't know whether to laugh at his squad-mate's wisecrack or kick his ass for pissing off their superior officer. Not that trying either right now, when they were all just trying to remember how to stand at attention, was anywhere near a smart idea.

Anyway, kicking Haldeman's ass would be too much trouble. *Especially* if this puffed-up little bastard Card socked them with extra punishment detail for his smart mouth. It wasn't as if pulling riverside security at the main Protectors Association supply depot was the sort of work that kept the sec detail a lean, mean, fighting machine.

Mostly what Reiser and his little bunch did was try to stop pilferage. Except, of course, by duly authorized pilferers. By which he meant quartermaster corps.

Sometimes it seemed like *that* bunch's assignment was doing its utmost to prevent potentially valuable supplies from being wasted on the troops. Not that Reiser and his buddies failed to snag their share of the loot. But they thought of it as getting back for the little guy.

Fort Thor was the grandiose name for a facility that was double-large, in the geographic sense, what with having to accommodate goods transhipments and storage, meaning flatboats and wags. Most of the personnel complement was just cargo handlers, which meant troops from the Protectors Army told to do pretty much the same sort of backbreaking grunt work for the barons they did in their civilian life.

As such, it wasn't a bad billet. Some of them got fed more regularly at the mess than back at the manor. And at least in Reiser's experience the chow was better. Or at least consistently moderately shitty, which was an improvement over what you got if the baron was cheap or had dropped an unusually large wad gambling with his or her bids, or the supervisors woke up on the wrong side of the cot that morning.

As the main shore-head and resupply point for the whole grand and glorious Protectors Army it would be a prime target for a sheepherders' attack. Except of course it was miles behind the front lines, with pretty much the whole of said army between the Uplanders and it.

Except this night. This new mercie squad the sheepherders had hired was supposed to visit them. Reiser had already heard that, too. Of course, scuttlebutt was faster than official military intelligence, and consistently more reliable.

"So is it true, Lieutenant Card?" Private Coonts asked. "The general's got a spy in the Sheepfucker HQ?"

Of course, dumb-ass, Reiser wanted to snarl. Just like Al's got spies in Jed's tent. It's not like we look any different from each other, or talk a different lingo or something.

Card smiled and laid a finger alongside his long nose. He had a long skinny face for a guy who appeared to be carrying that big a cannonball in the gut area of his blue uniform blouse, which was of course immaculate and fresh. Nothing but the best for the men in the rear with the gear. Reiser had no idea what that gesture meant and knew damn well Card didn't, either. Reiser had read about it in old books. For Card to have done likewise would imply he knew how to read, which Reiser wasn't ready to concede.

"I only know what little I pass on to you men," the lieutenant said importantly. "But I can tell you that the mercies are planning to sneak into the fort by hijacking a wag deadheading empty barrels back to the boats for hauling back downstream."

Which, of course, happened all the time, at pretty much every hour of the day or night. Making it, Private Reiser had to privately concede, at least a double-shrewd scam. Except for them blurting it out under the ears of Bismuth Toth's paid traitor in Baron Al's court, of course.

"Word is, they're gonna be hiding inside. Then in the middle of the night they'll creep out and blow the powder stocks. Just like the Trojan Horse."

He grinned. "Except they're never gonna get through the gate! A troop of First Battalion's gonna make sure of that!"

"So what do you want us to do, Lieutenant?" Coonts asked.

Card smiled wider. "Nothing at all, gentlemen," he said. "The higher-ups just didn't want you panicking when the balloon went up. For tonight, you can all stand easy and let the glory boys from the pony troop earn their jack!"

Reiser felt his eyebrows rise. "Well, that's a first, Lieutenant," he blurted. "You've given us some good news for once."

"READY," SERGEANT Clancy whispered as the wag approached the outer perimeter. The sprawling camp was ringed about on the landward side with double rows of razor tape and barbed wire, depending obviously on how much of what variety scabbie had been available when a specific section went up.

The idea, or so Trooper Brown and his eager comrades thought, was to crouch hidden in the dark behind barrels and stacked crates just inside the inner wire, while every fourth man from A Troop held his and his mates' horses in a space behind the blacksmith shop and a warehouse where they couldn't be seen from the gate. But where they were ready for the troop hiding in ambush to mount up and ride down survivors of their little turnabout surprise.

The covered wag rumbled forward into the lights of big lanterns that flanked the gates. The first set of guards pulled up the barrier, per routine. The wag proceeded into the ten-yard space between it and the next gate, which stayed shut.

The team of four horses bobbed their heads in agitation. Long-time veterans of the run, they knew this wasn't how it was supposed to go.

As barriers, neither was much, though wags loaded with sandbags could be rolled out to block the inner entrance in case of serious threat. For regular operations the barriers were pretty nominal: a couple of ancient metal light standards, too brittle to be worth chopping up for scrap. They wouldn't actually hold back much, certainly not the mass of a full-size cargo wag, even one carrying nothing but empty barrels. But horses wouldn't push against a visible barrier unless they knew it would open, the way they learned the gates of their stalls would. So the relatively flimsy barriers blocked horse-drawn progress as effectively as a reinforced-concrete wall.

At once the driver, a crusty old man with a hat battered to shapelessness with a ratty old cock-pheasant tail feather stick in it, started looking around, his eyes as wild as his bushy gray beard.

"That's suspicious behavior if I ever saw it," muttered Corporal Rollins, crouched to Trooper Brown's right.

"Stand your ground and prepare to be searched!" cried the troop commander, Captain Morris.

"Wait! No! Please!" The wag driver began to wave his hands desperately, causing his ragged sleeves to flap like cavalry pennons in a stiff breeze. "Please, don't hurt me! I'm not in this! They made me! I'm only doin' it 'cause they got blasters on me—"

In response to his words a muzzle-flash bloomed in unmistakable orange fire out in the black of the bottomlands. By the way the shot's sound hit Brown's ears a beat later, it wouldn't be more than one or two hundred yards out.

"We're under attack!" the captain roared. "Open fire!"

With enthusiastic obedience, Trooper Brown pulled the trigger of his longblaster. The brass butt-plate of his replica Spencer repeating carbine slammed his shoulder as a giant yellow flame and a big cloud of smoke erupted out the muzzle. He jacked the lever action, feeding in a fresh .56-caliber rimfire cartridge, specially loaded back in Hugoville, into the chamber from the 7-round tubular magazine.

The old wagoneer was still waving hysterically. "No!" he shrieked, his voice soaring even over the slamming blasts of the weps to either side of Trooper Brown. "Them barrels ain't empt—"

A white flash swallowed the old man, the wag, the team.

Before Trooper Brown could do more than blink at the glare and feel a kiss of warmth on his downy-bearded young face, the white light swallowed him, too.

AT THE ENORMOUS FLASH, followed rapidly by a head-splitting crack of explosion, J.B. turned a wicked grin to Jak, who was crouched beside him in the darkness at the water's edge.

"Oh, shoot, did Ryan say we'd steal a wagload of *empty* barrels in front of whoever the spy at Uplander HQ is? What a damn shame."

Jak grinned back. Like the Armorer, he had averted his eyes from the direction of the front gate of the compound they'd infiltrated by canoe, floating down the broad yet shallow Des Moines River, to preserve his night vision. Now they opened to mirror the orange dance of flames from the wreck of the powder wag.

It hadn't been even half a challenge to find a fully loaded powder wag, headed out from the supply base to the Protectors camp, given how insatiable an army's appetite for gunpowder was. And Jed was shrewd enough to stockpile what he could between battles.

Nor had it been hard to jack the wag, especially since they were miles behind the army's lines. And if there was any special alert it would concern the unloaded wags heading back south to send the barrels home to Hugoville to get filled up again. And it had been a breeze for J.B., cool hand that he was with explosives, to rig up percussion caps to the barrels in convenient locations to be hit by incoming bullets—from Ryan's Scout longblaster, if the fort's defenders inexplicably hadn't obliged. As naturally they had. Ricky had been a help, too, even suggesting a few little twists of his own. Handy, that boy, J.B. thought.

Now he was hiding in some weeds near the water with as good a lookout on the supply base's waterfront as J.B. had thought decent to give him. He was out of sight of both J.B. and Jak, but ready to give support while his two companions did the necessary.

The wag blowing up was the signal to commence. J.B. hoped the blast had killed enough of the troops hiding out to await the raiders—just as Ryan had predicted—and discombobulated the survivors enough Ryan could slip away safely into the night to where Krysty, Mildred and Doc waited with their horses. He had reckoned it was worth the risk to fire at least one shot from his longblaster to make sure the Protectors lying in ambush opened up first and asked questions… never, as it turned out.

But it was Ryan's plan, all the way. And even if J.B. had been a man inclined to worry, worrying about the one-eyed man was the last way he'd waste his valuable time. The man just had a way of surviving, no matter what.

Now it was up to J.B. and Jak. The Armorer checked the load in his Smith & Wesson M-4000 scattergun. Although to save their relatively rare and valuable smokeless ammo, they all were using scabbied black powder weapons as much as possible. Jak was toting a Schofield double-action replica revolver in place of his favored Python handblaster, which mattered little to him since he planned on blade-work alone this night. Where needed, they were still willing to burn up their more modern cartridges and shells.

"Let's go," J.B. said softly.

Just like that, they vanished into the darkness.

ALTHOUGH HE WAS pretty much the width of the whole sprawling supply depot away from the explosion, it stunned Private Reiser. No doubt it was the sheer sudden shock of the event, as well as the head-smashing noise that left his ears ringing and the flash that had left giant purple balloons drifting across his vision.

He was walking the usual beat around the wooden and concrete docks where the supplies were offloaded and the various empties were put back on the shallow-draft barges, pushed upstream by small steam tugs, for the much easier trip back down the Des Moines to Hugoville. They kept to the lantern-lit area between the docks and the warehouses. The perimeter extended much farther to the riverbank, for reasons nobody ever bothered to explain to Reiser. But the higher-ups didn't deem it worth anybody's trouble to patrol the empty grass and weeds along the bank, when all anybody would care about was the storage areas or maybe the shops where tugs in need of repair got fixed.

His partner this night was Haldeman. Smart-ass though he was, Haldeman was a pretty clever soldier. He'd seen combat in the Grand Army's infantry before a muzzle-loader ball glancing off his hip relegated him to light duty.

But as he thought about it, there was probably no better man in the Fort Thor sec-man contingent to have at your back when the shit-hammer actually fell. And for the first time in his stint there, Private Reiser found himself thinking about it, as he tried to gather his reeling senses.

At his side Haldeman was snapping into action despite the blood that trickled from his left ear beneath his kepi-style cap, the one nearer to his partner. He had his own Spencer in his hands—a personal blaster that he'd brought with him to Fort Thor, having somehow managed to keep it from being stolen by orderlies at the field hospital after he got blasted at Third Greasy

Creek—and was looking toward the flames brightening up the sky above the roofs of the buildings between them and the camp entrance, looking for attackers.

Suddenly his head snapped forward. He sprawled on his face on the camp road, which fairly constant resurfacing with gravel couldn't keep the far more constant wag wheels from wearing ruts into. He fell gracelessly atop his blaster and lay still.

For a moment Private Reiser just stared down at his buddy with his mouth hanging open. Even without the stupefying shock of the bomb blast to knock him double-stupe, he would've had a hard time assimilating that twist of events. For all the carillon going off yet in his ears, he knew he'd have heard a blaster going off nearby.

Haldeman's kepi had fallen off, and in the lantern light there was no missing the big round hole, dark and oozing darkly shining fluid, in the back of the veteran's close-cropped head.

Reiser wasn't that stunned. Whether he'd heard it or not, somebody'd just blasted his buddy in the brain-pan. He ran, stumbling, down the short block to the corner of a dark warehouse, around into the narrow space between it and a carriage shop. A terrible sight stopped him dead.

A ghost stood there—or somebody as white as one, with white hair hanging almost to the shoulders of a jacket that glittered strangely in the flame light. Somebody small enough to be taken for a kid stared at Reiser with eyes that showed unmistakably the color of blood.

His eyes traveled down and they took in the big bowie knife jutting from a chalk-white hand, its deepbelled blade dripping blood, and the body lying face-down by the intruder's feet.

They looked at each other.

"Run," the stranger ordered.

Reiser ran.

Chapter Fifteen

Baron Al staggered into his quarters upstairs at the Lenkmans' house. He was way more intoxicated by fatigue than he was the booze he'd taken on board during the course of the evening—even the extra bottle of what claimed to be scabbied Jack Daniel's Black he'd sucked down after another screaming fight with Jessie Rae at dinner led to her storming out to spend the night with some of her officers'-wives pals camped under canvas on the house's grounds.

So he was expecting to be alone when he entered his bedroom. It wasn't that unusual an experience, anyway. Jessie Rae didn't much care to pass the night in the same bed with her husband these days. Said his snoring and tossing and turning made it hard to sleep.

Come to that, she didn't spend much time in his bed with him for other purposes, either. But that was a situation that would have to wait for peace to get addressed. Like so many others.

It took him three tries to light the kerosene lamp on the chest of drawers just inside the bedroom door with his pocket striker. He scorched his right thumb in the process. Jessie Rae would have scolded him. He had orderlies to do such menial tasks for him, to say nothing of the Lenkmans. But he thought damned little of a grown man who couldn't tuck his own broad ass away to sleep at night. How could he manage a ville, much less an army, if he couldn't keep his own house in order?

Of course, that thought might raise certain questions in relation to his wife, which he would try to keep from his mind this night, thank you very much. He needed to sleep so he could address what seemed like the whole new world of problems the morning would dump on his doorstep.

He turned...and stopped dead, his blood temperature dropping like a stone.

It took him a moment to recognize the lone intruder sitting in his chair as the one-eyed boss of the gang of mercies he'd hired on to do commando-style dirty work against the Protectors. When it did, the fact little reassured him. The man was clearly a coldheart.

And the very nature of mercies was that their loyalty—and their blasters—were available to hire.

"Back away off the trigger, Baron," Ryan said quietly. "You and me need to talk. Man-to-man—and in private."

"RAD-BLAST IT!" Baron Jed screamed. "Rad-blast all of them. And rad-blast all of you triple-stupe bastards for letting them make idiots of us time and again!"

At some level Jed Kylie knew he was out of control, but he'd been working up a good head of rage recently. The fact that this night's vigil had been a time of growing anticipation of the best of news—not just that the marauders who'd been such a burr in the bunghole of his Grand Army had at last been zeroed out, but that the murderers of his poor dear boy had been brought to justice.

If he struck real luck, some of them would even be captured alive, and dragged back here to face the most protracted and painful retribution his fevered yet fertile mind could devise.

Instead it had all turned into a chamber pot full of fermenting shit. As their spy in Baron Al's camp reported, the raiders had struck Fort Thor, their key transhipment point for supplies dragged up the river from Hugoville. Only the reported infiltration attack hadn't been a Trojan horse—*that,* they expected—but a trap of a different sort.

The hijacked wag had contained full barrels of powder, cunningly covered in percussion caps, apparently held to the outsides of staves with windings of cloth, so that incoming bullets would set the whole thing off in one gigantic blast. It had wiped out a quarter of the elite cavalry troop he'd had waiting to ambush the raiders.

Worse, because he could get more men to fire blasters for him far more easily than he could the powder to make them blast, the concealed bomb had served as a diversion. While all eyes were on the front of the camp, a handful of coldhearts had slipped in the back, chilled the sec men who got in the way and blown up a whole warehouse full of gunpowder. A couple nearby warehouses had been flattened in the process, torching or scattering everything from replacement uniforms to a week's supply of hardtack.

The glorious anticipated success had turned into the worst setback yet. Worse than the whole Uplander Army had managed to hand the Association in open battle in a generation, in ways.

Hours after receiving the news, and the sun not yet daring to show its red eye on the baron's righteous wrath, Jed was still pacing his headquarters tent raging at subordinates. His fury wasn't near played out yet.

The only reason he wasn't having somebody tortured to death in front of him for allowing this whole colossal screw-up to happen was that he couldn't settle on who he blamed *most*. Though Jed was sorely tempted to hang the collar on that pallid scar-faced sec boss of his. Colonel Toth was looking even paler than usual, his seam scar nearly blue-white, and he kept half murmuring, half hissing excuses that masqueraded as factual observations in a way that was actually stoking his baron's nuke-red anger.

But the bloodless sec boss was useful. Not even in the throes of his tantrum did Jed lose sight of *that*. And also both the sec boss and his master had taken certain measures to secure themselves against each other. It was a sort of mutual assured destruction arrangement. Even though Jed Kylie wasn't a man to accumulate useless knowledge for its own sake, he was well aware how *that* turned out for the U.S. and its rival, the Soviets, back in the day.

"I've dispatched men to detain the commander of Fort Thor," Toth said. "Perhaps when he arrives you can find...*satisfaction* grilling him."

Jed's brows pressed down so hard in a frown he was hardly able to see out his own eyes, which he was well aware were on the squinting side to begin with. Major Gray Linds was the officer commanding Fort Thor. He was also a major Association landowner, a baron in his own right and one of Jed's key supporters. It was why he'd pulled such an ace billet.

What Jed wanted to do was turn around and rip his sec boss a new one for suggesting Jed scapegoat a

man he could no more afford to alienate than he could
Cody himself, a fact the too-elegant colonel was well
aware of. But no matter how tempestuous his nature
Jed Kylie never quite let himself lose control of it altogether. That part of him that kept him alive in spite of
the inevitable intrigue among the wealthy and powerful
Association—the landowners, rich merchants and argu-
able barons being the only ones who counted a spent,
bent casing, after all—reminded him now he couldn't
really afford to blurt anything about his reasons for not
stepping too hard on Lind's neck, either.

Toth was far from imperceptive. His own watery
blue eyes widened slightly at the laserlike focus of his
baron's fury. Impossibly his face got even whiter.

Then a junior officer appeared at his elbow. He whispered something into the colonel's ear.

Jed prepared to unload the full force of his fury
on this subordinate. The protection Toth had secured
for himself didn't extend to his flunkies. And Jed,
whose sec staff wasn't so vast he didn't know at least
a bit about all its members, was aware this particular
man came from a very modest family of little conse-
quence—scarcely better than a tenant himself. There
was very little downside to scapegoating him.

But even as he pried open his trapdoor lips to pro-
nounce doom on the junior officer, Jed noticed some
color had returned to Toth's gaunt cheeks. That checked
him at least momentarily.

Which was enough for the colonel, now smooth as
oil on raw sewage, to say in a much more assertive tone
than he'd been using previously, "Baron, I've been informed we have a visitor from the Uplanders' camp. I
think you'll want to hear what he has to say at once."

For a moment Jed glowered at his subordinate. He twitched the hot glare briefly to the junior officer, who gratifyingly seemed on the verge of bursting into flame from sheer horror. Then he fixed it rigidly on Toth, who bore up unwilting; he was used to it.

What are you trying to pull now, you sneaky little shit? Jed thought. But he said, "Bring him on."

Even in advance of Toth's imperious wave the subordinate scampered out. An eyeblink later he came back squiring a plump brown-bearded figure wearing a uniform turned inside out.

Baron Jed couldn't help it. He burst into laughter. He knew why his spy had done it—to prevent any random Protector patrols he encountered in no-man's-land from blasting him on sight, to say nothing of main camp guards whose trigger fingers were understandably most itchy after the night's escapades. But the fact he had literally turned his coat was just too much for the baron to keep his composure.

If he couldn't find outlet for his rage any other way, he'd laugh his fool head off like a hyena. He was the nuking baron, after all.

The major was a man who managed to appear mousy despite his portliness, a chubby mouse, mebbe. His brown eyes widened at his baron's outburst.

But Toth, having given his master a few moments until the edge of hysteria came off his laughter, smiled thinly.

"You might wish to wait to laugh until you hear what our Major Bear has to say, General," he said.

Jed choked the laughter right off. "Tell me," he snapped, all business.

▼ If offer card is missing write to: The Reader Service, P.O. Box 1867, Buffalo, NY 14240-1867 or visit www.ReaderService.com ▼

NO POSTAGE
NECESSARY
IF MAILED
IN THE
UNITED STATES

BUSINESS REPLY MAIL
FIRST-CLASS MAIL   PERMIT NO. 717   BUFFALO, NY

POSTAGE WILL BE PAID BY ADDRESSEE

THE READER SERVICE

PO BOX 1867

BUFFALO NY 14240-9952

Bear's Adam's apple rode up and down beneath his beard in a convulsive swallow. He nodded.

"It's Baron Al," he said. "He's...out of it."

"Wait," Jed said. "What? What do you mean 'out of it'?"

"Incapacitated," the spy said. "Mebbe dead, even. Nobody knows. It's all rumor now."

"What do you actually know, then, Major?" Jed asked, in tones that could have left the spy, already quaking, in no doubt that he was on thin ice.

"What I saw with my own eyes, Baron," Bear said. "When Cawdor and the others got back from their raid on Fort Thor, he got to partying hearty. You know how Al is, Baron. He started whooping and hollering and slamming the booze straight from the bottle.

"Until he stiffened like he got a 'lectric shock. His eyes rolled up in his head, and he fell straight down like he'd taken a ball to the back of the head. Was all thrashing and foaming in his beard when a bunch of staff monkeys carried him out. And since then the whole command structure of the Uplander Army's gone to shit.

"Nobody knows which end is up or who's in charge. It's total chaos, Baron. Total chaos!"

Jed stared at him for a moment, then looked around at the cloud of anxious officers hovering around him.

"Mobilize the army," he said. "Get everyone who can hoist a blaster up on his pins and be ready to march. Get the artillery and the supply wags hitched up and rolling north. Get the cavalry out screening them. The foot sloggers can march past them if they get rolling first."

"What are you doing, Baron?" Toth demanded in something like alarm.

"Putting an end to this war once and for fucking all," he said. "We'll smash the Uplanders so bad we can reclaim what the bastards stole from my granddaddy.

"Action this day, gentlemen! We march to final victory."

Chapter Sixteen

"Quo vadis, domine?"

Jed Kylie looked in frank irritation at Snake Eye, who had without ceremony—much less permission— just taken his place riding his gleaming black gelding flank-to-flank with the baron's chestnut stallion in the very midst of his cortege. The baron of Hugoville rode at the head of the Grand Army of the Des Moines River Valley Cattlemen's Protective Association, although he had a cavalry troop out scouting the way ahead.

"I'm not even gonna ask how you managed to get past all the aides and sec men who are supposed to keep the rabble away from my skinny august ass," Kylie said. "But I will ask what the glowing night shit that was you asked me?"

"It meant, 'Whither goest thou, Lord,'" Snake Eye said. "A classical allusion. A weakness of mine."

"I'm guessing you're not just along to help me enjoy the morning sunshine," the baron said.

"No, indeed. Although it is a fine, fair morning."

It was. The sky was blue and brushed with fluffy horsetails of cloud. The only off note was a line of cloud above the Western horizon, black with an ominous orange tint that the sun was just too high in the sky to explain away as dawn light. It might be that the valley was due for a thunderstorm, if not one of its infrequent acid-rain storms.

"Well?" Cody snapped from the baron's other elbow—his left.

He was visibly not pleased by Snake Eye's sudden appearance out of nowhere. Although Snake Eye found it hardly mysterious, to his own private amusement. The aides and sec men all knew the tall, lean man with the black hat, the yellowish cast to his skin and the black eye patch was the baron's personal hired assassin.

And there was that in Snake Eye's manner that didn't encourage forwardness of any sort in those whom he encountered.

"I came to ask a question," Snake Eye said. "Which I have duly asked."

"Let me ask a question," Jed said sternly. "Why haven't you chilled that bastard coldheart Cawdor and his murdering friends yet?"

"That is no easy task, Baron," Snake Eye said with his standard calm. "How successful have your shiny sec boss and all your brave soldiers been on that front of late?"

"Impertinence!" Toth hissed. "General, one word. One word and my men will have him down and be peeling the scaly hide right off him!"

Snake Eye bent his head forward to show the man a smile. "Feel free to try that, Colonel," he said, tipping his black hat.

An uncharacteristic grin warped Jed's rumpled features.

"I feel too good to take offense at what he says, Bismuth," he said. "Which is true, anyway. Not that that's anything a man should count on as an offense. A baron's privilege is the foundation of an orderly society. Without it we'd have anarchy."

"We certainly can't have that, Baron," Snake Eye agreed.

"As for what I'm doing, isn't it obvious? I'm leading my troops to put paid to the Uplands Alliance once and for all. Or hadn't you heard? Their commanding general, Baron Al, partied himself into a stroke last night when he heard about my powder warehouse blowing up, and fell down stone-paralyzed. Which, about now, the entire Uplander Army should be too."

"Indeed," Snake Eye said. "I can see how one would draw such conclusions, certainly. Still, don't you think a certain degree of caution is in order?"

"Caution?" Jed laughed. "When the greatest opportunity of a lifetime lies before me? I think not."

Snake Eye shrugged. "It is, as you say, your prerogative. So I'll take my leave of you, Baron. As for my contract with you, I continue to pursue it. At my own pace. And with guaranteed results. I always fulfill a contract."

He tipped his hat. "Good day, Baron, gentlemen… Colonel."

"Are you sure you don't at least want to stick around and watch?" Jed called after him as he turned his horse off the road to trot across a fallow cornfield. "It's going to be historical. The decisive stroke will be struck today!"

"No doubt it will be decisive, Baron," Snake Eye said, and spurred the black gelding to a gallop between the broken stalks.

SNAKE EYE FOUND a vantage point in the second story of a derelict barn. The associated farmhouse had had its

stone walls half-caved-in by cannonballs at some point
during the wars. A fire had completed its ruination by
burning through the ceiling beams and letting the roof
cave in. The barn, which was wood and corrugated
sheet metal, remained mostly intact, occupied largely
by dust, and the ghosts of smells of mildew and long-
rotted hay. Not a recent casualty, apparently.

The barn, like its ruined farmhouse, stood on what
passed for a height on these bottomlands—more a fold
in the grassy land. Its second-story hatch looked to the
east, where with the aid of his telescoping brass spyglass he was able to get a decent view of Baron Kylie's
army marching along the road a mile or so to the east.

Doffing his coat and spreading it on the warped
floorboards, Snake Eye sat to enjoy the show.

"WELL, MAJOR," Colonel Toth said, "are you eager to
see your former comrades get their comeuppance?"

The baron raised an eyebrow at that. It seemed his
sec boss was piling it on the turncoat Uplander. Major
Bear's round, bearded face, which was already damp
with perspiration—the morning, though far from hot,
was definitely humid with the river anchoring their
flank not a quarter-mile east—suddenly had its forehead dotted with fresh little domes glinting in the sun.

The head of the Grand Army had just passed the
halfway point between the rival encampments. Bear
had swapped his Uplander uniform for a dove-gray
coat over a dark gray vest and trousers. Though Jed
had told him he was accompanying the Grand Army
on its march in order to provide additional assurance he
brought accurate information, Jed had allowed him to
change clothes as well as getting himself a fresh mount

before setting out. Jed reckoned there was less likeli-
hood of him getting targeted in the heat of action—by
his new Protector friends by accident, or by his erstwhile Uplander comrades by vengeful design.

Bear stammered something Jed couldn't make out.
As part of his sec-boss duties, Colonel Toth was naturally the Protector spy-master. It came to Jed to wonder
just what hold his master spider had over the Uplander,
to get him to betray the very people he'd grown up
among. Whatever it was, Toth was tweaking him with
it now and smirking in sadistic delight.

"Frankly, sir," Bear said, working his way up from
mumble to bluster, "I feel—"

His head vanished. A roar like a full-bore twister
howled by. A hard blast of wind slammed Baron Jed
on the side of his head.

As his horse reared and he reeled in the saddle, he
saw blood shoot up like a red geyser from the stump of
Major Bear's neck. He heard a flat, hard crack like a big
board being split clean across by a sledgehammer strike.

The major's tubby torso still sat bolt-upright, reins
still prissily upheld in a gloved right hand. Then his red
roan mare jumped and hopped as the hot blood splashed
onto her neck. The body fell away. The pumps of blood
from the headless neck were dwindling visibly as he
fell out of sight.

A strong arm caught Jed around the waist. "Get the
general to cover!" Colonel Toth shouted.

With wiry strength the colonel hauled Jed out of
his saddle. The baron kicked and screamed curses and
threats. Holding the baron against his side, legs bicy-
cling, the sec boss rode his own horse off the road and
into the weeds of the ditch.

Jed snapped back into control of himself. Even as his sec chief handed him off to bodyguards who had already dismounted, he was screaming for the infantry and artillery to deploy, and for the cavalry to advance and wipe out the blasters.

Before a sec man unceremoniously pushed him facedown in the muddy weeds at the bottom of the ditch, he saw a horse torn in two as if by a giant hand, twenty yards ahead up the road. A second cannonball screamed by. It bounced again somewhere behind. The screams Jed heard then were from men and animals.

Nuke take it, he thought. He reckoned he knew what happened. The Uplanders, fearing just such a move from their mortal foe, had sent one or more of their pair of massive twentieth-century-made replica Parrott cannon south to delay the Protector advance as long as they could. Weighing in at over a ton each, the enormous beasts could hurl twenty-pound projectiles with some accuracy more than two miles. Though both sides relied mainly on a couple dozen Napoleon twelve-pounder smoothbores, backed by a couple of three-inch Ordnance rifled cannon, the Association possessed only one of the long-range Parrotts.

The weapons were well suited for indirect fire, to a map reference or in response to signals sent by a forward observer, by means of flag or heliograph. A week or two before both sides had bombarded the tiny ville of Taint in no-man's-land, each under the mistaken impression the other was about to occupy the place. That episode ineffectually ended a brief stint in which both armies maneuvered to try to gain an advantage over each other, at the unsuccessful conclusion of which they both pulled back to their existing lines to try to work out what to do next.

That fat bastard's Al's providential stroke had shown Jed what to do now.

The Uplander blasters were clearly set to fire down the direct road—like triple-big sniper rifles. Jed judged whomever had ordered them out had sent both, given how close together the shots came. They were muzzle-loaders, like all the cannon used by both sides. The rifling grooves in their over three-and-a-half-inch bores made them slow to reload.

Realizing at that point that another shot from the ambuscade was a ways off, Jed shook off the well-meaning bodyguards who were trying to keep him under cover, to look up the road. Spotting where the blasters were sited was no great task: two localized clouds of dirty white smoke hung to either side of the road, about three-quarters of a mile ahead.

He watched his cavalry sweeping forward in two blocks to left and right. Though an attack was only really likely from the west or left flank—and only remotely, under the circumstances—Jed had ordered half his horse troopers to cover the right flank as well, riding between the road and the river, about a quarter mile to the east. He wanted to be able to get all his cavalry into action as quickly as possible once battle was joined, which required them to be split in two.

As he looked, Jed saw a white flash from near the base of the left-hand cloud, from a green smudge that suggested a stand of trees, a woodlot or an orchard. The shot whistle-roared overhead to strike the long blue column a couple hundred yards south.

Though he knew that ball had likely smashed up

more of his men and horses, Jed smiled in grim satisfaction. Horrifyingly accurate though the big Parrotts could be, especially when fired by the wickedly proficient Uplander gunners, they didn't hit moving targets for sour-owl shit. Between that and his slowness, the Protector cavalry would certainly take them both down quickly without taking much damage.

And now that his marching troops were ducking off the roadway into the ditch they'd be much less vulnerable to the bounding projectiles. Both sides had explosive shells, which would be marginally more effective against troops in cover. But because they had access to nothing like predark fusing technology, the things were unpredictable at best—most likely to explode ineffectually in midflight or not at all. And occasionally in the barrel of the weapon that fired them. Or—potentially worse—a yard or so past the muzzle.

His supply wags—and his own artillery train, including his own giant Parrott blaster—were far more vulnerable. But he consoled himself that the enemy superblasters would soon be silenced. *Forever.*

"Now watch this, Bismuth," he said excitedly to his sec boss, who squatted inelegantly next to him with his spit-polished riding boots buried to the insteps in the mud of the ditch bottom. "Those rad-blasted rifled cannons have been a pain in our butts for two generations! Now they're going to be ours. And once my cavalry sweeps this delay away—"

Fifty yards ahead of both wings of cavalry, still too far from the concealed blasters to charge and advancing at a lope, the very Earth seemed to erupt in stabs of yellow flame and puffs of smoke. Horses reared and

fell thrashing to the ground. Others fled with emptied
saddles.

From the left came a bigger, brighter flash. A giant
invisible fist seemed to punch a hole in the advancing
cavalry line as twelve pounds of musket balls with random bits of metal scrap hit them.

Just like that the Grand Army's glorious cavalry
were streaming back south, far faster than they'd been
going north an eyeblink before.

Through the roaring of his ears, louder than the longblasters of his men lying in hiding, louder than the
blasters, louder even than the screams of unendurable
agony, Baron Jed heard Colonel Toth utter the most unnecessary words he'd ever heard in his life.

"It's a trap!"

WITH A GRIN Snake Eye snapped his spyglass back to
a short tube and packed it away in its protective black
velvet carrying bag.

He wasn't especially surprised by the turn of events,
although he suspected there were even more surprises
in store for his current employer and associates. Such
as when the body of Uplander cavalry he'd spotted a
few moments before, winging around to the west, hit
the disorganized and already demoralized Grand Army
in the left flank.

He didn't need to see any more. He enjoyed watching explosions and violence as much as any man, but
the script for this old-days action vid was too familiar.

Plus he had a good idea how it all came out.

Hearing the crash of battle—or one-sided slaughter,
to give it its proper name—crashing to a crescendo, he
turned, climbed gingerly down a rickety wooden lad-

der and reclaimed his black gelding from where it was tethered in the stall. He rubbed its soft muzzle and blew up its nostrils briefly to reassure it. The animal was used to blasterfire, but not exactly on this scale, even at some distance away. And not impossibly some shift in the sluggish breeze had brought a hint of the spilled blood of fellow equines to its sensitive nose.

Regarding the massacre's outcome, the only real question in his mind was what the Association would be able to preserve of its Grand Army. If anything. As to the fate of his employer...well, Baron Jed wasn't conspicuously lovable, even by the notably unlovable standards of barons. Nor did he seem to go out of his way to be so.

And whether Jed lived or died made little difference. Snake Eye would find more of his specialized kind of mercie work, in more abundance than even a craftsman at his level of mastery could actually handle.

He would carry out his contract, though. He always carried out his contracts.

But at his own time, as he had so recently told the unfortunate baron. Snake Eye had his own priorities.

With his horse's tail high in agitation he loped away to the west. He had treasure to find.

And prey to play with. Because in many ways, his name and slightly scaly skin notwithstanding, Snake Eye was more like a cat than an actual snake.

Chapter Seventeen

The soldiers, some in green shirts, most identified by the green rags tied around their upper arms, were finishing off the badly wounded with quick, decisive thrusts of fixed bayonets. Or occasionally strokes from a brass-clad blaster butt.

Mildred winced as she rode with her friends from where they'd watched the battle. It had been north of the line where Baron Al had deployed his infantry and lighter, smoothbore artillery along a shallow stream. It had also been east of the Uplander Army.

J.B. had expressed reservations about the possibility of getting caught between either a battle or a streaming rout and the river if things turned sour for their side. But Ryan wanted them in position to move on the enemy if they could do their employer some good. He wanted to be on the other side from the Uplander cavalry launching its sneak attack, and he was fully confident in their ability to travel along the riverbank as need be. To which J.B. nodded and concurred, and the matter was done.

They rode openly down the road. When Uplander foot soldiers examining chills or looting wags saw them, they stopped to cheer. Krysty smiled and waved. Doc doffed his hat and waved like a late-nineteenth century politician on a stump tour. Ricky looked as embarrassed as Mildred herself felt; Jak, J.B. and Ryan sat as stone-faced as if they were watching mud dry in the sun after a brief shower, only occasionally nodding acknowledgment.

Halfway down the column Baron Al, himself dressed in his shapeless trousers and a dirty undershirt, sat in the box of a covered wag. The surviving horse had been released from its harness and presumably run away. What was left of its teammates…

Mildred had to look away. It was irrational, she knew, but she was of necessity inured, relatively, to human suffering. The suffering of animals always hit her hard.

At least these horses weren't suffering anymore. And if the level of trauma was any guide—and though no veterinarian, Mildred was pretty sure it was—they couldn't have suffered long.

Despite the fact that he sat surrounded by the outcome of the most one-sided victory in a generation, possibly the whole family saga of a war, the winning commander was being harangued by his chief lieutenant, who stood in the road next to the wag with his hat off and a saber still in his gloved right hand.

"But how could you hold us back, General?" Colonel Turnbull was saying. His leanly handsome face was twisted in what seemed authentic emotional agony. "We could have smashed the Grand Army once and for all!"

Lips clamped stubbornly inside his black beard, which was even less kempt than usual, Al shook his head.

"That won't answer, Cody," he said. "And you know it. Once the cavalry came in they took off pretty fast. And some of the units toward the rear in the column in good order. Had we sent the cavalry against them, their blasters would've ripped our boys and beasts up bad."

"And to what end?"

He gestured panoramically with a big hand.

"We killed the devils, plenty of them. We got most of their supply train, most of their artillery. Even their own lone big Parrott. They're not a threat to the Alliance Army any more this year. Far less to the people of the Alliance herself. Not this season, not this year. Probably not for years to come."

"But we could have ended the war for good, General," Turnbull persisted.

"Is there really any such thing, Cody?" Al asked with a gentleness that surprised Mildred. "You know better than that. Even if we bagged Baron Jed, even if we caught him and all his barons, what then? Association territory is bigger than ours. We could kill every man who was on this road today, and their total population would still be twice ours or more. We couldn't conquer them. Not without bleeding ourselves dry in a hopeless never-ending war to beat them down. That could only end with us so weak they'd likely turn the tables on us, and we'd be back under *their* boot heels again."

Al stopped, then wiped sweat from his face with a grimy rag from a pocket of his drawers. He looked at the companions, who had drawn their horses to a halt a few paces from the debate and sat quietly waiting. Ryan wasn't one to yield readily to any man, but he was also smart enough to know better than to try to interrupt any argument between rival barons, which functionally Turnbull was as much as Al, without some compelling reason to do so.

"Where are my rad-blasted manners?" Al said. Mildred failed to miss the way Turnbull winced at a baron apologizing to mere hirelings. She decided she didn't much care for the colonel. "Sorry. We won big today, ladies, gentlemen, and you all made it possible. The Alliance is in your debt."

"Will you still be requiring our services, Baron?" asked Krysty, who sat on her gray mare at Ryan's right.

"No," Turnbull said. But Al laughed.

"Reckon so," he said, "though in what you might call a lower key. Jed, if he survived, his successor if he didn't, is going to dig in tight and start thinking they're in a stronger position than they are. Precisely because we can't *really* afford what it would cost us to finish them off—now, or at any time."

He added the latter without even having to look to see Turnbull opening his yap, undoubtedly to whine about how a good pursuit *could* have ended the Protectors after all.

Mildred was no history buff, no strategic or tactical mind—those were Ryan's and J.B.'s departments, and they were welcome to them. But just in these past few years she had seen enough of battles lost and won, of retreats, pursuits and sudden reversals, to know Al was basically right.

And that's yet another sad testimonial to what my life's become, she thought, though these days the realization was familiar enough to kindle little heat within her.

"We got a peace treaty to negotiate. So I reckon I need you to keep up the pressure. Just a bit, mind. Sting the Protectors' wide asses every now and then, to keep their minds right."

"And what might you have in mind in that regard, Baron?" J.B. asked.

Baron Al frowned. He looked around at the army, busy with the mop-up of action. From somewhere in the middle distance came the sound of a shot. Some of the young men of Al's ever-changing staff, who took on themselves the roles of sec men—as far as Mildred could see the Uplander commander had no official bodyguard—looked alert and started to close in from the discreet distance at which they'd hovered around their baron. Al ignored them.

"I think, what with one thing and another," Al said slyly, "I'll just leave that to you folks' discretion. Think of it as part of what I'm payin' you for."

Turnbull looked pained. "Speaking of which, Baron, is it really responsible, to make such outlays to…outland hirelings, given the costs the barons of the Alliance have absorbed already for this war?"

"Now, Cody," Al said, "wasn't it you, not hardly a moment ago, arguing we needed *more* troops runnin' around burning powder today? Whatever I paid these folks, even tossing in a nice reward for playing such a key role in this here little victory and all, it's less than the bill for powder burned in a couple minutes' decent artillery barrage, or even an average cavalry skirmish."

A troop of cavalry in green shirts and armbands came trotting up the road from the south. Their horses' coats were dark with moisture. The troopers' faces were flushed and running with the sweat of heat and exertion—and something more.

"Shadowed them back to their lines, Baron," Lieutenant Owens reported.

He had a smudge of burned powder on one cheek

and a bandage around his left forearm with some red soaking through. The battle hadn't been entirely one-sided. Then again Mildred knew too well by now, they seldom were.

"Just like you said, Jed had got 'em whipped back into pretty decent order by the time they were halfway there. Even left a few squads of foot sloggers to lay up in the weeds and snipe, keep us cautious. They're already digging in tighter behind their old emplacements."

"So Jed did survive. Told you, Cody. That little cuss is as triple-hard to kill as a cockroach."

Al nodded to the cavalryman. "Good job, son. Start spreading the word. We're shifting our own main bivouac down to the stream where we set our ambush. That'll add to the pressure on the Protectors, too."

He glared around at his young staffers, who were still holding handblasters and carbines at the alert.

"Some of the rest of you kids, too," he said, "seeing as you got nothin' better to do at the moment than protect me from imaginary Protector chillers!"

"One last thing, General," Owens said. Mildred noted that Turnbull frowned. Clearly it displeased him that a junior officer had not instantly obeyed his commander's order, for whatever reason.

But Al was unfazed. "Hit me with it."

"The Protectors pretty well rushed out of their lines this morning. That's going to work to their advantage. A lot of their supply wags and even some of their smooth-bore arty never made it past the perimeter. And even if between shooting it and losing wags they used up most of their ready powder supply, I reckon they got enough yet to make it triple-hot on us if we try to force things.

Plus it won't take all that long for Jed to get more barged back up the river from Hugoville."

"Right. Confirms what we reckoned, too. All right then, spread the word like I told you. Git!"

Lieutenant Owens and some of his fellow young officers turned to go, though large numbers of foot soldiers were drifting back to cluster around the wag where Al sat. Noticing that, the baron looked at them quizzically.

"Three cheers for the general!" a voice yelled from somewhere, "savior of the Uplands! Hip, hip, hooray!"

Hundreds of voices joined in the cheering. Hats were tossed in the air.

Baron Al grinned and nodded. When the applause subsided he rose clumsily on the wag box.

"Thanks, boys," he said. "Just doing what had to be done. Like all of you. And I must say we all did us a heap of good work today!"

They cheered that, too. Mildred noticed Ryan looking thoughtful.

As the fresh wave of acclaim subsided, Al clambered down from the driver's board. Mildred wasn't surprised to see him wave off the young staffers who had, presumably according to some kind of rotation, remained to attend him when about half their number rushed off to spread his latest orders.

"Baron," Ryan called.

Al looked up at the one-eyed man, sitting calmly on his bay horse.

"Just a word to the wise," Ryan said. "From one experienced hand to another. Once the war is won, some of the people closest to you start having second thoughts about you. Mebbe worth thinking all your enemies aren't necessarily back in the Protector camp."

Al shrugged like a tired mountain. Suddenly he *looked* tired. And old. Mildred wondered if postbattle letdown was settling in, now that the first fiery rush of combat—and victory—had passed.

"If the folks of the Alliance decide I've finished the job I got picked to do," he said, "reckon I'll abide with that. Meantime I'll go on doing what I can to secure our future, and our children's future, best I can. Always reckoned that's been my real job, all along. But thank you kindly, young man. I know those are wise words."

He turned away to put his head together with Colonel Turnbull. For all Mildred's growing dislike of the prissy officer, she did see his whole demeanor change to one of pure professional interest. At the core he was clearly a man who took his duty as seriously as his general did.

And that's supposed to be a good thing, she thought. Why does that make me think he's all the more dangerous?

FROM THE CONCEALMENT of a clump of trees by a fire-blackened field-stone chimney that was all that remained of the farmhouse, Snake Eye watched the small group ride away from the Uplander commander, south along the road a few hundred yards to the east.

With a smile he lowered his brass spyglass from his good eye and telescoped it back down to fit in its pouch.

"Enjoy your victory while you can, my friends," he said aloud. There was no need to keep his voice down; he knew no Uplander troops were within two hundred yards, and the wind carried from the river and the battlefield toward him.

He knew enough about battles, and their aftermath, to be thankful he had little sense of smell.

"You've earned it," he said, turning back to his horse. "But now *our* game begins in earnest."

Chapter Eighteen

A prairie chicken call whickered up the freshening breeze.

Sitting in a slight depression in the gently undulating grasslands between the army camps, Krysty looked up from the low yellow fire. Her hand fell to the butt of the Colt Lightning replica she had scabbied from a Protector cavalry sergeant who had no further use for it, or indeed anything.

The group, their horses and the grass alike were still damp from a rain that had fallen earlier, around the time the sun set. The smell suggested they might be getting wetter again sometime soon.

Krysty eased her hand away from her handblaster.

"Somebody coming," Ryan said. He seemed mostly to be explaining it to Ricky, who was hunkered down on the far side of the campfire next to Jak. The youngster was still getting brought up to speed on the group's protocols.

Krysty smiled. He learned quickly, though, which was one reason he'd stuck when so many temporary companions had fallen by the wayside.

Jak, who squatted next to his new friend, rose. He was almost quivering with eagerness for the chase, like a dog who scented a fox. J.B. was on watch, currently, as the group prepared to heat a supper of horse jerky and beans.

Ryan nodded in the direction from which the call had come. "Show him in," he said.

Jak vanished.

For his part Ricky jumped to his feet, clutching his beloved handmade blaster like some kind of talisman. "Where?" he whispered. "Why is everybody still sitting down?"

"Relax, son," said Doc, who sat braced on his arms with his long legs splayed out before him and the much-abused soles of his knee boots toward the wan flames. "That was no danger alert J.B. gave. Had he considered our still-mysterious nocturnal visitor a threat, he would have emulated a yellow-crowned night heron."

Ricky just looked blank.

"He's not gonna give it now," Mildred explained, "because J.B. and Jak would just think *we* were in trouble. Don't sweat it. You'll get it all figured out. All it takes is time."

From the darkness emerged not the ghost-white form of Jak Lauren, but the small yet sturdy figure of J. B. Dix. He cradled his M-4000 scattergun in his arms.

Right behind him came an old man with a white beard and hair sticking out any which way from his face, wearing a sorely battered slouch hat. He had a paunch pushing out the front of a wool shirt that had been red but had faded to pink. A pair of little donkeys, all but dwarfed beneath equipment and bagged swag, ambled behind him.

As if taken by surprise at the ancient scabbie's arrival, Ryan rose to his feet.

"Name's Ryan Cawdor," he said. "Welcome to our campfire."

"My handle's Old Pete, as in, old enough to know better. Don't piss down my leg and tell me it's raining, son. I know how the land lies. You sent this here pale young feller to escort me in whether I wanted to or not."

Ryan grinned. "Fair enough. You're still welcome— if your intent is peaceable."

"If I weren't I'd be triple-stupe to announce the fact to a campfire full of blasters," the old man said. "But it is, it is. Happens I've got a pot of cold beans and plenty of possum jerky to share, if you folks ain't et yet. And pleased at the chance for some company other than Bess and Hoovie, here."

"Possum jerky," Mildred said in tones dripping with sarcasm. "Be still my heart."

Krysty frowned at her friend in honest puzzlement.

"You talk as if you don't like possum jerky, Mildred."

"I know. What's wrong with me, huh?"

OLD PETE DROPPED the ceramic jug from his white-whiskered lips, which he wiped with the back of a liver-spotted hand.

"Ah, now," he said, amid and around a hearty belch. "That's the good stuff. Not for the young, though."

Seated next to the grizzled scabbie by the fire, Ryan nodded. He'd taken a swig of the man's Towse Lightning and promptly decided he was too young for the stuff.

Especially since he was intent on getting *older*.

Old Pete automatically passed the heavy stoneware vessel to the person who'd just squatted at his left. It was Ricky, who'd been fussing over the donkeys, where they stood hobbled and grazing near the party's horses. He had spent weeks every year traveling the southern part of his home of Monster Island with his father's trade caravan, through generally mountainous terrain where the best available transport happened to be donkeys. He clearly missed the little equines. And probably his home, as well.

Accepting the heavy jug, Ricky frowned down at it as if uncertain what to do with it. After a moment he looked up. His gaze hunted around the fire, settling on Krysty. Without changing expression the woman gave her head a slight shake.

Ricky nodded back and passed the jug to Doc, who accepted gratefully and guzzled generously, head back, Adam's apple bobbing.

Mentally, Ryan shrugged. It wasn't his concern if the kid drank the toxic stuff, as long as it didn't cause him to make mistakes when the shitstorm hit. Which was no different from how he regarded the rest of his friends. Fireblast, *he* was no stranger to gut-burning swill like that when he was the boy's age, but Krysty had her own way of doing things, and Ryan was way past questioning her judgment. If she thought the new kid should refrain, then fine. Anyway, it wasn't as if the boy didn't look relieved to let the cup pass from him.

Old Pete stared into the weak yellow flicker of the campfire as if seeing visions there.

"Just come back to these parts," he said, more as if talking to himself than company. "Got a rich trove of scabbie just lyin' out under the sun and stars, after that big battle a few days past. O' course, man's got to step pretty lively to avoid the patrols from both sides. They look on that brand of honest scabbie as looting. Take it for a shooting offense."

"You mean you've been robbing the corpses?" Ricky asked, with revulsion and outrage throbbing in his adolescent voice.

"Only makes sense, boy," said J.B., who happened to be sitting next to his apprentice. "We've done it a time or two since you been with us, remember."

"Yes, but we killed them!"

They all looked at him. Even Old Pete looked up from whatever he was seeing in the flames.

"Okay, slow down, Ricky," Mildred said. "You lost even me on that last turn, and I'm the squeamish one here."

"I—I—" Ricky waved his hands in the air. Ryan reckoned he was just outraged, and now floundering around looking for a way to justify it.

The kid was smart. Trouble was, much of that was book smart, and that made him think everything had a reason. He just needed to learn that stuff like most feelings didn't need a reason—nor have anything to do with what you knew or what you thought. They just *were*, mostly, like wind and weather. The difference was that you could sometimes control feelings.

"It's been a few days since the battle. Aren't the bodies, well—"

"Ripe?" Mildred suggested callously. When she called herself out as squeamish, she didn't mean about blood, guts or decay. Her predark training as a doctor had bashed all that kind of squeam clean out of her system.

"That's why we tend to get them while they're fresh, generally speaking," J.B. said, taking off his specs and polishing them. "Plus the fact that the early vulture gets the liver."

"But—but—"

"Give it up, kid," Mildred said. "That's a fight you'll never win."

"Amen," said Doc sorrowfully. *"O tempora, o mores!"*

"Got to admit," Pete said, "I don't much cotton to messin' with stiffs that're swole up and leakin', myself. But a man's got to keep himself from windin' up in that very state. And I need to do what I can to tide myself over."

He stopped, his old blue eyes flickering left and right.

Ryan knew trapped-animal furtiveness when he saw it.

"Here," said Doc, who had just taken another long and somewhat noisy pull from the jug. "Whet your whistle. Calm your nerves."

Ryan suppressed a grin. Old Pete was probably thinking Doc's own triple-grizzled appearance and age-husky voice made him relatively harmless. A common mistake, often made by, say, those who sat down across a gaudy-house table to play cards with Doc. Though those, at least, commonly survived the experience of underestimating the apparent old man.

Old Pete nodded and showed jumbled brown teeth in a grin. He accepted the jug and took a pull.

Ryan quickly did an eye-check to his companions. So well-attuned were they that each nodded ever-so-slightly. They quickly caught Ryan's drift, which amounted to: we've done all the drinking being sociable demands. Let's leave the rest of the liquid lubricant for our guest, see what it helps slide out of his mouth.

The only one who frowned slightly back was Ricky. J.B., noting that, put his head close to the boy's and spoke briefly. Then Ricky almost dislocated his neck bobbing his agreement.

Fortunately Old Pete was already in for a protracted swallow of Towse Lightning, and didn't notice.

The others sat and let him drink in companionable silence, which he did until he muttered, "Mebbe now we'll get peace that lasts a spell. And I can finally make the score I've been a-hopin' for for so long!"

Ryan twitched a finger. He didn't want anybody to press the old man on the issue. *Yet*. He reckoned the scabbie had something he wanted to share with others, no matter how good an idea his conscious mind knew it wasn't. He'd speak it in his own sweet time, once he'd sufficiently anesthetized his better judgment with repeated applications of rotgut.

Or he wouldn't. And Ryan and company would be no poorer than they had been before Old Pete wandered in out of the night, probably sensing their campfire despite their efforts to keep it discreet, and hungering for human companionship. But Ryan had never known a man, woman, or mutie to catch a fish by yanking the hook out of the water before the creature took it in its mouth.

"Found the mother lode, I did," Old Pete said.

Chapter Nineteen

"Or anyways," the ancient scabbie went on, "what might *be* the mother lode. An old-days fortification, buried underground. Don't reckon anybody's been in there since whoever was in it last from the time before the Big Nuke. Wandered inside with my lantern. Solid walls all of concrete. Found some offices and cubbies that still had stuff in the drawers and mugs on the desk. From the black crap caked at the bottom they'd probably been left still holdin' coffee, dried out years and years ago."

By reflex Ryan glanced at the weakest link, who naturally enough was Ricky. The boy's eyes were wide, as if he couldn't believe the old man was telling random strangers—to say nothing of random, heavily armed strangers—anything like this.

Ryan showed him a quick, tight-lipped smile. Just a flash. Kid, he thought, you've got a lot to learn about people. The feeling of knowing a secret nobody else does is one of the most powerful forces in the universe inside our heads and bellies. The gnawing thought that it's not really any fun unless somebody else knows it, too, was right up near second place. Especially when you spend enough dark nights with only the thoughts in your head and a couple of donkeys for company.

Old Pete shook his head. "Can't tell you how many

days since that one I wished I'd at least grabbed something. Have something to show for it. Some evidence it wasn't all some kinda triple-crazy fever dream. But then—"

The man shrugged. He seemed to be talking to the fire now, rather than his newfound friends.

"Then I likely would've rotted away to a skeleton long since if I had. Because something in the back of my mind made me go outside to check. And I heard, plain as day, the shouts of some kinda patrol riding into the little ghost ville, Heartbreak, it's called.

"Never knew which side they belonged to—greenbacks or bluebellies. Only caught a glimpse of them before my donkeys and I hightailed it outta there. They was wearing just normal clothes, not uniforms, and I couldn't make out no armbands. Not that it mattered even a teeny tiny bit. Even if they was deserters, which for all I know they could'a been. Whoever and whatever, they'd have been only too happy to chill an old coot and steal all that gorgeous old-days scabbie for themselves!"

He took another drink and shuddered. Since the awful throat-searing booze had no visible effect on him, Ryan guessed that was memory at work.

"Was away from here, when peace broke out last autumn," Old Pete went on. "Out a ways west, tryin' my luck in a less risky locale. Because for someone like me, just pure old-fashioned coldhearts are safer to deal with than armies. You can always tell what coldhearts'll do. Not so with armies. They can be your best friend one moment, and lookin' to see the color of your insides the next.

"Time I got back, the rad-blasted war was on again

like it had never so much as paused for breath. Not so much shooting and stabbing as such...never is. But all the time, patrollin', patrollin', patrollin', looking for the least advantage over t'other side, mebbe ambush their opposite numbers if they hit a strike. Even less chance than before to go back and grab some of that hidden treasure."

He upended the jug, shook it over his mouth, up-turned open like a hungry baby bird's.

A single drop of clear liquid, glittering in the fire-light, fell into his waiting mouth. Old Pete swallowed as if it were the size of a goose egg, then cast the jug into the night.

"Now, though, I'm just hanging around biding my time. Reckon things'll settle down for spell, after that there beating the greenies laid on the blues a few days back. Both sides are played out—ever'body knows that. Their barons most of all.

"So this go-round, I calculate, they'll have to make peace. Won't stick any more than the last one did, of course. Uplanders and Protectors just fight natural, like jays and hawks. But they both need 'em a good blow before they puff their chests up for another go at each other."

Without more rotgut to suppress his better judgment his blue eyes unclouded, ever so slightly. His white eyebrows bristled more than usual and he frowned in thought.

"And no, I reckon I'm a garrulous old fool," he said, "and run my mouth off more than is good for me. Just a bunch'a old-man crazy talk, my friends. Nothin' to it."

He blew his whiskers out in a sigh.

"Oh, well. Either I'll wake up come morning with

a second smile beneath my beard, or I won't. Not so sure what difference that even makes me, anymore...."

Old Pete's words ran down like a clock that needed winding. His chin dropped to his chest. He began to snore softly.

Several minutes passed. Out on the grasslands around them a litter of coyote pups clamored for attention until their mother shut them up with a sharp yip. Ricky looked around as if wondering what signal that was. But this time he noticed right off none of the others was reacting. It wasn't White Wolf, as Jak had been known in the bayous in his guerrilla days, but a canine of a different color.

Ryan smiled. The boy learned fast.

"Breathing's as regular as clockwork," Mildred said at last. "If he's faking it, he's too good for me."

"Thoughts?" Ryan asked softly.

"Not a lot to go on," Mildred said. "I suppose we could rouse the old geezer and try to get more out of him. This Heartbreak ville could be anywhere around here."

"On the contrary, dear lady," Doc said. In contrast to the other oldie—and his own too-frequent self—his pale blue eyes were bright, and he leaned forward keenly. He was on the hunt intellectually, Ryan knew. And that always stimulated him. "I believe we have ample data to go on. Do we not?"

"We know the redoubt's hidden in what was no-man's-land before we helped Baron Al redraw his lines," Ryan said. "We know its entry is underground, in some deserted ville called Heartbreak."

"We've been all over this country the past few weeks, lover," Krysty said. "There's a lot of deserted villes."

Apparently as the currents of the war ebbed and flowed over decades, settlements had sprung up, been abandoned, some resettled, some not, as new ones came into being. They'd found clumps of derelict buildings dotting the grasslands, some just a couple of shacks, some big enough to have possessed a street or two, all in states ranging from relatively intact to just a few rotting-away planks or stones sticking up above mounds in the grass.

It was testimony both to the relatively rich nature of this country, and the abiding nature of the conflict being waged over it.

"We could squeeze more info out of him," Mildred said with obvious reluctance, "since we're all out of liquid encouragement."

"Ryan's right," J.B. said. "Reckon we got enough and more to go on. Don't need more of his addled memories to help us find what we're looking for. If he's not just hallucinating, or making the whole thing up to entertain us and himself."

Ryan shook his head. "It doesn't smell that way to me," he said. "We keep hearing rumors about the place. This strikes me as a solid a lead as we could ask for. Plus we can keep hunting while doing our jobs for the Alliance."

He stood up. "I'm hitting the sack," he said.

"Are we really so eager to jump out of here, lover?" Krysty asked softly.

"What do you mean?" Ryan asked.

"We've got a gig," she said. "Right now, it's pretty easy. Sniping at the Protectors and picking off the odd supply wag isn't much more hazardous than just living day-to-day is normally. If any. Things seem to have settled down. Old Pete's right. Both sides need to make peace and make it last, a year at least, mebbe more."

"If they make peace," J.B. said, "Al's not so likely to want to pay us to shoot at the lowlanders, though."

"There're other ways to live, J.B.," Mildred said with a curious light in her dark brown eyes.

"Baron Al's as much as said as we could have a nice homestead right now," Krysty said. "Not as if there's plenty whose owners got no more call to use them. We could try, you know. Settling down. For a spell."

"You really want to live like a baron?" Ryan asked. "Lord it over the farmers like they do?"

"We don't have to act the same way they do, Ryan," she said. "We don't, anyway."

"Even in my time," Doc said thoughtfully, "the warning was most ancient, not to rely on the gratitude of princes." He looked up. "Does experience teach us that barons are any more reliable?"

"But Al's a good man," Krysty protested. "He's not like most barons. We all know it. Don't we, Ryan?"

Ryan knew how the dream of settling down, finding peace and security, was important to his lover. He hated pouring cold water on it when it flared into flame.

"He is," Ryan said. "That's a rare thing, we all know that. He seems square."

"But…" J.B. said. It wasn't a question.

"Yeah. Times change. Things change. Right now Al's riding on top of the world, as far as the Alliance is concerned. Fireblast, it wouldn't surprise me if he's a sight more popular in the Association territories than their own boss baron is right now. And not just only among the common folk.

"But he's a war chief. That's a temporary gig. He

talks about that himself often enough, we've all heard him. He says he's looking forward to nothing more than just being the baron of Siebertville. He's never shown me a reason to doubt he means that.

"And both sides got more barons than just the one. Right now you got to think Jed's subordinates are thinking once and mebbe twice about how hard it'd be to pull him down, set one of them up in his place. And you know what? Victory can cause that kind of thinking, almost as sure as defeat."

"But you said it yourself," Krysty said. "Al's a hero."

"To some," Ryan said. "And to some, that just gives them one more thing to feel jealous of him over."

"You don't think—"

He shook his head. "What I think won't load us any blasters," he said. "Or keep us from winding up with dirt hitting us in the eyes. We can't know how things are going to play out from here."

"When do we ever?" Doc asked.

"And you can stop looking at me like that, Krysty. You, too, Mildred. Like I just stomped your new puppy. I'm not saying we jump right ahead out of here. For one thing, it would be hard to do that before we find this redoubt, now, wouldn't it?

"So regardless of what you want, or what I want, or any of us want, we're stuck here for a while. I'm just saying, I want to find this redoubt, if it's real, as soon as we can, because when has it ever proved to be a bad idea to have an escape route close to hand?"

Krysty sighed. "You're right, lover. As usual. But promise me that if we find it, and it has a working mat-trans, we won't use it unless we absolutely have to get out of here in a hurry."

He barked a laugh. "I'm not triple stupe. Nobody hungers for an end to the wandering and constant danger any more than I do. Nobody. But I don't honestly know if that's to be found in this world we live in. I don't know if we can find it here. But the day I stop looking out for all of us, best way I know how, I hope that's my last day on Earth."

Krysty stood and kissed him on the cheek. "I'm okay with that. Now let's get some sleep."

SQUATTING BEHIND A bush several hundred yards away, Snake Eye grunted, then snapped his spyglass shut with a click.

Even had he been skilled at reading lips, he was too far off to make out what anybody had actually said around the campfire. Nor did he care to risk trying to creep significantly closer. He had a healthy respect for the senses and skills of his quarry.

That was why he so hugely relished having them for quarry. That Baron Jed was willing to pay him for bagging them was just a bright red cherry on top.

The wrinklie who'd stumbled into the camp was a scabbie—that much was clear—and he had told his listeners a story they obviously found worth trying to draw out. His lone eye had not failed to miss the way they all suddenly stopped taking their turns from the jug, and encouraged their guest to do all the rest of the drinking himself.

He didn't reckon any of them had any trouble saying no to booze. He'd studied them far too well for that. He also had studied them far too well to think they'd do anything quite so purposeful…without purpose.

He was smiling when he went back to his horse,

grazing in a shallow draw behind him. He undid the hobbles, stashed them in his saddlebags and mounted.

Snake Eye had what he needed. For now. Time for a much-needed break.

He could find his prey once again when he returned to the chase. He felt full confidence in that. They were being careful to keep themselves hidden, but not from him.

And when he caught up with them, he judged, they would be that much closer to leading him to that which he, and they, both sought.

Chapter Twenty

"Gentlemen," Baron Al said, rising from his chair in the Lenkmans' parlor and addressing the Protector negotiators, "it may not have much place in diplomatic wrangling, but I'm going to speak my mind and speak it plainly. We would make a damn sight faster progress if Jed Kylie were to come here and talk to me. Man-to-man and baron-to-baron."

The emissaries of the Des Moines River Valley Cattlemen's Protective Association traded uneasy looks.

"He knows I at least respect a flag of parley," the baron said. "Ask him yourselves."

The emissaries made noncommittal noises. For a fact, Colonel Cody Turnbull thought, they seemed to lack the authority to negotiate effectively. In any sense of the word *authority*.

It was a word the colonel took seriously.

As usual he tried to keep from looking at Jessie Rae, seated at her husband's side. As usual he failed. She was ravishing in a low-cut yellow gown. And also, tight-lipped with apparent anger.

He escorted the negotiators to the front door of the manor, where sec men took over the task of seeing them mounted and escorting them out of the Uplander camp. The three men, minor landowners as well as Protector staff officers, mumbled courtesy farewells. They seemed glad to be escaping from the presence of the enemy leader, even though Baron Al had been nothing but courteous himself. Far too much so, in Cody's opinion.

The men had seemed shaken and subdued throughout the short, unproductive negotiation session. Cody noticed that even in the yellow lamplight their faces had an unhealthy gray tinge, and their skin seemed to sag on them. Possibly they were still shocked by the abruptness and the scale of their defeat of a few days before.

Or maybe they were frightened by living under the shadow of their own baron's reaction to it.

He heard the ruckus before he even got back to the parlor. He felt his face go hot and his brows draw together.

"—coddle our enemies like that, Aloysius Siebert?" Jessie Rae's lovely voice was anything but lovely, pinched and shrill with outraged wrath. That somehow made its sound even more like silver needles going through Cody Turnbull's ears straight to his heart.

Steeling himself, he pushed on against the continuing torrent of her vituperation into the room. His commanding general sat in his chair, his big homely face a blank of puzzlement. His decades-younger wife stood almost nose-to-nose with him, fists clenched at the ends of arms held stiff by her sides. Her own pert and pretty—and to Cody Turnbull, illicitly precious—features were reddened and twisted by her unseemly anger.

"Lady," he said quietly, gliding up to take her gently but firmly by the elbow, "please. There's no point in your exercising yourself so."

She tore her arm from his grasp, and in the process turned the full fury of her wrath on him.

"Don't you *dare* lay hands on me, Cody Turnbull! If you were *half* the man I thought you were, you'd be demanding that our army finish the job of whipping those lowlander curs back to their kennels right this moment, too!"

"Now, Jessie Rae—" he began.

"Save your breath, son," Baron Al said. "I tried that tack already."

Jessie Rae sucked down a breath so profound Cody was astonished her breasts didn't simply explode out of the bodice of her expensive silk dress.

"Men!" With that final furious exhalation, she turned and stamped from the room in a most indelicate manner.

Al shook his head. "Poor girl," he said sadly. "Sometimes she just lets her hate for that sister of hers get the better of her."

Cody sighed. "Ah, well. It's not like she means anything by it."

He looked up from under bushy black brows at his second in command. "If you got no further business with me tonight, Colonel, feel free to take yourself off to bed. It's been a long day. Funny how peace can take it out of a body almost as hard and fast as war does. At least when the fighting's on full-bore, a man knows where he stands."

He dropped his chin to his palm to brood. For a moment Cody stared at him, feeling his cheek flush hot and unable to do anything about it.

How must the poor girl feel, he thought, shackled to a brute like that—forced to submit to the fumbling caresses of his paws? Yes, he's a capable leader. Yes, he brought us all glorious victory. But late at night, when she slips out of that yellow dress…

He turned on his heel and walked out. He wouldn't finish that thought, not when there was danger of betraying his deepest, darkest feelings to his general.

"A MOMENT OF your time, Colonel?"

Though he billeted in the Lenkman manor along with the general and other key officers, Cody Turnbull had decided to take a last turn around the grounds, hoping to clear his mind—and cool his raging passion—with night air still brisk from the season.

He stopped on the graveled path that led from the front door of the stately two-story house to the stables and cocked a quizzical eyebrow at the men in Uplander uniforms who had accosted him.

"Walk with us, if you will," said the shorter, older and stouter of the two in his customary deep, lugubrious tones. He was Captain Phineas McCormac.

Turnbull moistened his lips with his tongue. "Certainly."

They strolled away. After a few paces where the path curved off to the stables, Cody's two new companions led him straight on, across grass already damp with dew.

"We have some concerns we'd like to share with you," said the taller, thinner and younger of the two. His long sideburns were trimmed close to his narrow face and clipped into points that emphasized the vulpine look of his jaw. His name was Captain Phil Asaro. Like the older man, he was among the landowners with the most substantial holdings in the Uplands, a powerful baron in his own right.

Like his companion, he also never seemed to contrive to rise higher than company command in the Alliance Army. They were known to resent the fact, which Cody could understand, if not truly sympathize with. It was an affront to men of their standing. Yet the chain of command was sacrosanct; without it they'd have anarchy, and be no better than stickies or tech-nomads.

They were well away from the buildings now. The grounds were fairly well kept, and the perimeter was carefully watched by the stout but assiduous Oliver Christmas's sec men riding patrols. Whatever the status of relations between the rival powers, generations of experience had taught the Uplanders never to take for granted Protector brutality and treachery. Nor the cornered-rat cunning of their current baron. The men were safe enough out here, in their footing and otherwise.

"We speak on behalf of a group of concerned citizens of the Alliance," McCormac intoned. "Fellow officers, as well as certain others who—good patriots all—find themselves compelled by age, infirmity, or unbreakable obligation to serve the Alliance in a purely civilian capacity."

"Men of our class," Asaro added brightly and not altogether necessarily.

"Of course," Cody murmured, frowning. He wondered where this was going. He frankly didn't like the direction he foresaw it might take.

"To be candid," McCormac continued, "we find ourselves concerned, specifically, about the conduct of Baron Al. He seems to be behaving in an increasingly autocratic and arbitrary fashion since our smashing victory over our hereditary enemies. And he seems to feel the popularity his success—to detract nothing from its brilliance and glory—has bought him from the unthinking rabble, gives him license to do whatever he pleases."

"Increasingly without regard for the concerns of responsible men," Asaro said. "Men of our class."

Cody's brow-furrowing deepened to a scowl. "Gentlemen," he said briskly, "I have sworn an oath to serve my commander loyally and without hesitation. As have we all."

At that Asaro got a wild look in his pale eyes and opened his darkening face to rejoin. McCormac stilled him with a wave of a plump, peremptory hand.

"Indeed," he said. "And indeed, we all have sworn to serve the baron as commander in chief. For the duration of the emergency, I might hasten to add."

He looked at Turnbull. "But the emergency, can we not all agree, has now passed? With the crushing blow that the baron dealt the lowland scum—again, nothing but praise to him for that feat—surely the Grand Army has been rendered incapable of posing further serious threat to the welfare of the Uplands for the season. Or for years, possibly a generation."

Cody started to say something, but it came out as a sigh. He knew that was true; though his own first profession was a sheep-farmer and baron, he took his enforced secondary profession as a military officer of the Alliance with utmost seriousness. And he understood what the fat man said was perfectly true, well enough.

And still, he thought, I mourn for the opportunity Al let slip through his clumsy fingers—to crush the Association serpent for good and all!

Phil Asaro still looked hot beneath his high, starched

collar, but he managed to offer, "The baron's time has passed," in what could pass for a civil tone.

Well enough at least for Turnbull, a man as punctilious about his honor as his appearance, to allow it to pass as such.

"So you see," McCormac said, nodding with even more than his usual gravity, "what we encompass is fully in accordance with our law, both civil and military, as well as morality. However unlikely either the present general commander or his bumptious security chief are to see it that way."

Which was true. For all that Al was unusually forbearing for a baron—dare Cody think, *weak?*—he was also justly famous for his volcanic passions. Especially rages when he found himself seriously crossed. He might be almost as livered in his treatment of the Protectors as Jessie Rae accused him of being—his face went hot and his jaw tightened, and he swallowed as he fought not to envision the way her own passionate outbursts had made her full white breasts surge from her bodice—but he had an abrupt way when faced with outright opposition.

And for all that his obesity and slovenliness betokened what could only be an equally disordered mind, Turnbull couldn't deny that Oliver Christmas had shown himself time and again to be a zealous and shrewd defender of his ward. Even though he came of a house that had long been somewhat bitter rivals of the Siebert clan, he owed loyalty to the commander of the Alliance Army, not Al's own person.

Cody Turnbull's heart lurched. His stomach rumbled in sympathy. However he hated to hear them, he couldn't deny the heavyset baron's words were true.

Those very concerns had been eating at Cody Turnbull and robbing him of sleep ever since Al had, to his mind, inexplicably refused to deal the deathblow to which the Protector scum lay helpless—and the army cheered him for it.

My honor is my loyalty, he thought, and vice versa. Yet which way did true loyalty lead?

Loyalty to the Uplands Alliance had to supersede all, of course. That much was obvious.

He cleared his throat. "Gentlemen," he said with a quiet assurance he didn't altogether feel, "I admit that, despite misgivings, you have interested me. Please continue."

After all, he told himself, what could it possibly hurt to listen to them?

Chapter Twenty-One

"You what?" Snake Eye shouted at the old man's reddened, water-streaming face. "You told who?"

"Gah!" Old Pete said, and vomited a thin stream of slurry of water, dinner grits, beans and rotgut into the green algae soup in the stock tank from which his captor had just yanked his head.

The abandoned farmstead on the western fringes of the no-man's-land between the Uplanders and the Protectors was still dark, although a thin line of pallor showed in the west. Concerned to make sure his primary quarry hadn't headed off somewhere in immediate response to whatever information they'd pumped out of the grizzled old bastard, Snake Eye had continued to shadow Ryan's party for a couple of days. He reckoned the scabbie was headed in to sneak around the battlefield and grab what he could from the corpses, bloating slowly in the sun and river humidity. He doubted the pickings would be fat—the armies and their camp followers would've looted the ace swag, plus grave details from both sides were burying the corpses, although that was a task that would take some time. Snake Eye calculated he'd have plenty of time to scoop up Old Pete for the conversation they were having now.

Except it had also, apparently, given Old Pete time

to hit a gaudy to spend some of his meager take from the war zone. *And* run his white-bearded face.

"They seemed like nice fellers!" the wrinklie sputtered when he stopped gagging and started breathing air again instead of the water Snake Eye had pumped into the concrete tub. It apparently saw somewhat frequent use from passersby, since there was more water getting thick and green and scummy in the bottom than the season's rains would account for. "Anyway, I was drunk, and it seemed to me like I was seein' the faces of, you know…all them poor chills. All swole up and blue, staring at me with empty eye sockets and all. It felt like I owed 'em an apology or something."

"An apology?" Snake Eye demanded. "How did that possibly translate into telling a bunch of strangers in a saloon about the treasure? A secret you'd kept for years?"

"Well, since I already done told them other young folks about it, I thought to myself, 'Pete, where's the harm in it, really? You done broke the ice already—'"

He probably tried to finish the word, but if he did, he did so underwater as Snake Eye thrust his head under it again.

"Corruption!" he swore. He was as furious as he could remember being.

The wrinklie thrashed and struggled futilely against the mutie's iron strength. Snake Eye ignored that as an obvious byproduct of the process.

Sure, he was mad at Old Pete—hot past nuke red. But most of all he understood the proper target of his rage was himself.

He was the best. The best blaster for hire in a world full of blasters, where hiring out your piece and your trigger finger—and your willingness to use them both in concert—was one of the few ways to advance yourself in the face of universal want, privation and general despair. Just staying alive as a mercie was a brutal challenge that claimed most of those who tried it at a young age. Staying alive at all in the Deathlands was a challenge the majority of people born failed at.

Yet Snake Eye hadn't just survived, he'd clawed his way to the top, despite the potentially lethal disadvantage his mute put him at, of that bloody pyramid. He was the best. No question.

Well, yes, he made himself remember—one question remained. The man who lived in a thousand whispered campfire yarns and gaudy-house whispers, the invincible one-eyed chiller and his band of mysterious travelers. Some said he was the best: Ryan Cawdor. And if a man looked into the matter, as few dared to do—and Snake Eye had—he could find abundant evidence to back that claim.

"To be the best," a wise man who'd mentored Snake Eye loved to say, "you got to beat the best." Which of course was why eventually Snake Eye had to chill *him,* as another step up that bloodstained pyramid.

Snake Eye reckoned he was better than Ryan Cawdor. He was willing to stake his life on it, which of course was exactly what he was doing.

And one key element of Snake Eye's surviving, let alone making that triple-hard and brutal ascent, was total, ruthless objectivity. Especially about himself.

When something this bad happened to Snake Eye, Snake Eye's unpatched eye never looked far for whom to blame. It was him.

Because to be the best, you had to beat yourself. If

you played at that level, your worst enemy was always you. That was the conviction Snake Eye formed at an early age, and had lived by ever since.

Nothing was done to Snake Eye. Nothing happened to him. Not since he'd been born with just enough of a taint showing to ensure he'd never be able to pass as human, even if he covered up his yellow serpent eye. He either did it to himself, or permitted it to happen.

He noticed the old scabbie had stopped struggling.

"Corruption," he said again, softly. He hauled up the oldie. The man was as limp as a half-full bag of wet gunpowder and twice as useless.

Snake Eye had let himself get so caught up in his anger and his thoughts he'd drowned the old bastard.

He let the deadweight drop. The balding head lolled on one side, tongue sticking out, its blueness showing as unnatural darkening in the starlight that gleamed on the curve of one old eyeball that would continue to stare at nothing until it rotted to slime and dissolved in the water—or, more likely, some enterprising raven picked out for a tasty snack.

He went back to his horse, who grazed in the grass nearby, taking a moment to unfasten the two pack donkeys he'd tethered to a post of a corral fence. He dumped the packs from their backs and left them free.

Snake Eye was ruthless, but he wasn't cruel. Not without reason, anyway.

With the sense of comfort knowing his goal and taking action to win it always gave him, he rode south as a sickly gray light stole across the grassland.

CODY WOKE SUDDENLY to find the thin chintz curtains in his quarters on the second floor of the headquarters just barely lightening with a hint of dawn. By reflex his hand sought and found the .44-caliber Schofield revolver on the nightstand beside his musty feather bed.

Al had shifted his quarters to be closer to the new Alliance lines. He now occupied another farmhouse that had lain derelict for a year or two. It had serious artillery holes, hastily patched to keep the rain out and the floors and stairways not too unsafe. Nothing could be done about the general air of decay, though, the smells of dry rot, dust and mold.

"Wait," a husky female voice said from the gloom at the foot of the bed. "Turn on the lamp."

His heart seemed to jam itself in his throat. "Jessie Rae?" He hardly dared to breathe the syllables.

He hardly dared to imagine he wasn't dreaming.

"Turn on the light and see" came the answer in kittenish tones.

Laying down the handblaster Turnbull used a flint-and-steel striker converted from an old-days cigarette lighter to spark flame to the wick of the kerosene lamp beside the bed. Turning the flow up to a low ochre glow, he turned to behold his nocturnal visitor.

His heart, which had been fluttering like a trapped bird in his throat, now seemed to stop.

It was Lady Siebert. Her voice had already told him that. But Jessie Rae Siebert as he had never seen her before—except in his waking dreams, of course. And even there he'd only permitted himself to indulge sparingly. So it was fair to say that the vision that greeted his wondering eyes exceeded his wildest dreams.

She was clothed. Her negligée was short and silky, blue to match her eyes, which were huge and round with emotion.

"I need help," she said, gazing into his eyes. As he saw with a stab through the belly of guilt when he tore his eyes away from the little peaks her stiff nipples put in the low-cut bodice of her frilly garment. "Your help, Cody. Please."

"J-Jessie Rae," he croaked. "Lady. You shouldn't be here."

She came to the bed. Her breasts swayed like sea waves as she threw herself to her knees beside him.

"You won't send me away!" she begged. "Please! I—I have nowhere else to turn!"

The touch of her palm burned like hot iron on his thigh.

Cody Turnbull was no virgin, but he had never sated his lust with a woman of his own class, and especially not illicitly with a married woman of good station.

Especially not one married to his general.

Passions he couldn't have named had he even dared try clogged his throat. He shook his head mutely.

She took that as refusal to send her away, apparently, because she twitched the comforter off him, and as he gasped as if she'd hit him with a bucket of winter-cold water, swarmed up to straddle his thighs with her own. The touch of bare skin on skin was electric; her inner thighs were soft flesh bedding over firm muscle.

His penis, standing straight up in defiance of all that was decent and right, practically vibrated with forbidden lust.

"You know I've always wanted you, Cody," she said. Her fingers closed around his rod. His body jerked involuntarily and he moaned.

Cody moaned again as she began to pump her little

firm fist up and down on his dick. "But I can't lie with you yet," she said. "Not until Al is out of the way."

"I can't—" he managed to choke out. "Disloyal—"

With her free hand she grabbed the front of her nightie and yanked it down. Her breasts bobbed free. They were full and as sweet as ripe pears—how well he knew that—but he was unprepared for the creamy perfection of them. Or the way her pale-pink aureoles had contracted to nothing as the nipples pushed forth, as if begging for his mouth.

"I can't raise a hand against my general," he moaned. It was the hardest thing he'd ever done to say those words to her here and now, with her leaning forward, jacking him off, a lock of hair swinging by the side of her pertly perfect face, her breasts bobbing in time to the exquisite illicit motion of her hands. Harder than leading a charge of cavalry against the Protector guns last summer at Holmun's Ford, even after a blast of grapeshot sprayed his best friend's blood and guts all over his face and the right side of his body. "Swore… oath—"

Smiling angelically, she shook her head. "I'd never ask you to harm him," she said. "Your loyalty does you credit, my love."

He moaned again, this time with a whine, when she let go of his cock. He was *that* close to spending the lust that threatened to burst his body like an overripe cherry.

Then she scooted her round rear down his legs and leaned forward. Her big breasts flopped onto his crotch to either side of his rigid tool.

"But I'm calling on your greater loyalty," she said, as she used her hands to squeeze her breasts together around Cody's erection and work them up and down.

Her eyes never wavered from his shocked gaze. "You swore an oath to serve the Alliance and its army. Not one man. Not even my husband. And you can't know what it's like to be bound to a brute like him! His booze-reeking breath, his clumsy paws mauling my tender flesh. Not like your strong and lean and manly hands, Cody Turnbull!"

He clutched handfuls of the sheet beneath himself and groaned aloud.

"Tell me you'll help me! Tell me you'll help the Alliance against my husband's overweening pride."

"Uh, I—"

"Please," she said, rolling her shoulder to add an entirely unknown dimension to the wonderful sensation her breasts were giving to his cock. "Please, tell me you will! When at last Al's deposed and put aside, I can give myself to you. That sweet thing, my love—"

She stuck her posterior in the air with abandon that even now shocked him. The green lacy fabric slid onto the small of her back, giving him a glimpse of the two white, apple-round mounds of her cheeks.

"Yes. *Yes!*" he screamed. His body vibrated like a tuning fork hit with a ball-peen hammer.

She showed him a delighted smile, which she proceeded to wrap around the swollen purple head of his cock. As she sucked in with delicious pressure, her tongue played sweet music where shaft met head. With a gargling cry he spent himself in violent spurts.

As his cock, slick and wet, bobbed out of her mouth, the dawn air caressed it with cold fingers.

"So we have a deal," she said in a businesslike tone. She sat up and stuffed her breasts back into captivity. "We must strike quickly."

Cody Turnbull uttered a sound like a sob and let his head fall helplessly back onto his pillow.

"TOP OF THE MORNING to you, Baron," Snake Eye said, setting his black gelding alongside the Protector commander's high-stepping chestnut. "Lovely day, isn't it?"

The early-morning sky showed brilliant blue through breaks in high white clouds. The sunlight glittered on the dew on the grass that clothed the low-rolling countryside south of the Grand Army camp, where Jed Kylie had chosen to take his morning exercise in company of his sec boss and a quartet of guards. They stared at the mercie, who had apparently sprung directly from the green landscape, as if he'd appeared out of a purple puff of smoke.

Jed Kylie showed him a wearily cynical blue eye. "You again? How in the name of glowing night shit do you manage to keep materializing out of nowhere like that?"

"You impudent beast!" Colonel Toth hissed from the baron's other side. "How dare you show your scaly yellow face around here! I'll have that hide off you in a—"

"Pipe down, Bismuth," Jed said, turning his face forward. "If the bastard wanted to chill me, I'd already be staring at the sky, and there's nothing you or your boys could have done about it."

"Precisely!" Snake Eye said heartily. "You're a wise one, Baron.

"And the answer to your question is 'proper reconnaissance.'" He looked past Kylie to Toth, who continued to glare blazing death at him.

"I recommend it to the attention of you and your men. It's a trifle too late, alas, to do anything about the disaster the want of proper reconnaissance brought on your army a few days past. But in five years or so when you're ready to resume your campaign, it could come in handy."

Snake Eye expected more rage from the little baron. Instead the creases in Jed Kylie's face grew deeper until his eyes vanished into slits. But his teeth showed yellow in a grin of sorts.

"If you're gonna come here and rub my nose in my biggest failure," he said, "I hope for your sake you bring me news of your own success."

He spoke with a certain mordant humor. Snake Eye smiled, mentally noting not ever to underestimate the banty-cock baron. As famous as his tantrums were, he evidently never lost control so far he couldn't reel it right back when he needed to. That suggested to Snake Eye that the rage fits were an indulgence Baron Jed was doubtless not above using purely to calculated effect.

"Neither," Snake Eye said with equanimity.

He couldn't see Kylie's eyes, but he could see his face harden. "Then give me one reason I shouldn't let Colonel Toth loose his dogs on you. And don't bother threatening my life. It's not quite as damn dear to me as it might be, just now."

"Because I bring you something that will prove of far greater value to you than vengeance."

"What could possibly interest me more than hearing you've skinned those child-murdering bastards alive and are bringing me their dripping hides in a wagon I ain't seen yet?"

Snake Eye laughed. "Not yet, Baron," he said, "although I assure you that's coming—for as everybody knows, I *always* fulfill a contract. But what I bring is something unlooked-for—information."

"He's lying," Toth hissed.

"In turn, Colonel," Snake Eye said, "I might remind you that my reputation is a commodity of great value to me. Without my hard-earned name for probity I'd starve. I mention this purely for informational purposes, but a word to the wise, eh?"

"It better be information," Jed rasped, "that can help me turn the tables on these Uplander sheepfuckers and in the process, get my own honor back."

"It is, Baron," Snake Eye said. "Oh, it most certainly is."

Chapter Twenty-Two

Snake Eye was riding a high-class slut when the bedroom door opened. Without pausing, he grabbed his handblaster off the table by the bed and leveled it. The intruder's eyes flew wide as a scaled, black-taloned thumb clicked back the hammer.

The slut, sensing something other than her own distress, looked toward the door. She moved as if trying to escape. Without glancing away from his three-dot sights, Snake Eye grabbed her offside cheek with his free hand, digging in his claws until she squealed in pain.

He recognized the intruder. It was the gaudy-owner's youngest son, Micah Savage, his naturally somewhat pendulous underlip quivering and his face blank beneath a mop of brown hair.

"What is it?" Snake Eye demanded. He kept the handblaster leveled between the boy's wide brown eyes.

"There're...people," the boy said. "Like—like what you told us to be on the lookout for."

"Five men, two women," Snake Eye said, "led by a tall man with one blue eye, a patch like mine, shaggy black hair and a scar down the side of his face?"

The boy swallowed and nodded. "'Cept one of 'em's a boy, more correct. Mebbe two, though t'other's a mutie, with skin and hair white as snow." He moistened his lips with a pink tongue. "They say he has bloodred eyes!"

"He does," Snake Eye said. "But he's no mutant. I'm a mutie. He's an albino."

"Yuh-yuh-yessir," the boy stammered.

"What are they doing?" Snake Eye demanded.

"Got lodgings for the night," the boy said. "They're in the main room, now."

His eyes had wandered to the naked woman sweating on the bed, her fists knotted in the sheets, her fine features partially obscured by strands of black hair that had escaped the elaborate bun her employer insisted she bedizen herself with to make her more alluring to the customers. Snake Eye was no expert in juvenile psychology, but it seemed to him the kid was on the young side to be hypnotized by the heavy, swaying breasts. But they were definitely preferable to looking down the 9 mm maw of death.

Snake Eye tipped the muzzle toward the room's low ceiling and engaged the safety with a clawed thumb.

"Go back and keep an eye on them, boy," Snake Eye said.

The boy stared at the naked woman for a few more moments, then he vanished like a rabbit down his hole.

And now, to the business at hand. Snake Eye carefully replaced his handblaster on the nightstand, then reached for the gaudy slut.

"ALL RIGHT, RYAN," J.B. said, coming in with Ricky, Mildred and Doc. Jak and Krysty already sat with Ryan at a table near the gaudy's long, polished-hardwood bar. "We've got the gear stowed in our room."

Holding both hands on the knife-scarred wood tabletop, Ryan twitched his left forefinger. J.B. instantly clammed up and sat down.

"It'll sure be good to sleep with a roof over our heads for once," Ricky said cheerfully. "I won't mind a break from those hit-and-run raids, either."

"Hush up now, boy," J.B. said under his voice. He nodded at Ryan's hand. "Next time, know the sign."

Ricky's olive face went white, but he shut his mouth and sat down. Sitting on Ryan's left, Jak gave his buddy a quick grin, half gloating, half commiseration.

"So this old beezer told you *what?*" demanded one of the wag drivers as he bellied up to the bar. There were four of them, three men and a woman. Their clothes were rough and smelled of dust and old sweat of men and animals. Their hair was shaggy, their faces as coarse and weathered as their voices.

"Triple-damnedest thing I ever heard," the woman said in a gravel-crusher voice. "Said he'd found this secret underground place, all stuffed to the rafters with the choicest scabbie! Weps, ammo, self-heats, meds, fancy-ass old-days tech."

"Just a buncha oldie B.S.," said a balding man with a black billygoat beard. "They stay out in the sun long enough, makes 'em crazy as a stickie with a bag full of lighters."

Doc's blue eyes, which had been looking rheumier and dreamier than usual as the fatigue of a few weeks dragged his lids lower and lower, suddenly went wide. He sat up straighter in his rickety wood chair.

"Oh," he said softly.

"Damn straight—*oh,*" Mildred said.

The female wag driver was shaking her head. "Not this time, Leo," she said. "Least, that ain't how I read it.

Oh, sure, the old guy was crazy enough, and not just on the rotgut he'd been sucking down. It was like he was talking to someone who wasn't even there."

The woman paused to down a rotgut shot of her own. Even as she shivered in reaction, she went on, her voice a couple degrees raspier. "When he snapped out of it, he admitted he'd been out robbing the chills from that last big battle between the sheep boys and the cow-people."

The black man she'd called Leo hunched farther over the bar and the shot glass enfolded in his own big hand.

"Don't remind me of that, Cissy," he said. "That sawed-off little fuck Jed's been on a tear ever since. Bad enough for us trader types. He's been having those tenant drivers the Grand Army uses for their organic transport whipped bloody on the slightest excuse."

He shot back his own drink. "Or just whipped to death, when he's feelin' triple-cussed. Most days, actually."

A shape loomed up on Ryan's left. By the gust of eye-watering smell that had blown in before the approaching figure, Ryan already made it for the gaudy owner. The scent, which she may have bathed in—possibly instead of water—had that unique combination of throat-clogging sweetness and eyeball-stinging rancidity of scabbied predark perfume that had gone off over the intervening decades.

"So, name your poisons, people!" she said in a bellow Ryan judged was supposed to be hearty. He didn't look her way as the newcomers gave their drink orders.

They were in Wolf Trap Creek, which was the first stream of any size west of the Des Moines. The Association capital of Hugoville had been built where it met the main flow. As such, the gaudy built on a ford that gave it half its name of Storm Crossing served as a major watering hole for trade flowing between the rival river-valley powers and points west, and for trade between them, whether legal or, as more commonly, otherwise.

The other half, of course, came from the owner-operator, Storm Savage, whom Ryan felt no need to look at now because once was enough. It was possible, he supposed, that if you subtracted the extra beef that showed in the vast jowls that flowed down pretty much uninterrupted to an even vaster bosom squeezed horrifyingly into—and out of—a tight black corset, and the child-bearing hips, plus the garish red paint on the lips and the raccoon-smears of kohl around beady eyes and the brown and ash roots of the unnaturally bright red hair piled atop a beer-keg head, she might not have been hard to look at in her younger days. If you squinted. And the light was bad. And also you were drunk.

"Anything not on the menu," she added, "is negotiable."

Meaning mostly the gaudy sluts she ran, as a normal part of such operations. They had a reputation for being top-notch, as such went; and from the glimpses Ryan had caught of various items of what seemed to be the stock in that part of the trade, by and large didn't seem to require much by way of low light and strong drink not to scorch the eyeballs.

Then a bovine elbow-nudge to Ryan's right biceps forced him to look up. "That goes double for you, handsome," she said. "You got a right dangerous look to you."

He reached ostentatiously to pat Krysty's right hand,

which happened to rest on the table. "This one here gives me all I can handle," he said. "Thanks."

"Well," the proprietor sniffed, "when you decide you're man enough for a real woman's curves, you know where to find me."

"Nose in feed trough," Jak said, deadpan, when the gaudy-keeper had waddled far enough away into the barroom clamor to be beyond hearing.

J.B. raised an eyebrow. "Did you just make a joke?"

Jak blinked red eyes at him innocently. Ricky snickered.

Ryan held up a finger, reckoning the new kid would spot that. The wag drivers had finally quit carping about the various inconveniences peace had imposed on independent contractors in the region and returned to the subject of the oldie's lost trove.

"Anyways," Cissy said, "when he came back to the present time and noticed we was all staring at him, the old bastard as much as told us he'd been looting the battlefield. Said he'd let the drink get the better of him, and all he could see was the swole-up faces of all them poor young dead boys. Explained to them he had to do what he was doin', and hoped they didn't mind, but that this was the last time he'd have to, because what with the fighting all wound down now and all it was safe for the first time for him to make his big score."

The fourth member of the group shook an upended mug over his upended mouth to get the last few drops of beer. Apparently because he'd paid for it, or so Ryan thought. Sometimes these random gaudies homebrewed real top-quality stuff; from the sample Ryan had tried, Storm Crossing was clearly not one of them.

"Nuke shit, Cis," he said. Nobody'd mentioned his

name. He was a morose fat man in suspenders, with sandy hair that was still squashed down on top and kind of flared out to the sides from wearing the slouch hat he'd set on the bar.

"Now, why you got to go and say a thing like that, Gus Tarmac?"

"You just said he was rambling on like a man got a whiff of gas. He was just another stone-crazy old coot. Kind likes to build castles in the air, then live in 'em."

Mildred snorted at that for some reason. Ryan gave her a look. If nothing else, it was poor policy to let people in a gaudy like this know you were eavesdropping on their conversations, even when they weren't exactly making an effort to be covert about it. She stifled, but her chocolate eyes still danced; some old-days joke of hers or another, he decided.

But the wag drivers were paying no mind to any business but their own. "You sure about that, Gus?" the goateed man said. "When I left the new Uplander camp just before noon today there was some kind of ruction. Nobody'd tell me what it was, and I reckoned when a buncha men with blasters start to get excited, the prudent place for an outsider to be is elsewhere, double-fast."

"Now ain't nobody can argue with ya there, Cal," Leo said. "Them Uplanders may not be suffering the perpetual red-ass quite as nuke-hot as the Protectors, but it doesn't mean they won't look at you and realize how much use their little army could get out of your trap, your team and your own personal ass than you could on your lonesome."

"So I wonder if that might've been that news hitting their camp," Cal went on. "It'd get me going."

Cissy downed another shot, then pounded her shot glass on the bar with such loud conviction that even as stoutly built as it was, Ryan was surprised it didn't at least crack.

"All I know is what I saw and heard," she said. "And that was like one of them deathbed confessions. Plus his oldie eyes were clear when he 'fessed up to the rest of us. I think he told it to us straight, and like it really happened, not like he imagined. But that's just me."

"So," the black guy said, "*will* it get you going, Cal? You gonna go off in search of buried treasure so's you can retire? Provide you get to it before that loco old bastard does."

"Damned right it will," Cal said, jutting his bearded chin. "Get me going clean outta the territory, fast as I can deadhead my rig. They say three people can keep a secret if one of them's a chill. In this oldie's case, even one knowing the secret wound up being way too much in the end."

"If he's telling the truth," Gus said.

Cal shook his head. "Makes me no nevermind. You all do what you will. But I reckon, if anything's gonna get both rad-blasted armies out in the field again, full-force and loaded for bear, it's a tale like the one we all just heard. True or not don't enter into it, any more'n it ever does in politics."

And taking up his own black hat from the bar, he stuffed it authoritatively on his balding head and swaggered from the gaudy.

The others watched him go, then turned back to mutter with their heads together over the bar.

Ryan looked around at his friends. It seemed to him

Doc summed the whole thing up best with an eloquent shrug.

"So, Ryan Cawdor," a voice said from the shadows in the nearest corner of the bar, "what about you? Will you and your friends go off in search of this fairy gold? Or should I say, this lost redoubt?"

Chapter Twenty-Three

The whole gaudy went dead still. Not more still than Ryan himself, though.

Slowly he turned his head. A shadowed figure sat alone with a bottle at a table beneath a particularly low-hanging garland of age-tarnished tinsel.

As Ryan turned, the figure stood up and stepped into the light. Ryan heard a hissing intake of breath, possibly from one of his friends.

The man was tall and lean. His head seemed oddly short and wide beneath the black Stetson. A black patch covered his right eye.

But that wasn't what probably startled the onlookers. The tall, thin stranger's face was yellow. It had a hard, waxy cast and the slightest suggestion of...scales.

His hands, their thumbs hooked to either side of a silver belt buckle cast in the shape of a diamondback with wide-open fanged mouth, showed black talons in place of nails.

The stranger was a mutie, and made no attempt to hide the fact.

Ryan immediately took note of the fact he was allowed inside the gaudy. A lot of gaudy owners wouldn't allow even a suspected mutie through the door, which sometimes provoked unpleasant and sometimes volatile incidents concerning Jak. Storm Crossing had either an unusually lenient policy on muties, or its proprietor and this particular mutie had an understanding.

"You seem to know me," Ryan said, "but I don't know you."

"Perhaps you've heard of my work," the stranger said. He had a pleasant voice, baritone and well modulated, and spoke in as educated a way as a big East Coast baron's son, that Ryan, who *was* a big East Coast baron's son, was well-equipped to recognize. "I've certainly heard of yours. They call me Snake Eye."

He looked around the group. His visible eye was light brown and unexceptional. Ryan wondered what injury mandated the patch over the other. Unlike Ryan, Snake Eye's face showed no visible scar to go along with the blinding.

"Krysty Wroth," he said. "Your beauty is as luscious as all the stories make it out to be. J. B. Dix, often called the Armorer. Dr. Theophilus Tanner—good to meet a man of education. As an autodidact, I still admire your academic achievement."

"A what?" Ricky asked.

"Hush, son," J.B. said. "Doc'll explain it later." His tone suggested, there might not be a later. Ryan could tell at first glance this mutie was bad, bad news even if he hadn't worn two blasters at his hips. J.B. was at least as sharp that way as he.

"The erstwhile White Wolf, Jak Lauren. Mildred Wyeth, noted crack shot and healer. I have often wondered, do you ever patch up the victims of your marksmanship?"

"If I shoot them," Mildred said grimly, "they don't usually need patching."

He smiled. His teeth were clean and white. It came

as almost a shock to Ryan that he had normal eyeteeth instead of fold-out rattler fangs.

"Point taken. And you, young man, I gather you must be the newest member of this illustrious troop. Still a new enough phenomenon to remain a mystery, aside from being wrapped in the enigma of the group as a whole."

"You used a word a moment back, Mr. Eye," J.B. said.

"Snake Eye is fine," the stranger said. "Which word?"

"I think you know the one he means, mister," Ryan said. He wasn't too eager to have the word tossed about like a ball among ville kids. It was too much to hope for that the whole damned gaudy, including the sluts and their customers hadn't heard about what the wag drivers were not so secretly jawing about at the bar. *That* bullet wasn't going back in the blaster anytime soon. But the fewer specifics about the real nature of the so-called trove that came to light, the better.

"'Redoubt'?" Snake Eye asked. "Ah, yes. That's what's being discussed, isn't it? And after all, you and your illustrious crew are known to have something of a fascination with them. As well as a remarkable, if hard to credit, propensity for being reported in widely spaced parts of the continent at close to one and the same time."

Ryan felt as if the mutie had driven a black-clawed fist with pile-driver force into his gut. Could the bastard be on to their deepest secret, the existence of the mat-trans network and their ability to use it?

It was possible.

"How do you come to know so much about us?" Krysty asked. Her natural manner was friendly and disarming, and she wasn't above using that to advantage when her or her friends' survival might be at stake.

Snake Eye raised a hairless brow. "Why, I should think it plain as day. I've made a study of you," he said. "Quite lengthy and comprehensive, you'll agree."

"Why would you do a thing like that?" Ricky blurted.

Snake Eye smiled again. "Because we're in the same profession, you and I," he said. "Most especially, your distinguished leader and myself."

"What profession might that be?" Ryan asked.

"Chilling men," Snake Eye said. "Me for pay, but always for advantage. Even if it's only continued survival."

"Plenty of folks do that," J.B. said, scratching the back of his neck. Without making a show of it he had stood up. He had leaned his M-4000 scattergun against the table when he sat; fortunately Storm Crossing wasn't one of those places where the proprietor had a hair up her butt about the customers carrying weapons. "Dark night, plenty get paid for it, too."

"Ah," Snake Eye said, "but very few do so at a level at which they might arguably be called the best. And that's the reputation you possess, my friends. It's what caught my attention years ago. It's the very reason I began to study you assiduously—to actively seek out and collect as much information on you. Even the wildest gossip, which perhaps unsurprisingly, overwhelmingly predominates provable fact."

"All right," Mildred said suspiciously. "Why?"

"I wanted to study your methods," he said. "You're artisans—craftsmen and -women. As am I. He or she who would be a master takes teaching where it's to be found. Don't you find that so?"

"I'm not accepting any pupils," Ryan said, "if that's what you're aiming at."

"Oh, no, Ryan Cawdor. You misunderstand. I have already learned from you. And learned quite well, I will add, since false humility befits a would-be master as poorly as bravado. No, it has to do more with the nature of the concept of…the best. As a vid from long ago puts it so very well, there can be only one."

And he raised his right hand to the patch over his right eye.

Ryan was already in motion, flinging himself left, away from the table and from his friends, most of all Krysty. His own hand was drawing his SIG-Sauer P-226 handblaster with puma speed.

The clawed thumb whipped up the black patch. The eye revealed was a rattlesnake's eye in all truth: yellow, round and glaring, with an evil slit pupil.

Ryan noticed that only out at the edge of things. His vision was focused on the black vest buttoned over a gleaming white shirt, where the center of mass—and best handblaster target—could be found. And far more than the terrible staring inhuman eye he was aware of the left hand drawing a black semiauto handblaster faster than Ryan had ever seen a man move in his life.

Ryan was fast on the draw, but even so, Snake Eye cleared leather and fired before Ryan even had his blaster out.

A hammer hit Ryan in the upper right chest. He didn't feel much pain—not then—but the impact itself seemed to momentarily red out his vision.

Shit happened.

Shit happened, as shit so often did, shit-*fast*.

As Ryan's left shoulder hit the boards, he heard the roar of J.B.'s scattergun. He rolled, and even the numbness that often followed a significant wound didn't stop his chest from hurting like blazing nuke death. He heard more shots and shouts, saw flashes of flame in the gloom.

He fetched up against the bar, unarmed. The downside of dodging to his left was that it made more of a target of his gun arm. The bullet shock had caused his hand to lose its grip on the P-226, and he wasn't sure where it had wound up.

He heard scraping sounds as his companions pushed their chairs back from the table across the sawdust-covered floor, then a scrape of shoe leather and a creaking of floorboards under major weight. He looked up into the cavernous barrels of a sawed-off side-by-side shotgun, and right behind it, Storm Savage's fat, painted face staring down at him like an unlovely moon. Her plump finger was in the guard. So apparently she decided to side with the snake boy.

Pap! Pap! Pap! Ryan heard the loud but somehow peevish-sounding reports of Krysty's snub-nosed .38-caliber handblaster going off right nearby. Through the ringing the blasts left in his ears he heard her yell, "Get away from him, *bitch!*"

And Storm Savage was going away, but it wasn't like she had much choice. Blinking his good eye, Ryan saw red spray from her capacious boobs, fat neck and heavily rouged cheek as a result of shots fired upward from Krysty's blaster.

The smoothbore scattergun let go as reflex convulsed Storm's finger on the triggers, both barrels, but not directly into Ryan's helpless, upturned face.

Instead, as its wielder fell away, the shotgun had swung up. It discharged its lethal load at random into the gaudy. The huge flare and roar left Ryan dazzled, half-deaf and his face feeling sunburned. Unburned powder stung his chin and neck like tiny pissed-off bees.

Through the ringing in his ears he heard screams, hoping none came from his friends.

But there was nothing he could do about that, but plenty he had to do, and in a hurry. Despite the flash-bang stunning effect of the blaster going off about a foot from his face, Ryan was recovering from the initial physical reaction to getting hit.

He forced himself to roll onto his belly. From the sloshing behind his washboard abs, it felt as if his stomach was a half roll behind. But he'd been wounded enough in the past to expect that. Nausea wouldn't chill him. As for the bullet that had hit him, that hadn't done the job yet, either.

Ryan began to crawl toward where he thought his SIG-Sauer had flown when he lost his grip on it. He found right off the bat that his right arm wasn't much use, but he made do anyway.

Down in the sawdust, the stench of the vomit and spilled brew it was meant to soak up was nearly over-whelming, but he was able to ignore it after a first whiff or two came back double-strength. It didn't do his stomach any good. Shots flash-cracking from nearby were enough to keep him focused regardless.

His head and vision had mostly cleared when his stretched-out left fingers touched cold steel. He made himself lunge forward despite the pain shooting through the comforting numbness of his right shoulder and chest. His fingers closed around the grips.

Blaster now in hand, Ryan rolled onto his back to perceive a vision out of old-days stories of hell: a haze of greenish black-powder smoke, already dense filled the room, turning all shapes to phantoms, shadowed and indistinct, lit in patches by the already inadequate yellow glow of kerosene lanterns and stabbed randomly through by orange muzzle-flares.

Movement drew Ryan's eye down the bar, past his scuffed and upturned boot toes, to where a burly young man with long brown hair, dressed in a foully stained apron over a T-shirt and jeans, stepped out and raised a double-barreled scattergun.

Ryan had already formed a flash impression of the tactical situation: his friends, crouched behind two overturned tables in the middle of the gaudy floor and shooting toward the end of the room that was now behind his head. He had no time to puzzle over the wood plank top that was somehow providing them actual shelter against the bullets that slammed into it in return. The key fact that exploded into his shock-clouded brain: the newcomer was about to blast his friends from behind.

Chapter Twenty-Four

Ryan had already pushed his arm straight out along his body, pointing above and between his boots. Though he got the briefest picture of the new shooter in soft-focus blur above the front sight, it was mostly point-shooting when he started cracking off rounds. Skilled and seasoned a blaster-handler though he was, it took an active force of will to squeeze off the shots rather than just yank the trigger in frantic desperation to save his lover. That would have scattered the slugs all over the hell's fractional acre the barroom had become, and only stopped the threat by sheerest strike accident.

After the third yellow bloom of fire from the P-226's muzzle, the indistinct figure of the burly youth fell away. By sheer momentum—and to make sure—Ryan blasted off two more shots. Modern ammunition might be as precious as blood and as scarce as antibiotics, but there was a time to conserve ammo, and there was now.

A big ball of fire appeared from the farther of the two tables. From the shape of it, the shot was directed in Ryan's general direction; from the sound it was a big-bore handblaster, either Doc's .44 LeMat replica or the Webley double-action revolver Ricky toted, cylinder rebored to take the same .45 ACP cartridges as his DeLisle.

Ryan's first thought was that whoever it was had

popped a shot at someone threatening to shoot from behind the bar. Then he heard the tinkling of broken glass—and the *whoomp* of some kind of spilled accelerant catching fire. Even as those facts registered, the same handblaster flared off toward the end of the room past prone Ryan's head, where most of the hostile fire was coming from. A second lantern exploded, drooling yellow flame that quickly became a pool that spread and danced with blue and yellow light.

"Dark night!" Ryan heard J.B. roar. "What'd you want to do that for, kid? You set the place on fire with us pinned in it!"

A figure loomed up in the fog bank right over Ryan's supine body. He started to swing his handblaster to bear, but at the last instant he somehow recognized the presence, possibly by smell. A strong yet unmistakably nonmasculine hand gripped his wrist.

"Krysty," he croaked.

"Let me help you up, lover," she said.

"I won't say no."

As she draped his gun arm around her shoulders, he was aware of having heard Doc bellow out, "The boy gave us cover, by the Three Kennedys!" Followed by the boom of the stubby shotgun tube slung beneath the barrel of his enormous LeMat handblaster.

On shaky legs Ryan tottered alongside his lover, as she steered straight for the gaudy's front door. He had the impression of movement around them, shouting as well as shooting. Then Jak appeared at his right, firing his big Colt Python back toward the entry into the main room from the back. The potent muzzle-blast of the .357 Magnum wheelgun was near enough to make Ryan wince.

Mildred was at his left, on the other side of Krysty, popping shots from an unfamiliar-sounding hand-blaster—probably one she'd scooped up off the floor—from her left hand. Jak, now walking backward, fired two more shots toward the rear.

The door stood open, casting a rectangle of orange torchlight from the yard outside in the clotted gloom within. Ryan caught a whiff of fresh air that smelled like honey, then coughed in reflex. He realized how much stinging smoke he'd sucked down without being aware of the fact.

Suddenly a shadow intruded into the oblong of relative brightness. Ryan saw a big figure, a hint of wild beard topped by wilder eyes. A right hand was cocked back over one wide shoulder ready to smash something down on Ryan—or one of his friends. The newcomer was probably just reacting in blind panic rather than being deliberately hostile. But it didn't matter.

In dire need Ryan found the strength to launch his right leg in a stiff-legged kick. It had to have been fair strength, since the impact of shinbone into crotch lifted the bearded man up onto his toes. He dropped whatever it was he was wielding and bent over to clutch his violated balls as Ryan sagged in Krysty's firm grasp.

Krysty half dragged Ryan outside. Five paces from the door she let him drop, almost gently, to catch himself as best he could while she wheeled to cover with her .38 handblaster against possible attack.

"Sorry, lover," she murmured.

Ryan shook his head. He'd caught himself on his knees and a stiffened left arm. He'd had sense to take his finger off the trigger of the P-226, though his weight squashed his thumb uncomfortably on the hardpan beneath the blaster's grip.

"Don't be," he rasped.

Once they'd gotten outside the gaudy everyone seemed to lose interest in attacking them. For the moment, anyway.

Mildred knelt by his side. "Let me give you a hand."

He shook his head. "I can stand on my own, so radblast it, I will." He thrust himself to his feet, then staggered and almost vomited. Mildred grabbed him around the waist. She may not have been as strong as Krysty, but the stocky black woman was anything but weak herself.

He pretended not to hear her muttered, "Macho son of a bitch."

Ryan steadied himself, then, although he didn't pull away from the physician's support. He glanced back over his shoulder.

"Where's J.B.?" he asked in a voice that sounded as if he'd been gargling lye. He meant to ask about Doc and Ricky, too, but had trouble forming more words.

"Here, Ryan," the Armorer said. "Doc and I got our traps. Ricky and Jak went to the stables to round up our rides." Grunting with relief, he dumped a pair of heavily stuffed backpacks on the ground.

"Stay here," Krysty said. "I'll help the boys."

"Move me away from in front the door," Ryan directed.

"What?" Mildred said. "Oh, yeah." She helped him shuffle several steps to his left, out of the direct line of stray shots coming through the door—or right in front of the blaster of anybody coming out.

J.B. took a position near the door with his shotgun.

He let several fugitives, two men and a woman, stumble out although the woman clutched a cap-lock revolver in her hand. She wasn't looking to use it, as J.B. correctly read in a flash. He had that much faith in his own judgment, and reflexes, and as usual was right.

When another figure loomed out of the smoke, J.B. let loose a head-splitting blast. The figure fell back inside to become visible only as a pair of worn-through boot soles, drumming on the door stoop.

Ryan didn't ask, he didn't need to.

He felt strong enough at last to pull away from Mildred. She held on briefly, then let go. He wobbled a bit, swayed some, then managed to stand upright. Or close enough.

Ryan was still better than halfway out of it. It seemed a moment when Krysty appeared on her mare right in front of him, leading his horse by the reins. "Can you ride alone?" she asked.

"Help me up," he said. Somebody did, he didn't register who. He realized someone had relieved him of the SIG-Sauer and stuffed it back in its holster as he managed to more or less solidify his perch by hanging on to the saddle horn like the rankest greenhorn.

Then they were riding out through the open gates of the barbed-wire compound, across the starlit prairie. The wind felt as cold as winter and bracing as a shot of good shine.

From behind came a shouted challenge: *"Run, little rabbits!"*

The voice, heard only recently for the first time, had already become unmistakable. And hated.

"Shit," Mildred said in grunts between strides of her horse. "I'd hoped we'd chilled that motherfucker."

"Run far, run fast, little rabbits!" Snake Eye called. "Run and hide! But you'll only die tired!"

STANDING IN THE DOORWAY with the blaze of the gaudy heating the back of his black duster through the doorway like an open furnace, Snake Eye laughed a loud and melodramatic laugh.

His quarry vanished into a fold of the deceptively flat-appearing land.

"I wonder," he said aloud, "if I may have overacted, just a trifle?"

He decided it didn't much matter. "It's not as if they were in any frame of mind to critique my performance, after all."

He stepped out of the doorway and began walking toward the stables. It was time to reclaim his own mount and follow—at a discreet distance, of course.

Now I've put double pressure on them, he thought. Lots, if those fool Uplanders take the bait and begin to hunt the hidden redoubt, as well.

Ryan Cawdor and his friends would have little choice: either lose the redoubt to others, or give over everything in a single-minded pursuit of finding it before whole armies of eager searchers did. For all his research, Snake Eye didn't know just why the band valued the ancient facilities so highly, although he entertained a surmise or two. That they did was an unmistakable thread running through the whole patchwork narrative of their joint careers he had contrived to stitch together.

As he neared the stable doors, a short, sturdy figure lunged at him from within with a pitchfork. Without apparent haste he drew his left-hand blaster, and without appearing to aim, he fired. The pitchfork and his attacker fell separate ways.

"Consider that your reward for valor, lad," he said as he sidestepped the late gaudy-owner's youngest son, who had brought him warning earlier, and now lay howling and clutching a shattered shin. "Whether you prefer living in pain to having died game is a choice you'll have to make for yourself."

He loaded his saddlebags on his gelding's back and rode it out into the cool night air. If they lead me to the treasure, I'll chill them and take it for myself.

If they don't, I'll chill them and get on with my life.

In either case, he would collect his bounty from the baron of Hugoville—whether Jed Kylie or an as-yet-unspecified successor. Because as he'd told Jed, he *always* carried out a contract.

But as he'd also told the volatile baron—at his own time.

Chapter Twenty-Five

Jak's whistle brought Ryan's chin up short as it sank toward his chest. The chestnut's steady pace had lulled him into another brief nap, despite the dull throbbing pain of the wound in his upper-right chest, which Mildred had cleaned and bandaged as best she could by the light of a small, quick fire.

A hint of dawn glowed pale along a rolling range of hills toward the west. His friends rode in pairs along a rough rutted track that if a body was feeling generous might just be called a road. They had no reason to stay covert. Above some more low ridges ahead and to their right showed the faint light of the watchfires of the defensive line along the creek where the Uplander Army had waited in ambush for the Protectors, and where they had dug in since.

Silhouetted against that faint amber glow were the lead riders of a cavalry patrol. Presumably Uplanders, since it would be a major violation of the cease-fire truce for Protectors riders to venture out of sight of their own front lines. Given that fact, the patrol seemed pretty hefty to Ryan, perhaps twenty horsemen, he judged.

"Good," Krysty said from his side. She rode at his right and had been trying and failing not to make it

obvious she had been watching him like a hawk every
step they'd ridden since Mildred had tended to him.

She reached now as if to pat his arm, which he carried in a sling, then thought better of it. "It'll be a load
off my mind to get you proper medical attention once
we hit camp."

He grunted. "Mildred did fine," he said. "Thought
you trusted her more than any of the Uplander Army
healers, for sure."

"Well, yes." She smiled, but her eyes flicked back
to where her friend rode right behind her, side by side
with her own lover, J.B. She clearly feared that in her
worry for Ryan she'd inadvertently insulted Mildred.
"But she'll have better light to work by. And plenty
of alcohol and hot water to make sure the wound's really clean."

Ryan grunted. He felt a bit woozier than he thought
he ought to, given the severity of the wound. The mutie
mercie's round had missed smashing his shoulder joint,
and missed nicking a lung, both of which were undis-
guised boons.

But the big reason it hadn't pierced Ryan's right lung
was that after punching through the pectoral muscle,
it had skated along the outside of his rib cage before
exiting at the juncture of the infraspinatus and teres
major muscles—if he'd heard Mildred's medical gob-
bledygook correctly.

"Our bones are really pretty good armor," she had
told him cheerfully, as he set his jaw against the necessary pain of her probing the raw wound. "It's not
uncommon for bullets to bounce off. Handgun bullets
especially, and doubly so for the sort of round-nose
soft-lead slugs that freaky bastard's probably loading."

The bullet had done enough, as far as Ryan was concerned. There was some muscle damage, which Mildred judged would likely heal. It had also likely cracked a rib or two. One way or another he'd be a spell getting back full strength and use of his arm. Meaning his gun hand.

She'd dumped in one of their precious few scabbie sulfa packets. Now Ryan was a little concerned infection might be setting in despite the antibiotic.

"Omega," called the lead rider. In the starlight he seemed to wear a uniform tunic, and he carried a scabbarded saber, marking him as an officer or at least a sergeant.

"Glory," Doc called back, completing the challenge-countersign.

"No like," Jak whispered as the troop split to ride down either side of the line of companions. Ryan frowned.

"Fit to fight, Ryan?" J.B. asked below his breath from right behind.

"No," Ryan said, with a grin his friend couldn't see. "But I can manage anyhow. Eyes skinned, everybody."

"Why…?" began Mildred, then clamped it down as the first of the Uplander riders came abreast of Jak and Doc in the lead.

"Good evening, gentlemen," Doc said. The lead rider grunted something that might have been a return greeting and swung his mount aside. The rest kept riding, parting like water around a rock to avoid the companions, but otherwise scarcely acknowledging they were there.

Even half out of it Ryan could almost smell the tension in the cavalrymen, and not just their boots and unclean clothing, the oil on their weapons and the sweat of man and horse.

"What a relief to see an Uplander patrol," Krysty said. "We have a wounded man, so—"

The trooper leader whipped out his saber. "Take 'em down, boys!" he screamed. "Remember, the reward goes for dead or alive!"

"ALL RIGHT," Baron Al Siebert said, trying to cram an arm clad in off-white long johns into the sleeve of his uniform tunic as he lumbered into the parlor of the house where he was headquartered. "What was worth rousing me out of bed for at this indecent hour of the morning? The sun's not even up, gentlemen, and I haven't yet had my coffee."

Colonel Cody Turnbull compressed his lips to hold in a retort. He himself had been up an hour already, had washed and shaved himself before turning out in his customary immaculate uniform.

But he had little trouble letting it past. Leaving aside how much practice he'd gotten in overlooking his general's inexcusable slovenliness, excitement thrilled like a jolt in his veins. He found it hard to stand still, and kept shifting his weight from boot to polished boot. A slogan from one of his idols from the history books sang over and over in his brain: action this day.

Still, the colonel hadn't expected action quite this soon.

"It's important, I'm afraid," said Oliver Christmas, his sec boss. The big fat man was, as usual, even more rumpled than his boss, with a wing of his white shirt hanging untucked from his black civilian trousers and a lock of his comb-over standing straight up from his cannonball head like a weird bird's crest. He had, or claimed, no military rank, so his habitual sloppiness had at least that justification. Though Turnbull felt inclined to cut him little slack. Although Christmas was undeniably zealous in his job of protecting the Uplander commander in chief, and had proved quite effective at the task, Turnbull couldn't shake his conviction that such exterior untidiness could only reflect a disordered mind within.

"What do you mean, Oliver?" said Al, with his big homely face rumpling into a fierce scowl.

The sec boss gestured. One of his men, identified as a sec man by the white armband above the green one on the sleeve of his checked flannel shirt, came in supported by one of Christmas's personal crew in full green uniform. The left side of the staggering man's face was a mask of blood, with fresh flow shining crimson above a darkened stain of blood that had begun to dry.

"We were riding picket not half a mile south of the lines and ran into a probe by Protector cavalry," he said. "The fight's still going on."

"If you listen, sirs," his escort said earnestly, "you can just hear it."

Big Al's frown turned from fierce to thunderous. His beard bristled as his small pig blue eyes practically disappeared beneath bushy brows.

In the stillness—not usual in HQ, where at least a buzz of conversation was almost incessant—Cody heard it now. Convenient, he thought in surprise.

The iron had grown hot earlier than anticipated. Would his fellow…patriots be alert enough to strike it while it glowed?

Christmas blew out a gusty breath through big pink-and-gray lips. "I better go see what's going on, General," he said. "Stiffen up the perimeter security. This might be a feint to cover a strike from another direction."

Then he frowned and passed a hand over his pate. The rebel lock of hair smoothed down, then sprang defiantly back up.

"Though mebbe I should stay in case they mean to make a play for you here," he said worriedly.

"Sir," the green-coated sec man said, "we're here. We can handle it—in the unlikely event those lowland cowards get that bold."

Al waved a hand. "Go on, Oliver," he said. "I'll be fine."

Though he personally seemed to like his sec boss, and Christmas seemed to return the feeling, the baron resented security and was always eager to be relieved of any reminder of it. He usually insisted on his bodyguards, except for Christmas himself, at least staying out of his sight. He hated being nursemaided, as he put it.

"All right, Randy," Christmas said to the man who'd shown the wounded trooper in. "You're in charge here while I'm gone."

Despite the unmilitary address, the officer braced and snapped off a salute that warmed Turnbull's soul.

"Sir! The baron will be safe in my hands."

"Whatever." Christmas lumbered out like an annoyed grizzly.

An aide came in with a big steaming mug of something that was only coffee by nature of dash added, for the principle of the thing as much as anything else, and handed it to the baron. He sipped and nodded appreciatively.

Cody nodded approval to the aide. He had personally selected the staff duty roster for today. He could rely on this lad to do what needed done.

With Christmas gone, the stage lay open, awaiting only the proper players for history to be made. The "probe" was remarkably fortuitous, since just such a diversion had been planned for this morning, to get the potentially troublesome Christmas out of the way. Did my associates stage this? Turnbull wondered with a twinge of something like alarm, since they should, for courtesy at least, have informed him what to expect. Or does Providence truly guide our hands?

In walked Captains McCormac and Asaro. Baron Al looked at them through the steam rising from the mug he held to his lips.

"Phil and Phin, eh?" he growled. "What brings you to brighten my morning? You usually are less likely to see this unearthly hour than I am."

Asaro's long lean face darkened beneath his razor-cut sideburns, but his shorter, wider companion laughed his standard jolly laugh and patted Asaro's arm.

"Relax, my friend," he said. "For you see, things are about to change."

With a waft of lavender scent and the air of a queen, Jessie Rae Siebert swept in, holding the skirts of her green silk dress off the floor. Haughtily she took her place in the chair reserved for her beside her husband.

"Good morning, my dear," Al said, looking a bit surprised.

"We'll see about that," she said with a smile.

"What are you talking about now?" he said. "It's too early to be cryptic."

"Allow me, Baron," McCormac said. If Al noticed the slight implicit in the use of his civilian title as opposed to his military one from an officer in uniform, he didn't show it. He likely hadn't noticed, Turnbull reflected.

"You see, a lot of us men of standing and influence have long been concerned about your refusal to take the steps—obvious and readily available steps, honesty compels me to add—to end the threat of the treacherous Association cattle herders to our Alliance forever."

"Not to mention the way you're giving them a free shot at the treasure," Asaro asserted. Turnbull shot him a worried glance. He was clearly doing an even poorer job of holding back the anger that always simmered just beneath his skin than usual.

Then again, Cody reassured himself, what could go wrong at this stage?

The thought made him want to laugh out loud in relief, but he refrained. Unlike Asaro—or their mutual commanding general—Turnbull was well experienced in controlling his emotions, as a man of gentle breeding.

Baron Al snorted. "'Treasure,' my big fat fanny," he said. "If Jed wants to waste his few remaining resources chasing after a mirage, so much the better. Works to our advantage. Not that I'd put Jed as the type to fall for such a triple-stupe fantasy. But I suppose desperation can do that to a man."

"Phil," McCormac said smoothly, "please. Allow me."

Asaro jutted his foxlike jaw but nodded almost convulsively.

"Our men don't believe the story of a fabulous trove of predark technology and wealth is a fable, Baron," his fat fellow baron said. "They're grumbling in quite a discontented way."

Al laughed. "When did you start paying mind to soldiers' gossip, Phin McCormac? You always dismiss them as no more than rabble, anyway."

"What I'm telling you is that we—men of standing in the Alliance as well as the army who take our responsibilities seriously—"

That seemed to penetrate Al's rhino hide. "Are you saying I don't?"

"—have been concerned at your refusal to take decisive action against our vile foe since you failed, inexplicably, to give pursuit on the day of our glorious victory on this very spot. And you have continued to coddle our enemies in the negotiation, rather than forcing them to heel. And now—" he cocked his head and held up a hand toward the south, where the blasterfire murmur suddenly cut off "—we see the price of what we may charitably call your incompetence. You refused even to act when General Kylie mobilized the Grand Army in clear violation of the cease-fire to hunt this treasure you stubbornly refuse to believe in."

"And now the devils are openly attacking us!" Asaro almost screamed.

His associate's lips tightened, but he forced them to curve into the tight semblance of a smile, and his side whiskers bobbed as he nodded.

"Just so."

"What are you saying, gentlemen?" Al asked, with what struck Turnbull as astonishing calm, given his volcanic nature. "It's time to start walking all around the muzzle of the blaster and get to the damned trigger."

"Very well, Baron," McCormac said formally, sticking hands behind his back and puffing out his chest. "We have come in our capacity as officers and barons to make a much-needed change.

"You are herewith relieved of command over the army of the Uplands Alliance, Al Siebert. We thank you for your service."

Chapter Twenty-Six

Even as the officer shouted his treacherous command, Ryan had his horse in motion. Guiding it with his knees, he turned it right and sent it racing straight at the line of troopers riding in what was even more obviously an envelopment move down that side of his own little party.

Along with his SIG-Sauer in a shoulder rig beneath his left arm, he had a scabbied Peacemaker in a holster on his left hip. He drew the wheelgun fast with his good hand.

A clean-shaven rider, eyes wide in the still-dim light of dawn, tried to raise a sawed-off scattergun. Ryan stuck his own big handblaster over the neck of his prancing chestnut and blasted him through the base of the throat. His target fell backward from the saddle, discharging both barrels in a shout of flame and flash of noise.

The rider he'd shot had been on the left. The one who had just passed was now on Ryan's right as his horse bolted. The greencoat—whose sleeve wore the white brassard of Al's bodyguard detail—was hauling out a blaster and trying to turn to get a shot at Ryan.

Holding the burly Peacemaker across his body, the one-eyed man fired three times, holding back the trigger and slipping the single-action trigger with his thumb. He saw trail dust fly from at least two hits on the back of the sec man, who slumped over his horse's neck as she bolted.

Ryan raced his mount a few paces into the weeds, hearing hoarse cries, some turning to screams, and blasterfire behind. He reined her in and turned. He had a clean getaway before him, but that would mean leaving his friends, and that he wouldn't do.

Unlike the time the Protector patrol had gotten the drop on them, relaxing by their campfire, his people had already been alerted by the sec patrol's odd behavior that things might not be right. Following the standard principle that the best way to handle an ambush was to charge straight into it, his friends had all clearly done just the same thing Ryan had. With a quick count he saw to his relief that all six of them had made it off the road.

They'd broken out to both sides, though. As Ryan did his check, he saw Doc stab a sec man to his left and then blast one to his right with the shotgun barrel of his LeMat and then he joined Krysty and Ricky on the far side of the track.

Ryan blasted off the final two shots in his wheel-gun's cylinder. Then, holstering the blaster, he fished out the SIG-Sauer and cut loose. His friends joined in.

Horses screamed and bucked as the companions shot into the now totally confused scrum of cavalrymen. A couple went down, one pinning the leg of its howling rider beneath it. It was unfortunate to have to shoot the beast, who didn't have any blame in this fight, but even a lightly wounded horse could take its rider out of a fight as surely as a bullet through that rider's head. It had to be done, and Ryan and his friends all did.

The troop leader had somehow kept both his saddle and his wits. Now he brandished the sword and bellowed, "Pull back up the road and regroup! Ride, damn you!"

Then he jerked and swayed in the saddle as a shot hit him. Ryan wasn't sure which of his friends had tagged him. It might have been one of his own men, who were shooting wildly in all directions including right into the lightening sky. Fortunately they were too occupied with their panicked mounts to aim anywhere near properly.

Ryan caught a flash bead on the officer and shot three times. The man vanished from the saddle even as his men got their horses' heads turned back the way they came and began galloping out of the death zone.

"To me!" Ryan shouted. "Let the horses go and form a defensive circle!"

Spattering a few shots after the departing riders, his friends complied. Ryan swung down from his saddle, yanked his pack off from behind the cantle and slapped his horse on the rear. It raced away.

Ryan heard Jak yell, "Coming back!" and knew that the lure of whatever reward they'd been offered for this sudden betrayal was great enough to overcome even their fear of death.

"What do we do now?" asked a big-eyed Ricky, who'd emptied his Webley and now clutched his fat-barreled carbine to his chest.

"Fight a lot, son," J.B. said. "Mebbe die a lot."

He chuckled dryly as he checked the load on the Uzi machine pistol he'd unshipped from his own pack.

"You weren't planning on living forever, were you?"

FACE FLUSHING HOT, Cody Turnbull stepped forward.

"Lieutenant Peters," he said formally, "kindly take this man into custody."

"Sir!"

Al turned to look at his second in command. His face drained of color and his burly shoulders slumped.

"*Et tu,* Cody?" he said.

Cody stiffened. "My duty is to the Alliance, Baron," he said. "That overrides all other concerns."

A shrill caw of laughter followed that statement. Its note of wild malice—and madness—sent shivers down Cody Turnbull's spine.

Scarcely less taken aback by its source, Al turned his ashen face slowly toward his wife.

"Jessie Rae? Sweetheart—"

"Don't 'sweetheart' me, you filthy boar hog!" she yelled. Her lovely face was bright red beneath high-piled gold curls and twisted into a shape that was anything *but* lovely. Had he not seen the woman herself walk into the room mere moments before, Cody would never have recognized this demon-masked creature as his light of love.

Al sagged back in his chair at the fury of her verbal assault. She leaped to her feet.

"You've pawed my naked flesh for the last time!" she shrieked. "You've poked and prodded my cunny with that nasty cock for the last time."

Cody's jaw fell open. Even Asaro was looking aghast, his normally dark features sallow. Only Phineas McCormac seemed to take Lady Sierbert's shocking outburst in stride. He had his hands in the pocket of his gold-striped uniform trousers, leaning slightly forward on the balls of his booted feet, watching with a sort of detached interest.

At least Cody hoped it was that.

"Now you've fumbled and mismanaged your way

out of command," she shouted, "and now I get to wash my hands of you! Do you hear me? We're done! And we're going to march the army right out of camp before the sun is high, hunt down that little asshole Kylie and hang his hide up to dry, then take the treasure all for our own! And you won't have any part of it, you miserable *fuck*."

"But Jessie Rae," Al protested. "Why are you acting like this? Haven't I loved you? You can't be part of this dirty scheme."

"Part of it? Whose idea do you think it was?"

From the corner of his eye Cody saw a side of Mc-Cormac's mouth twitch up in a smug, fat smirk. Cody refused to think that might imply anything.

"But," the baron said, "I tried to give you everything."

Jessie Rae's small right fist came up from within the folds of her skirt. It held a two-shot derringer, which erupted with a colossal crack and a ball of flame that set the baron's eyebrows smoking.

"Yes," she said, looking straight into eyes with a blue hole suddenly between them, "and so you didn't give me what every woman wants—a man strong enough to tell her *no*."

For a moment Colonel Cody Turnbull could only stand rooted. "Wait," he said weakly, then louder, "Wait! This wasn't supposed to happen."

"Don't be such a pussy, Cody," Jessie Rae said, turning a look of luminous contempt on him. "It was always supposed to happen this way. We just didn't tell you because you're so weak-livered."

"I heard shots!" a new voice cried. "I— *Baron!*"

Cody turned to see Lieutenant Owens standing in

the door to the parlor. His hat was off, his blond hair in disarray. His green eyes were wide in horror.

And in his hand he held a Peacemaker.

RALLIED BY GREED—and mebbe equally by fear of the consequences failure might bring them—the ten or so surviving troopers came swarming back toward the companions.

"Down!" Ryan shouted. Whether they were badly trained, or just too caught up in the frenzy of the moment, the troopers were clearly not going to do the smart thing: get off their horses and shoot when they had a chance to hit something. Instead they clearly meant to overwhelm the companions with speed and superior numbers. And probably crush them under their horses' hooves.

The cavalrymen started spattering shots as soon as they began moving. Ryan saw a horse rear up shrieking, then fall straight forward onto its face and lie still, tumbling its rider over its neck. Ryan didn't hear a shot from his group, then realized the animal had been downed by Ricky with that tricky silent longblaster of his.

When first Ryan had laid eye on the homemade De-Lisle, he'd dismissed it as a gimmick. And once again the weapon—and the kid who carried it—had proved him wrong.

A ball sang like an angry bumblebee past Ryan's right ear, and he felt a slight tug. From the corner of his eye he saw a curl of hair, clipped free by the projectile, flutter away.

Then he was landing hard on his belly. It felt like his right upper side exploded. He felt wet, and realized he'd probably torn the half-cleaned wound open all over again.

Well, he was unlikely to bleed out from it. They'd either win this somehow and he'd get it bound up again. Or, well, a still heart didn't pump blood.

Ignoring the pain and the leakage, he rolled onto his injured side to bring his SIG-Sauer to bear on the charging horsemen.

Chapter Twenty-Seven

"Till!" Cody Turnbull shouted. "Hold on!" Though he couldn't see a reason on Earth why the eager young officer *should* hold on.

Tillman Owens began to swing up his handblaster.

Two shots roared out. The flashes came from Cody's right. As the young officer spun down, still clutching his blaster, Cody spun to see Lieutenant Peters standing with a look of satisfaction on his flamboyantly mustached face, and a line of blue smoke drooling upward from the muzzle of his handblaster.

"What have we done?" Cody could only ask weakly.

Phineas McCormac rolled into amiably ambling motion. He tugged at the derringer in Jessie Rae's hand. She clung to it a moment, then let go.

"Convenient," the baron and nominal colonel said conversationally as he walked toward the fallen lieutenant. Owens was lying on his chest with his face turned to his right and a look of horror still in his wide-open eyes. A pool of blood spread around him.

Grunting with effort, McCormac hunkered down at Owens's left side. His left hand was down by his hip, fingers up. Gently McCormac pressed the derringer into his palm and folded his unresisting fingers over its small curved grip.

"Here's how it happened, you see," he said, plac-

ing his hands on his thighs to aid in the considerable
project of heaving his bulk back aloft. "Maddened by
his general's inactivity, the gallant young Lieutenant
Owens snapped. He assassinated Baron Al with a hideout blaster, then tried to shoot his way clear before
being felled by the heroic Lieutenant Peters."

He turned a sanctimonious smile to Cody Turnbull,
who had begun to tremble with reaction.

"Or should I say, *Captain* Peters?" the fat baron said.
"How can you do anything less for the avenger of our
noble, if toward the end tragically misguided, commander in chief, General Turnbull."

Jessie Rae moved to stand smiling beside the pre-
sumptively promoted Peters. He slid his left arm around
her narrow waist. She rested her golden head on his
shoulder.

Outrage erupted from Turnbull. "What's going on
here? This is outrageous. I can't—"

"And then again," McCormac said with a shrug, "we
can always revise history again. On the fly, as it were."

He turned, holding a slim Colt blaster in his hand.
The weapon was leveled at Turnbull's lean gut.

"In the new version," McCormac said, still smoothly
smiling, "Colonel Turnbull becomes the cowardly assassin of his beloved commanding officer, and young
Owens the hero who died trying to stop him. Does that
version of events appeal to you more, Colonel?"

Cody turned an accusing glare on the true object of
his wrath. "You mean you'd go along with replacing
me again," he told Jessie Rae, "the way you replaced
me with *him?*"

"Oh, I didn't replace you with anybody, Cody honey,"
Jessie Rae said. "Randy's been my man all along."

"Then what about your promise—" Cody stopped dead. He realized there was no way he could finish that sentence.

She laughed. It was venomous music.

"You're being offered a sweetheart of a deal, Cody Turnbull," she said. "Swallow your pride and your principles—if you still pretend to have any—and accept a role as figurehead commander in chief of the Alliance Army. Or—" she shrugged "—be dead. It seems a pretty straightforward choice to me, but then again I'm only a woman. Weak-willed and simpleminded."

It was as if Cody deflated. His shoulders sagged forward. The military starch left his spine. His bony chin sunk toward his collarbone.

This is how it feels, he thought, *to have all your pride drain out of you at once.*

He sighed. Then straightening, he pulled back his shoulders and raised his head.

"What are my first orders to be, then, since I gather you're the ruling junta?"

Asaro looked to McCormac. The portly colonel nodded in turn to Jessie Rae.

"What that fat fool Al should have ordered long ago. The whole army up and on the march."

Cody nodded. "To bring the Protectors to battle and destroy them."

Her laugh was shrill. "Of course not. That can wait! The treasure first, you fool.

"Once it's in our hands, we'll have no trouble crushing Kylie and his pathetic Grand Army—then conquering the whole wretched Association. And maybe just getting rid of that bitch sister of mine once and for all."

SHOTS MOANED OVER Ryan's head. He held his SIG-Sauer up, gritting his teeth against the agony pounding in his wounded shoulder. He was a decent shot left-handed, not the ace he was with the right, and the P-226's 9 mm projectiles didn't have much punch at longer ranges.

He saw another rider go down, without the accompanying noise of a shot from his side, now spread out and spread-eagled in the grass. The new kid's steady, all right, he thought with approval.

The Uplander cavalry—sec men—were pretty hardcore. They'd taken losses bad enough to send most units running for cover. But still they came on, whooping, shooting and waving their big curved swords in the milky dawn light.

To Ryan's right, J.B. got up on one knee. He hosed the approaching riders with quick bursts from his Uzi. One horse reared, screaming, and fell. Another fell forward, tumbling into a flailing of limbs. The rider screamed in turn as his mount's weight crushed him. The beast itself heaved violently and lay still. It had broken its neck.

That was too much at last for the Uplander forces. They now outnumbered their quarry scarcely, if at all. They turned their horses' heads around and rode for camp as fast as the animals could run.

Silence fell heavy over the dewy grass. Slowly, Ryan lowered his blaster.

His friends began to rise like phantoms from the grass. Awkwardly Ryan thrust his blaster back in its holster. J.B. joined him, his stubby machine pistol slung and bouncing against his hip. He stretched down a hand. Gratefully, Ryan gripped his forearm and hauled him to his feet.

Ryan swayed. J.B. caught him by the arm and without comment helped steady him until he nodded.

The others were standing with weapons lowered but ready to swing into action should trouble abruptly return. Ricky Morales kept turning left and right, surveying the carnage in blank-eyed wonder.

"Twenty of them," he said. "Twenty men. On horses. And we won."

"If we survive, we win," J.B. said. "That's pretty much the whole story, right there."

"But none of us are even wounded," the boy said.

Ryan frowned. He was too messed up from the wound he'd suffered in the showdown in the gaudy.

"That true?" he demanded. "Everybody fit to fight?"

Everybody was. Jak had a bruised face but shook his head when asked if he needed help.

"Jak," Ryan said, "start rounding up the horses."

Jak nodded and moved off.

"We're good at what we do," Krysty told Ricky. "And we work well together."

She looked over at Ryan critically. "You need to sit and let Mildred take care of you."

Even though he'd just gotten up, Ryan was glad to sit down again. He was still a bit light in the head and loose in the joints.

Mildred bustled up. Krysty helped her remove Ryan's coat and open his shirt. The bandages beneath had come loose, and Ryan's side ran with blood.

"We'd better find this redoubt soon," Mildred said, cleaning the wound with a fresh rag form her pack and water from a canteen. "This is going to come close to using up our bandages, if nothing else."

"Best move on soon," J.B. said, standing watch

nearby, looking in the direction of the Uplander camp. "Those boys might come back with some buddies."

Ryan nodded, then raised his right arm slightly to allow Mildred to wrap a fresh turn of bandage around his shoulder and chest. It hurt, but he was still alive to feel it, which was most of what counted.

"So what now, Ryan?" Mildred asked as she cut the bandage with her knife.

Ryan chuckled, then winced. "Well, we're sure not going back for our pay."

Like the Armorer, Krysty was standing guard as Mildred worked on Ryan. "Would Baron Al really put a price on our heads after what we've done for him?"

"You know as well as I do how far a body can rely on a baron's gratitude," Ryan said. "Which is as far as you can throw a war wag. Usually. I agree about Al, though. I doubt he had anything to do with this."

"Okay, let me help you get your shirt on," Mildred said. "And I sensed there was a 'but' in there."

"Somebody sure as nuke shit offered those men a bounty for our hides," Ryan said. "Fact they were sec men doesn't strike me as a good sign. I'd say that means either somebody's replaced Al, or somebody pretty high up feels strong enough to make a play like this on his own hook. Which in turn suggests it's only a matter of time until Al's replaced for sure."

"Surely not so soon after he won the battle for them?" Mildred said. "And probably the war?"

"Politics," Ryan said. "Especially in alliances of barons like the two sides are made up of, everybody's always got one eye skinned for his own interests. Or even his own ego. I'd say somebody calculates Al's just about used up his usefulness. And a lot of important people may worry Al's gotten too big for his britches. Too powerful with the grunts and the peasant types."

Mildred shook her head. "Back in my day," she said, "we hoped humankind would evolve out of that sort of petty behavior by this time."

"One might argue human behavior has followed a retrograde path," Doc said sadly. "Although I suspect the truth to be, we act much as we have always acted since coming down from the trees. Although humankind's present circumstances do conduce to an added degree of ruthlessness."

Feeling stronger, Ryan pulled his shirt the rest of the way on after Mildred helped feed his right arm into a sleeve. It was bloody on the right side but he'd live with that. He stood up by himself. She refastened the sling that had come loose from his arm during the fight, and stayed slung about his neck.

Jak came back riding his horse and herding their other mounts. Ricky was with him. He had his DeLisle slung and a dazed look on his young face.

"Right," Ryan said. "Time to move."

"Where to?" Krysty asked.

He swung up into the saddle and shrugged. "Away. Find a place to lie up and rest during the day, take stock when we're in a bit better shape."

"What about you?"

"I'll live," he said. "Been hurt worse, got less care. Don't feel as sick as I was for a bit despite the fight. Some sleep's what I need now."

Mildred muttered her take on that but said nothing openly.

"One thing's sure," Ryan said as his friends began to circulate, quickly shaking down the chills for useful plunder. "We need to find the redoubt now, get stores replenished—if any are available there—and shake the dust of this whole little war off our boots."

"Won't be easy with two whole armies out looking for us," Krysty said.

J.B. laughed. His companions all looked at him.

"Don't forget," he said, "however angry Baron Jed might be with us, and whoever's after our hides in the Uplander camp, it's not gonna be *us* they're looking for."

"The redoubt?" Krysty asked.

"The rumor's out," Ryan said. "We learned that back in the gaudy. The kind of supplies Old Pete made the place out to have could put whoever grabs it on top of the whole heap, regardless of how things stand now."

"So fill me in," Mildred said. "Doesn't this mean we're racing these two armies to find the redoubt? While making sure they don't find us?"

"That's one way of looking at it," J.B. said. "Another is, why should we look when we got hundreds of people to do it for us?"

"But how can we possibly get into the redoubt if a whole army is holding it?" Mildred asked.

"It is unlikely to be an entire army that actually uncovers it," Doc said. "They will send out small parties of scouts, unless I miss my guess."

"That's how I see it, too," Ryan said. "What we need to do is wait until they find it, then move in while they ride back to get the rest of their crew."

His horse was starting to bob its head and step nervously in place. "Mount up, folks. I think my horse may sense others coming. We may've worn out our welcome here."

"I still can't believe we got away so lightly," Ricky said as he clambered, quickly if not gracefully, onto the back of his mare.

"Don't get too many ideas, kid," Ryan said. "The last easy day was yesterday. Let's ride."

Chapter Twenty-Eight

"He still there?" Mildred asked.

Ryan lowered the navy longeyes from his face. "Yeah," he said.

He made no move to pick up the Steyr Scout longblaster laid on the low knoll beside him. While it lacked the extreme range and accuracy of his last longblaster, it still gave reliable hits out to several hundred yards in the hands of a master marksman. Like Ryan Cawdor.

The problem was, their shadower knew that, and kept carefully just out of the range at which he judged Ryan would be willing to waste precious cartridges in hopes of a hit.

"One thing's for sure," Ryan muttered, glaring toward the distant figure sitting quite openly, silhouetted against a blue sky. "He wasn't lying about knowing a lot about us. Too much."

He had also managed to elude Jak when the longhaired albino youth—a master of stealth—had sought to sneak up on him, nor had he fallen for several of the cleverest explosive booby traps J.B., with the able assistance of his protégé Ricky, who had a gift for such things, had set for him.

"He is good," Ryan said. "And that's the bastard of the thing."

"He's smart and he's sneaky, granted," Mildred said. "That doesn't mean he's better than you, Ryan."

Ryan shrugged and winced slightly at the pain that sent throbbing through his injured chest and shoulder. In the past few days of playing serial cat-and-mouse games—Ryan's band stalking the search parties sent out by the Uplanders and the Protectors, Snake Eye stalking *them*—the infection that had initially dulled Ryan's wits had faded.

"Don't know," he said. "He just about did for me back at that gaudy. And I can't shake the feeling he deliberately cut me some slack."

"One thing is certain," Doc said, "he is not smarter and stronger and faster than all of us. As we shall demonstrate to him, in the fullness of time."

"Why would he have held back with you, Ryan?" Mildred asked.

"He thinks we can do better finding the treasure than he can solo, just the way we reckon two whole armies can do a better job searching than us."

Mildred shook her head. "I don't understand how Baron Al could be so stupid, even if that asshole Jed is. Why on Earth are both sides restricting themselves to a single search party when they could have hundreds of men combing the countryside?"

Doc uttered a caw of laughter. "Never underestimate the power of baronial rapacity, dear lady," he said. "Nor of baronial paranoia."

"He's right," Ryan said. "Neither leader trusts his own men any farther than he can throw them. They're each figuring they can keep closer tabs on a single search team than a bunch of them, so they're holding back their armies as reserves, to storm in and grab the redoubt when its found—and keep the freelance looting to a minimum."

He shook his head. "Which comes pretty close to convincing me Al's out of the picture. Mebbe he's really no less grabby than any other baron, but this kind of shortsightedness... I can't see that from him, no way."

"Does it matter?" Mildred asked.

Ryan frowned a moment, then shrugged.

"Reckon not," he said. "Dead's dead. All I care about is that none of us take the last train west anytime soon."

He pulled back from the crest of the low rise to scan the countryside to north and south. He had Mildred and Doc to keep an eye out for patrols—in particular Uplander patrols, since the three of them were currently just a few miles west of the end of their lines.

As stupid as he thought both commanders were being for sending out only a single search team each, they weren't equally stupid about everything. Since as far as Ryan knew they had no better idea than he and his friends did where the redoubt lay, it made decent sense to search the easier, safer zone first.

If the place happened to be hidden in the enemy's region, well, that was one halfway sensible reason to keep the bulk of the armies together and ready to move out as one to grab and hold the objective.

"Ryan," Mildred said as he scanned the flood plain to the south. "Something."

He instantly swept his single gaze to the north. "What?" he asked.

"Jak and Krysty riding back like their hair's on fire," Mildred reported.

He caught dark specks, just moving down a shallow slope at least half a mile distant toward them. The two of them were making good time. A quick glance through the longeyes confirmed Mildred's judgment.

"Stay sharp, people," Ryan said. He swung the longeyes up to sweep the horizon behind them. "We still don't know whether they found something, or if they're riding flat-out because they got greencoats on their tails."

"If they are pursued, it would seem by not many," Doc said. "Inasmuch as they are leading them straight to us."

"Yeah," Ryan said. If it was the pursuit scenario, that could only mean their pursuers were few enough to give the three waiting an opportunity to empty their saddles from ambush. Had it been a good-sized patrol after them they would likely have tried to lead them far afield and then give them the slip, then sneak back and join their friends.

Mildred shifted to skulk behind a grassy lump that was probably a predark car or even truck grown over. Doc took the reins of their three horses and led them behind a screen of trees growing along a creek.

Ryan put the longeyes away. Taking up his Steyr Scout, he stretched himself prone on the grass to wait. He didn't bother looking through the telescopic sight. He could cover more ground quicker with his one unaided eye. And if anybody was chasing after Krysty and Jak, they weren't exactly going to be sneaky about it.

But no other riders appeared anywhere along the northern skyline. Still, Krysty and Jak pushed their mounts hard. Both horses were wide-eyed, lathered and blowing hard when the pair approached. Ryan stood up out of the grass as they got within fifty yards. He still kept a hold on his longblaster, and a keen eye skinned, in case anybody joined the party late.

"Not getting chased?" he called as Krysty turned her mare's head and galloped toward him.

She reined the horse in a few feet away. "No," she said. "We got something."

"Where?"

"Abandoned ville mebbe five miles west and a little south. Pretty sizable place."

"Can find redoubt easy," Jak said, pulling his paint to a stop. "Find sentries, find place."

"Which side, my friend?" Doc called, leading the horses back toward the group.

"Greencoats."

"We weren't able to ambush them the way we hoped. They took off at an angle away from us. There're six of them, so we couldn't likely take them if we'd been able to catch up with them."

"Good call. How many left behind?"

"Start day, twelve riders," Jak said.

"Whoo," Doc said. "They must have found the mother lode indeed, to leave half their number behind."

Ryan nodded briskly. "Ace."

"Mebbe not quite so ace," Mildred called.

"What do you mean, Mildred?" Krysty asked.

Mildred pointed to the west. The skyline lay empty. Unbroken, specifically, by the infuriating black blotch of horse and rider that had been there since the sun came up, a couple hours after Ryan had sent his two teams to shadow the search parties north and south.

"So our shadow appears to have deserted us."

Ryan showed his teeth in a snarl.

"So the bastard learned all he needed to know. Fireblast!"

"Lover," Krysty said, "I'm so sorry—"

He waved a hand to cut her off. "Not your fault," he rasped. "No other way to play it."

He went to take his horse's reins from Doc.

"Jak," he called, "go get J.B. and Ricky back from ghosting the Uplanders. The rest of us'll join you outside the ville. Any decent cover there?"

"Hills west," Jak said. "Go north and south."

"Find us."

Jak didn't bother to answer. Instead he turned and nudged his horse into a gallop to the northwest.

"Well," Ryan said, swinging into the saddle, "I've got good news as well as bad."

"You mean good news other than finding a possible escape route from this debacle?" Doc asked.

"What good news do we have other than that?" Mildred asked suspiciously.

"Well," Ryan said, "the good news is, I don't think we're going to have to take out six troopers to get to the mat-trans and get out.

"The bad news is, we'll be going up against one man who's worse."

Chapter Twenty-Nine

"I suppose it's truly no great surprise, Ryan," Doc said with a resigned sigh.

Ryan grunted. "Not really a surprise at all. In fact, this is what I was counting on."

He moved his face aside from the Leupold scope of his Scout longblaster. "Well, not this *exactly*, I'll admit."

Doc and Mildred, who were lying next to him on the top of the low hill, murmured their agreement. Though the ville lay a quarter mile to the southwest, no one needed vision enhancement to recognize what stood just outside the collection of buildings that had probably been little more than a collection of tumbledown shacks even before a few years of utter neglect had taken their toll.

It was a sizable two-wheeled cart that had been up-ended. The wooden bed had a man in a blue shirt pinned to it in a spread-eagle position by big nails through his wrists and ankles.

"The snaky guy sure went to a lot of trouble to do that," Mildred said. "That took a lot of time, and it has to be purely to send *us* a message that's he's here and waiting on us. Cocky bastard, isn't he?"

"Yeah," Ryan said. "And that's likely the lonesome edge we got."

"Is he truly that formidable?" Doc asked.

"I hate to admit it," Ryan said, "but my shoulder says yes. He's not just triple-fast. He's triple-*smart,* and that makes him dangerous."

"So what now?" Doc asked.

Ryan sighed. "For now, we wait for our friends to do their jobs and hope like hell they survive. And that afterward, mebbe, we do, too."

"So the key, here, boy," J.B. said, "is to hide your trap in plain sight."

"How so?" Ricky asked, hunkered down beside him by the road.

He actually reckoned he had a fair head start on the answer, but he wanted to hear it straight from the Armorer's lips. A lover of tinkering and intricate mechanisms in general—and weapons and traps in particular—he recognized the awe-inspiring nature of an opportunity to learn from a true master of the craft.

"You know you don't want them to spot the trap," J.B. said. He had opened the uppermost of the heavy dispatch bags mounted tandem behind the saddle and spilled its contents onto the road. He was busily replacing them with messages of a different kind.

"Obvious-like. But in country like this, where it's not that easy to hide the trigger, you need to bait your victims to draw them in. And to take the bait, they got to see it."

"Ah."

They had been riding toward the Uplander camp, looking for a promising site and keeping eyes skinned for the Alliance Army, when a lone rider had come pounding hell-for-leather toward them down the road. Ricky guessed he was taking a message to his comrades guarding the entrance to the lost redoubt, and that that message was the army was on its way.

J.B. had them ride straight on to meet him as if nothing unusual was happening. As they approached within forty feet, the Armorer said, "Now."

He'd swung up his M-4000 scattergun, and Ricky had aimed his Webley at the man.

Unfortunately the trooper had recognized them— unfortunately for *him*. He yanked his horse's head sideways, apparently intending to turn the animal broadside to block their path, and made a grab for his own handblaster in its flapped holster.

Ricky and J.B.'s first shots had hit the hapless horse. Even as the animal squealed and went over on its side, the cavalry trooper got his handblaster out and started blasting. The horse, wounded and flailing about to get to its feet, pinned his leg to the rutted road. With the same more-balls-than-brains valor that got him into this mess, the Uplander trooper kept blasting the air— until a couple close-range blasts of buckshot quieted him down for good.

A quick swipe of J.B.'s belt knife across the animal's throat had stilled it, too.

"SON?" J.B. SAID after he'd worked in silence for a few minutes.

"Sir?"

The Armorer snorted. "No need to call me a thing like that. Not until I'm old enough to have a snow-white beard grown down to here."

He snorted brief laughter. "Yeah. And while I'm talking about things that won't ever happen, wait until

I can fly by flapping my arms, too. Anyway, I been thinking some. About this sister of yours."

"Yes… J.B.?"

"So, you do know the chances of us ever running into her, or even cutting sign of her are about the same as a solid diamond meteorite's going to fall from the sky and land at your feet. Right?"

Ricky nodded. He didn't trust himself to speak.

J.B. bared teeth in a grimace. "Fact is, odds are good she's dead."

"We are hard to kill, she and I."

J.B. stopped. He looked up at his protégé, then flashed a grin.

"Good point," he said, "if she's like you. But don't fill yourself up with hope so far you spring a leak and just collapse."

"I manage to keep plenty busy thinking of other things," Ricky said, gesturing at the open saddlebag.

J.B. nodded and got back to work.

"Why just one saddlebag?"

"Well," J.B. said, working without looking around, "we've got to conserve our limited store of plas, which is why I'm packing the contents of our boy's spare-powder flask in around the block of C-4, on the off chance it'll detonate the black powder when it goes. Won't add much to the actual blast, but could add some nice, showy smoke and fire.

"And, see, there's no real need for much explosive anyway. Whoever's in charge down this road has several hundred men. We're not going to put a big enough dent in that without a lot more explosive than we could haul around with us."

"Why are we doing this, then?"

"Delay," J.B. said. "Put the fear into them. Buy some time for Krysty and Jak to do their part. And Ryan, Doc and Millie theirs."

"So…"

Ricky paused. J.B. not only didn't mind his questions, but he also encouraged them, just the way his uncle had. And when he didn't want Ricky chattering he made it clear fast and plain. But Ricky was always self-consciously eager to avoid coming across like he thought he knew more than this small and not-very-imposing-looking man, whom he idolized almost as much as he did Ryan.

"Spit it out," J.B. said.

"So I know we want them to see the bait," Ricky said. "But isn't this, well, too obvious?"

"Would be," J.B. agreed, "if they had the least little reason to expect a booby, here and now. But that's not the way they and the Protectors have been playing their little game for all these years. And even if they figured out it's how we fight—dirty—what do you think the odds are they expect us to have done anything but hightailed it out of here fast as we could ride, after we settled accounts for a whole platoon of sec men?"

He closed the saddlebag gingerly and stood, waving absently at the flies that had already begun to swarm around the still-warm carcass.

"No," he said. "They won't suspect a thing. Not this time."

He gazed east and frowned, then nodded. "Right on schedule."

"What do you mean?"

"Check it out. Dust."

Scrambling to his feet, Ricky stared down the road. Above the horizon rose a brown plume.

"But it just rained a day or two ago," he said. "How can the road be so dusty already?"

"Stick around with us long enough," J.B. said, "you'll learn that's how it always goes with armies. They always seem to march in either mud or dust. Don't know why. Just is."

He gestured at the chill, who lay on his side in the road, fortunately facing away.

"Time to roll up the road a ways," he said. "Let's load our dead friend here on the back of his horse and go."

Ricky stared at him. He wasn't superstitious about handling the dead. Much, anyway. Nor was he squeamish...not really.

"Why?" he asked. "What do we need him for?"

He stopped short of pointing out the man was dead. J.B. was a patient tutor, but had little use for simps and stupes. And pointing out the obvious tended to put a person in one or the other category, if not both.

J.B. already had the chill under the armpits and was dragging him toward where J.B.'s horse was tethered to a peg, eating weeds by the ditch.

"'Cause we got a use for him," he grunted. "Now grab his rad-blasted boots and give me a hand. They don't call it deadweight for nothin'!"

THE ROAD STRETCHED across mostly level land for a mile or two. Level enough for Colonel Cody Turnbull, riding at the head of the army of the Alliance, to spot the black shape of the horse lying sprawled across the road a good ways off.

He frowned.

"What's that?" demanded Captain Randolph Peters, who rode at the colonel's side. Turnbull had refused to accept the rank of general without a full meeting of the council, although he had agreed to take command of the army.

The young officer had attached himself to the new supreme commander as aide-de-camp, if not actual second in command. Cody was uncomfortably certain he was there to ride close herd on him on behalf of Mc-Cormac and Asaro, even though that pair of plutocrats were riding right behind.

And for the treacherous temptress Jessie Rae. Cody still couldn't believe how his sweet-faced angel had played him like a violin. How could she allow this... this callow fool to sully her fair white flesh with his touch? How could she choose him over a gentleman of breeding and proved valor like Cody Turnbull?

That the blond-headed lady—now baron of Siebertville in her own right—had offered to let him assist the younger officer in...pleasuring her... He cut the thought off midstream. He wouldn't allow himself to think such things. Much less imagine them. What troubled him most wasn't the sickness that caused in his stomach, but the even more pronounced effect it had in regions south of there....

"Looks as if our messenger has met with some accident, Captain," Turnbull said, stammering a little at the outset. Fortunately the sheer habit of command kicked in and he finished, at least, sounding like a leader of men instead of a blushing schoolboy. "Send a small detachment to investigate, if you will, Captain."

Peters's long yellow locks swung as he twisted in

his saddle to shout orders. A quartet of soldiers from the squadron of sec men riding right behind the new commander put spurs to their steeds and galloped past.

That Oliver Christmas rode at the head of the commanders' bodyguard didn't bother Cody much. The sec men were mostly new faces. And even though most of the sec men McCormac and Asaro and their faction had secretly suborned had by sheer bad luck gotten themselves chilled by the mercie coldhearts Al had employed, Cody didn't worry about the men still loyal to the sec boss, either. Suspect what he might about the sudden demise of Baron Al, Christmas loyally served the office, not the man—as he'd said all along.

Then again, Cody had few illusions the fat sec boss would protect him against the machinations of Jessie Rae and her cohorts any better than he had her husband.

He continued to lead the army forward at a sedate walk. Jessie Rae had quit her carriage twice already since the army set forth to ride up on a borrowed mount and harangue him to force the army to go faster. But he had refused point-blank, and McCormac and Asaro backed him up. There was no point getting the men and horses exhausted, to say nothing of getting the horse troopers separated from the plodding infantry. The whole point of the exercise was all to land on the ville where their objective lay in one force, and let Baron Jed or anyone else do what they pleased.

He was skeptical of this whole treasure thing, at best. What quickened his pulse was the chance to draw Baron Jed to the decisive battle Al's misguided sense of mercy had denied them. And end the lowland threat once and for all.

And maybe, he thought, if I truly bring us final victory—and give her vengeance over her sister, unseemly as that may be—Jessie Rae will look with favor on me. And me alone.

The four horsemen reached the unmoving shape and dismounted a few yards short of it. One held the animals and another stood guard with a Springfield at the ready. The other two went to examine the dead animal.

"I don't see the rider," Peters said. "Where could he have gotten off to?"

A flash of orange fire enveloped the two men kneeling by the dead horse. Cody caught a glimpse of the sentry being flung like a rag doll into the ditch before a giant cloud of dirty gray smoke hid the scene.

The horses turned and ran in wild panic back toward their herd—the rest of the cavalry. Somehow the man who was holding them got his arm tangled in the reins and was dragged up the road between the middle two.

The sharp, flat crack of a detonation hit Cody with such force he actually felt it on his face, like a brief gust of wind.

The dragged trooper's shrill shrieks of agony went on and on, gradually getting louder. Until one of the stampeding horses stepped on his head.

Chapter Thirty

"Riders come!"

Seeing the way her own mare pricked up her ears Krysty already knew the animal was sensing other horses even before Jak called his warning. She didn't know how he'd detected him. Possibly by reading the reaction of his own scrubby horse, although his own senses were almost as sharp as a wild animal's.

She grinned at him. "Ready?"

For answer he sent his mount galloping straight ahead, in the general direction of the Grand Army of the Association.

Krysty galloped after him. They'd pushed their horses hard to get to this encounter in time to have a hope of doing some good. And they'd need to push the animals harder still to pull it off—and maybe even survive. But there was no help for it. They had to play it this way or not at all.

No more than a quarter mile ahead horsemen abruptly appeared against the afternoon skyline. First one, then three, then a dozen or more riders. Some of them wore blue shirts, but the fact that they were visibly armed and the direction from which they appeared identified them positively as a Protector patrol, presumably screening the main body from blundering without

warning into the Uplander Army. Or marching blithely
into another ambush.

Krysty's heart raced. There's not going to be any
strike reverse-ambush where we all ride away un-
scathed here, she thought. The numbers were too great,
the enemy too aware.

So naturally she turned her mare straight toward
them and rode at full speed, Jak right alongside.

While they weren't the least-distinctive-looking people in the Deathlands, it was unlikely the Protector cavalry could possibly recognize them at this range, even if
any of the patrol's members had glimpsed them during
their brief yet eventful stay among Baron Jed's troops.
But weapons came out. Carbines were brandished and
a few sabers winked in the sun. While on a hunt for
fabled treasure on the edge of enemy territory, the soldiers were inclined to prepare for the worst.

They didn't shoot, though. Not that mounted men
could muster enough accuracy to hit mounted targets
except by lucky accident. The problem was, there were
a lot of them, and it wouldn't take much for their luck to
hit, and Krysty's and Jak's to go straight south.

She let the looped reins fall to her horse's neck and
waved her arms. The mare continued to close with the
cavalry.

"Hey!" Krysty shouted. "It's us you're looking for!
We chilled the baron's son! Us! Come and get us if you
can, you bastards!"

At her side Jak raised a wolf howl. The sound sent
a chill down her back.

Whether their enemies could understand the words
she couldn't know, but they knew a challenge when they
saw it. They reacted the way cavalry troopers naturally

would: cotton balls of white smoke puffed suddenly
from longblaster muzzles.

Slowing their mounts, Krysty and Jak wheeled about
and headed away. A quick glance over her shoulder
showed Krysty that the bluecoats were racing in pursuit. They stopped shooting as some officer or noncom
doubtless snarled at them to quit wasting the baron's
good powder and ball, but they began to whoop in the
sheer excitement of the chase.

Leaning well over their horses' necks, Krysty and
Jak led the troopers on a wild chase, but not exactly
back the way they had come. Rather, they angled
slightly to the northeast. Now all they had to do was
keep the Protector cavalry interested—and not die,
which might be the tricky part....

"THEY'RE GOING right," J.B. said.

The sun was halfway down the western sky. Ricky
lay on his belly on the grass beside the Armorer, peering through a tall clump of weeds beside the partly ruined farmhouse.

Five hundred yards to the southeast, the advancing
Uplander column slowed visibly. It wasn't any great
mystery why. The body of the chilled messenger lay
in the middle of the dirt track—right where J.B. and a
mystified Ricky had left him.

The column's lead riders turned well shy of the
corpse and rode along the ditch. It had a couple of
inches of water trickling among the weeds at the bottom, as Ricky knew well, since he'd recently been wad-
ing in that same ditch, helping the master at his work.

J.B. had his minisextant out and was using the little
telescope he used to shoot the sun when they needed

to know where they were. He lowered it and showed a
quick, rare smile to Ricky.

"Watch this."

Ricky felt his pulse pick up its beat. He had an idea
what was coming, but he didn't see the flash. Smoke
billowed from the ditch, throwing out clumps of dirt
and sod. It swallowed at least two riders and their
mounts. A third horse following a few paces behind
simply fell onto its side in the ditch and lay still.

On the road horses reared and bucked. The crack
of the booby's blast reached Ricky and J.B.'s lookout,
along with the screams of horses. And, more faintly,
men.

Officers were trying to regain control of their troops
when an explosion erupted in the far ditch, then two
others on the same side.

As the heavy, hard sounds reached them, J.B. looked
thoughtful. Then he shrugged.

"Four out of five," he said. "Not too shabby for this
kind of work."

The multiple blasts—coming from off the road,
where the column had gone to avoid what now looked
like an obvious trap—had induced complete disorder
in the first half of the long column.

J.B. watched through his minisextant as a figure on
a black horse gesticulated with a saber. Troops were
dismounting and deploying, gingerly, into the untended
fields to either side of the road. Infantry squads came
up at the trot, longblasters at port arms. They likewise
spread out to the flanks into skirmish lines.

"Ace on the line," J.B. said. "The commander's cautious. He doesn't know yet whether those were all boo-
bies or somebody's shooting cannon at them. Mebbe

more ambush. It's that skinny prissy-pants character. Al's second in command. What's his name?"

"Turnbull," said Ricky. "Cody Turnbull. Colonel."

J.B. tucked his minisextant away. "Never would have reckoned he had the sand to make a move on old Al. Then again, I don't pretend to know how people work."

He came up to a crouch and moved back behind the cover of the house. Ricky followed, carrying his longblaster.

J.B. was untying the horses from the posts that held up the sagging roof of the back porch.

"More I see of people," he remarked, "better I like machines. Come on, kid. We've done our job here. These fellas won't sort things out for a good hour. Mebbe two.

"Time to get back and lend our friends a hand."

KRYSTY FELT her mare's strength begin to fail beneath her.

She and Jak had managed to stay no more than a hundred yards ahead of the pursuing cavalry. Because they'd left their packs with Ryan outside the deserted ville, their mounts were more lightly laden than the Protector horses. But the truth was the cavalrymen were more experienced riders, and just better at getting the most out of their mounts than their two intended victims were.

Krysty could feel her mare trying to keep up the pace, but her steps were beginning to falter; she could feel it in their rhythm.

Then Jak, who had pulled ahead, called back over his shoulder, "There!"

He pointed ahead and to the right. Beyond a deceptively easy rising slope of grass, waving in a stiffening afternoon breeze, rose a brown cloud. Dust.

Already leaning forward over her saddle horn to reduce drag, Krysty stretched out even farther. "Go, brave girl!" she shouted to the horse. "Just a little farther! Then you can rest."

Whether she understood the words or simply the encouragement in her rider's tone, the mare's head and ears came up. Her strides neither lengthened nor became faster, but became stronger.

They reached the top of the rise. There, several hundred yards off to her right, rode the Uplander cavalry vanguard under the green and white banners of the Alliance. Behind trudged what looked to Krysty as their entire army, including their smoothbore artillery on its caissons.

Well, she thought, since the whole point of this scheme was to get well and truly stuck between the hammer and the anvil...

She rode straight at the marching army, whose hundreds of blasters made the menace of the relatively small party closing in hungrily on their horses' tails seem like a mouthful of warm spit.

At her side Jak gave voice to another uncharacteristically loud and piercing cry. This one was a serious of shrill yips, like a coyote.

Whether Jak's call had anything to do with it, Krysty saw a ripple pass through the column. Arms pointed. Soldiers began to unlimber weapons, although few pointed their way yet. A pair of riders was no threat to an army, no matter how crazy they acted. If they acted as if they were really going to charge, a volley could easily vaporize them both before they got close enough even to sting the larger force.

Then heads seriously began to turn. Krysty heard shouts with frantic notes. Trumpets blared hastily. She glanced back. The pursuing Protector patrol was coming over the low crest no more than fifty yards behind. They reined in their horses so hard they almost stumbled as they got a look at just exactly what *they* were riding toward.

The Uplanders, for their part, were getting seriously excited. Infantry had swung about and knelt to present their longblasters. Officers pointed with swords and shouted. Trumpets blew again and what looked like a hundred cavalry with green pennons rode out in a ragged mass. Toward Krysty and Jak.

"Jak!" she screamed. "Veer off!"

Now was the crunch time. If the two blood enemies were more excited at the sight of each other than of a pair of random riders—and she doubted any of the Uplanders would recognize them at this distance, even if some of the Protectors may have—they'd have a chance. Otherwise the hammer and the anvil were going to hit, and they'd be like a couple of ripe tomatoes caught between.

Jak had already turned his horse's head left and rode hell-bent west, paralleling the road. Krysty's mare needed little encouragement to follow. Now she did pick up her pace, sensing her mistress's urgency and fear if not recognizing a threat on her own.

Krysty heard a few black-powder blasters pop. She winced, bracing her body for impacts. The huge soft-lead slugs moved much slower than the smaller, pointier slugs launched by more modern weapons, but they tended to act like battering rams on human flesh and blood, smashing huge and hideous wound channels through limbs and bodies. While she'd already been aware of the fact, they'd seen plenty of evidence over the past few weeks in the form of mangled chills. And worse, the wounded.

Next came a rattle of at least semiorganized blaster-fire. She didn't hear so much as feel the moan of a fat bullet passing slower than sound.

She looked around again. The tails of the Protector patrol's mounts were just vanishing back over the rise in furious pursuit of Uplander cavalry.

Nobody seemed to be looking at her and Jak. They just weren't interested anymore.

"We can ease off, Jak!" she cried. He was already sitting up straighter and bringing his horse to a trot with gentle pressure on the reins. Krysty did likewise.

Her mare blew loudly. Her sides were drenched with sweat and quivering.

"Good girl," Krysty called. "Now get us back to Ryan, and your work is done!"

Chapter Thirty-One

Struck by the nail of a strong and well-scarred thumb, the match flared into blue-and-yellow light. By its brief small glow Ryan read the sheet of paper he'd plucked from the cart bed, where it had been nailed next to the twisted and now-stinking corpse of the Upland soldier.

You have to face me, it read in almost fussily precise cursive. *Come with friends and watch them die first, or come and die alone. But you will come and you will die.*

He uttered a grunt. It might have been a laugh.

"Nice of you to warn me," he said quietly. "Never would have worked that out on my own."

He had felt no hesitation striking the match. Though the moon wasn't up, the stars gave some illumination, enough to see him walk openly down from the hill where he'd parted company with his companions. But not enough to read.

That tiny match flame, flickering its brief life away, would give a blaster as skilled as Snake Eye all the light he needed and more to drop Ryan in his tracks.

But he wouldn't.

His enemy hadn't set up this whole scenario so he could snipe Ryan down from the shadow of a derelict store. He wanted to savor the moment and he wanted his victim to be looking into his eyes, the human one and the snake one, when he died.

The mutie mercie wasn't the only one who understood his enemy loud and clear. He may have spent a lot more time studying the companions than vice versa, but Ryan was a quick study, especially when survival was at stake.

He whipped the match dead just before the flame reached scarred and callused fingers and flung it down. The bare dirt, pounded so hard by years of feet and hooves and iron-bound wag wheels that it had so far resisted the efforts of rain and temperature to break it down, offered no tinder to risk starting a blaze that might burn the ville down around their objective.

He surveyed the dark derelict structures, mostly made of wood scraps and other scabbie, that leaned together in the dark like drunken wag-drivers turned out of a gaudy after drinking down their pay. Somewhere in there, he didn't doubt, his enemy watched. Waiting. Smiling.

Ryan said nothing. He cared to waste words no more than bullets—or blood. He merely hitched the scoped Scout longblaster on its sling, muzzle down over his left shoulder, and walked into the waiting ville.

He knew that would send his message to the mercie far louder than any blustering shout: *challenge accepted.*

A BEAT OR TWO after the thump of Ricky's DeLisle longblaster, nothing happened. The boy said nothing. But lying beside him in a sort of hollow that overlooked Heartbreak's nearest structures from no more than fifty yards away, Krysty could see his young pale face go dark in furious frustration.

The bolt clattered as he threw it. Unlike most "silenced" weapons, the carbine he had lovingly helped his uncle craft over an ancient Ishapore-made Enfield rifle truly made next to no noise when fired. The locked bolt kept gas from escaping the breech, there was no associated clack of a semiautomatic action reciprocating to eject the spent casing and slam home a new cartridge, and the .45ACP projectile traveled slower than sound, meaning it never produced a loud crack when it passed some object in flight.

He aimed over the iron sights, squeezed the trigger again. This time one of the riders approaching the ruined ville's eastern outskirts threw up his hands and pitched from the saddle. The other five Uplander riders never glanced around.

"They don't even know it happened," J.B. murmured from his position kneeling to Ricky's right. "Couldn't hear squat."

That was enough for Krysty. She grabbed the lever-action Winchester Model 73 replica that lay by her side. Pressing the steel butt-plate against her right shoulder she quickly took up aim from her prone position on the lead rider and shot.

The black powder .44-40 cartridge produced a big red flame and a lot of noise. Nothing happened initially, but as Krysty levered a new cartridge from the tubular magazine slung beneath the twenty-four-inch barrel, the second rider in the loose formation reeled in the saddle, clutching his gut. She threw a second fast shot, scarcely bothering to aim.

At this range, under feeble light cast down by the half-moon that had recently crept over the horizon, it would have been a tough shot even for Ryan the master marksman, with his scoped blaster. For Ricky to

have scored two hits in however many shots—Krysty
lost count what with the noise and flash of her own
weapon—and over open sights was a testament to skill
beyond his tender years. Or his triple-strike luck, which
was almost as good.

Now the Uplander troopers knew they were taking
fire. They reined in their horses. Even at this range,
their body language told Krysty they were feeling surprise and uncertainty.

Naturally enough. They were expecting opposition
to their dash into the ville to try to secure the hidden treasure trove to be opposed, if at all, by opposite numbers from the Protector army. Baron Jed's men
had hunkered down along a rutted wag-track several
hundred yards south. The two forces had spotted each
other, approaching the ville almost simultaneously, by
the blood-colored light of the setting sun. The Uplanders had likewise halted a similar distance away. And
in the hour or two since, each army had simply sat,
doing nothing much the five companions could see at
this range. Each was obviously waiting for the other to
make the first move.

Now the Uplanders had. Krysty blasted off a third
shot. That one missed like the rest.

But hitting anything wasn't the point. Realizing that
at least one "enemy sniper" had them under fire, they
turned about and ran for the safety their own lines.

"Whoever's in charge over there," Mildred muttered
from right behind Krysty, "isn't going to thank those
boys for running."

J.B. chuckled softly. "Lot can happen in a face-off
like the one they got with Baron Jed's bunch. They'd

rather take their chances with a pissed-off baron than face a shooter who's already thinned them by a third."

He turned to look at Ricky. "That was some shooting, boy."

In the dim moonglow Krysty saw a hint of the dark color that had drained from Ricky's face when he scored his first hit return to his cheek.

Threat averted—for the moment—Krysty took a quick check of her little party, under cover in a sort of bowl nestled among the little hills. Ryan and J.B. thought that this little spur of rises, at least, was probably not natural. They, and perhaps the whole set of hills, probably came about when the ruins of some predark ville got covered over by dirt and vegetation in the course of a hundred-plus years.

Jak hunkered right behind Krysty, his Python gripped in one hand. His foxlike jaw was clamped shut so tightly Krysty could practically hear his teeth creak against the anger of being denied the chance to perform his trademark creepy-crawling in the derelict ville to help Ryan. But the one-eyed man had expressly forbidden his companions from trying to rescue him no matter what the outcome of his crazy duel to the death with Snake Eye. And under his steely blue glare, each had sworn to do his will.

He had left up to them the question of whether to hang on to their horses for an escape attempt in the event Ryan lost. They had instantly and unanimously agreed to unload the horses and set them free to shift for themselves. They were on a one-way mission into Heartbreak.

It could only end, now, in a getaway by mat-trans jump or death.

"So what happens now?" Mildred asked.

"Same as we been doing," J.B. answered. "Wait. Try not to die."

"And pray," Mildred added.

J.B. shrugged.

Krysty said nothing. She didn't need to. Her friends knew her well enough to know she'd been praying silently but ceaselessly since her Ryan had left them.

As if to torment her she heard blasterfire from somewhere in the cluster of thirty-to-forty buildings, which the rising moon had turned into a horrific wasteland of jumbled, jagged shapes and threatening shadows.

But she didn't get long to dwell on what that might mean for Ryan, because Jak whistled low and pointed south.

A group of cavalry was riding hell-for-leather from their own temporary positions to the south. At least a dozen troopers this time.

And they were clearly not making a dash at the ville Krysty and the others guarded.

They were riding straight at them.

IN THE CORNER of his eye Ryan caught a splinter of movement.

To perceive was to react. He hurled himself to the left, smashing into a closed door. At the same time he flung out his right arm and fired two shots toward the motion, which had come from a darkened doorway half a short block ahead and to his right.

For all his panther quickness, fire flared yellow before he got his first shot off.

The door was largely dry-rotted. Instead of smashing his left shoulder it virtually exploded at the impact of his body. The instant before he vanished into the darkened building, his SIG-Sauer kicked his hand for the second time. At the same instant a second muzzle-flash bloomed.

Ryan had no clue where the first bullet went, other than that it didn't hit him, which was what really mattered. He heard the second shot punch into the door frame. Dropping his left shoulder to hit the floor first, then rolling with the impact to slide along the warped planks on his back, he actually saw shards of broken wood fly away from the impact.

In a moment Ryan was on his feet, shifting left until his shoulder hit a wall. He sensed he was near the back of the room, well away from a spill of moonlight from a window from which the glass had long since all been broken out. If Snake Eye decided to follow up, he didn't want to be an obvious target, nor yet in an obvious location, such as crouched beside the window.

Ryan dropped to a knee to reduce the target he offered. Holding the SIG-Sauer out left-handed, he watched the blank blackness between the paler, differently shaped oblongs of window and door, ready to blast if a silhouette appeared. Not that he expected one. But he wasn't going to miss a chance at an easy win because he overestimated his opponent, any more than he intended to let underestimation chill him.

That was too nuking close, he decided. His own thoughts were scarcely audible above the pulse pounding in his ears. He drew deep breaths into the pit of his stomach, ignoring the smells of dust and mildew and rotting wood.

He couldn't help wondering just how seriously his enemy had been trying to nail him. Back off, he ordered

himself. As seldom as he felt it, he still recognized the
sense of helplessness and the dangerous sense of fatal-
ism that could engender.

When a handful of heartbeats had trip-hammered
by, he got into a crouch. Ryan slid back until the wall
touched his back, then shifted until his questing right
hand felt an edge and then emptiness.

He slipped into the back room. There didn't seem to
be any furniture in the building, which helped, since
he wasn't about to strike any kind of light to help him
make his way.

Moving quickly to clear the doorway, the one-eyed
man turned and took stock. Faint light showed another
doorway at the back of the room.

He moved quickly to the wall to the right of the doorway. It proved to be the frame of an old screen door,
with just a few pathetic rags of fine mesh still hanging
around the edges.

A quick look around the frame at waist-height
showed an alley ten feet across with a heap of some
kind of trash, indistinguishable in the darkness, between Ryan and the end of the alley toward where the
shots had come from his left. He sprinted a few steps
to the opposing wall and hunkered down, then looked
left and right.

From the left end of the block he heard the faintest
scrape and swung the SIG-Sauer that way one-handed.
He was saving the very limited strength of his right
arm for when it would count. Not for steadying his
aim at phantoms.

After a long moment the noise wasn't repeated. He
doubted it would be. Snake Eye was careful, and knew
how to move that way.

In his mind's eye Ryan formed a flash impression
of the alley. Back behind him he'd spotted what looked
like another open door on this side. He emerged from
behind his mound of assorted decaying crap and moved
toward it.

Does the bastard have any external ears? he wondered. He hadn't noticed any in the confrontation at the
gaudy. Then again it had been brief, the light was poor,
and Ryan had other things to think about.

He also was a man who had trained himself to miss
few details. He didn't think Snake Eye had ears.

That might mean he didn't hear triple-good. Not like
he saw, anyway. Ryan's ears were exceptionally keen.
And while Snake Eye was meticulous, Ryan was highly
skilled in moving through built-up areas—or rubble, or
any stage in-between—without making a sound.

Ryan didn't know how much of an edge that gave
him over his chillingly efficient foe, but he was going
to work it for all it was worth.

Smiling slightly he ducked into the open doorway.

THE WINCHESTER ROARED, vomited fire and kicked
Krysty hard in the shoulder with the butt-plate. Barely
twenty yards away an Uplander trooper dropped the
revolver from his hand and toppled backward over his
horse's rump.

Light strobed to her left. J.B. ripped short bursts
from his Uzi with head-splitting noise.

The surviving greencoats had had enough. They
turned and raced back toward their own army. It was the
third probe the companions had fended off that night,
yet none of her friends was seriously hurt. They'd gotten dings or scrapes; she had a cut on her cheek where

a near miss had sent a flying rock chip her way. J.B. had had his hat shot off, although when that attack was driven off he'd imperturbably collected it, dusted it off and crammed it on his head again.

And that couldn't last.

She jacked the action. The tubular mag was empty. The last of the captured black-powder .44-40 cartridges had dropped the soldier.

Krysty threw the weapon away. She'd be relying on a black powder Peacemaker now, with her little Smith & Wesson 640 blaster as backup.

At her side Ricky was sorting through his preloaded mags and loose cartridges, looking as if he'd bitten into a burrito to find a fresh dog turd.

"Leave that for when it'll do the most good, son," J.B. told him. "Use this while it lasts."

He handed the boy a scabbied Smith & Wesson Model 3 reproduction revolver chambered to shoot .44-40 cartridges, like Krysty's Winchester repeater. Of course, the six in the cylinder were all it had.

"Why don't they just rush us en masse and be done with it?" asked Mildred, who was also using a Peacemaker to conserve their store of .38 ammo hers and Krysty's handblasters both used. She wasn't happy about it—her ZKR 551 target pistol was a tool tailored specifically toward her needs, and what she was used to using. The Peacemaker was heavy and balanced differently, along with being single-action, meaning Mildred needed to cock it manually for every shot.

J.B. laughed. "Fear," he said. "They want to commit minimal men to taking us down, 'cause they're afraid if they send too many troops against us, the other army'll take advantage of the split to jump them. Same reason they don't just say, nuke it, and all charge headlong into the ville at once. There's no knowing how that kinda goat-screw would shake out. And neither baron intends to come away empty-handed. Or chilled."

He glanced from one enemy camp to the other. They weren't hard to see. They had built campfires, presumably to feed as many troops as they could while the waiting game played out.

"Then again, the bastards know they don't need to send a big force against us," he said. "All they have to do is keep pecking at us. Sooner or later, they'll get unlucky."

Jak whistled softly and touched Krysty's arm from behind. She looked up to see a new force riding out from the Protector encampment.

"Could be now," J.B. said.

"So let's take as many of them as we can," Krysty said, as thirty enemy horsemen charged their tiny clump of shielding hills.

Chapter Thirty-Two

Ryan stalked through the surrealistic angles and blackness of the abandoned ville. His senses, especially his hearing, were tuned as sharp as he could get them. His passage made no more noise than his own shadow, cast irregularly by the rising half-moon.

He was doing the unexpected.

It wasn't as if being on the short end of the odds was anything new to him, and what he'd learned long ago was that when the smart odds said you were chilled, the triple-crazy thing was the way to go.

Of course, it had to be the *right* triple-crazy thing.

The smart thing to do would have been to try to keep as much distance between himself and the inhumanly efficient killer as possible. But what good would that do? Even if Ryan could somehow find the redoubt entrance and fort himself up inside so well Snake Eye couldn't get at him, the mercie could just pick off Ryan's companions when they tried to join him. Which eventually they would do, to find and help Ryan—if they weren't overwhelmed by the tiny little fact they were facing not one but two entire armies bent on seeing the color of their insides.

The smart thing, maybe, was to blow this whole ville, forget about the redoubt and try to escape overland. The companions had already rejected that option as a bad play.

And anyway, Ryan saw Snake Eye as a problem that needed solving now. His obsession with Ryan and company wasn't altogether sane, and that was the root of the thing. He knew too much about them. While the Deathlands were large, and the companions could pop up in any part of them at any time, Snake Eye had a feel for the kind of situations they tended to find themselves in, as he'd shown over and over already during their brief acquaintance. There was a chance they would cross paths with the reptilian mutie mercie again. And next time he might go directly for the kill, rather than dick around for his amusement as he was doing now.

Snake Eye had set the terms out plain as the hand at the end of Ryan's arm: the only way this ended, *truly* ended, was with either him or Ryan Cawdor staring up at the sky.

So Ryan meant to settle it, here and now, whichever way it shook out.

He was circling back toward where they'd had their first encounter. He was sure Snake Eye had moved on from there. He also suspected the mercie thought Ryan would move away from him, best he could.

It was the smart thing to do. The only sane thing to do.

Ryan was staking his life on the fact that the mutie wouldn't be able to hear him coming, and that sooner or later Ryan would hear *him*. It wasn't much of an edge, but it was the only one he had.

He moved in short, swift rushes, cover to cover, mindful of silhouetting himself in the open. It was something he couldn't avoid, but could minimize by carefully picking his route. He would have had more and better options had he been willing to scale ancient fences or random stacks of trash that had accreted in the narrow streets and narrower alleys, but he couldn't do that without unacceptable risk of making noise. So he went around; and if he couldn't go around, he went elsewhere, and when he went through a building he moved very deliberately and stayed near the walls where the floor was less likely to creak and betray him.

The ville wasn't large, but it was still a daunting maze in the moonlight, offering a bewildering variety of hidden ways—and hiding places.

By moving to the outskirts, Ryan got around behind where the shots had come from. Now he was working his careful way inward, following the same path he'd taken before.

As he paused at the exit of another junk-jumbled alley he heard a whisper, as of a hip brushing a chunk of half-rotted timber.

While his hearing wasn't any more precisely directional than any other normal human's, Ryan had a good notion where the noise came from: down the street to his left. Strain as he might, he saw no movement that way.

Another sound—the crunch of something beneath a boot heel. Snake Eye might not even be aware he was making those noises. They were the kind of noises only an expert could avoid in a setting such as this.

An expert like Ryan Cawdor.

He slipped around the corner of a building and into the street, then crossed quickly. Keeping to the shadows, he moved as quickly as stealth allowed toward the building with the fallen-in roof at the block's end.

If he's doing this to sucker me, Ryan thought with a certain grim amusement, it's working. But this was his only high card, so he was going all-in with it.

Ryan reached the corner. He could smell a trace of ancient charring. The frame of the window he'd just past had been turned to charcoal by a fire that had somehow left the outer walls mostly intact. He paused, drew a deep breath. Extending the blaster in his left hand, he leaned around the corner.

A shadowy form of a tall, lean figure in a long frock coat stood not thirty feet away, bolt upright, his back to him.

Ryan took a flash sight on the center of that back and triggered a double-tap.

Impossibly the tall shadow was already moving. It ducked and whirled into a doorway, out of the line of fire.

Ryan threw himself backward as two lightning shots blasted back at him. He landed on his butt, then scrambled to his feet. He heard the crunch of boots walking on the hardscrabble street with no effort at keeping quiet.

"I have you now, Cawdor," Snake Eye said. "If you stand and face me, I'll make it quick. My word of honor."

Fuck that, Ryan thought. The crazy thing was, he reckoned the mercie meant it.

Not that he intended to do what he was told and find out. He turned and raced back along the street, ducking into a doorway just ahead of another gunshot. This one missed by so little he felt its hot breath on the back of his neck.

LOOKING CAUTIOUSLY AROUND a corner, Snake Eye glimpsed a tall shape in a long coat duck into yet another doorway. He laughed quietly to himself.

"Enough fun," he said softly. "Time to end this charade."

He walked openly down the street. He was unconcerned that his enemy might pop up and shoot him. He knew for a warm certainty now that he could blast first, before even Ryan Cawdor could loose a round.

Because he was Snake Eye, and he truly was the best.

"Let me sweeten the pot, Cawdor," he called as he strolled slowly toward the doorway into which his quarry had vanished. The buildings on this street block were one-story structures, with flat roofs. He kept alert to the chance his prey might manage to scramble up and pop a shot from a rooftop.

It wouldn't make any difference. He held a blaster in either black-taloned hand, and was equally proficient with both.

"If you stop running and stand and face me, I'll make it quick for your friends, too," Snake Eye said. "Don't think I forgot about your sweet-cheeked little redhead bitch and the rest. I took a contract on all of you, and I always fulfill a contract."

He came to the door. "Ready or not..." he began.

And stepped around into the doorway.

By the faint moonlight filtering in through door and window he made out the gleam of an eyeball, the curve of a scuffed boot toe. He even could make out the shape of a tall man.

Unbelievably, his victim was sitting in a chair passively awaiting him. Snake Eye didn't know whether to be disappointed or impressed: pathetic resignation, or final act of supreme bravado?

That didn't matter, either. He didn't even bother ducking out of the doorway's fatal funnel. He had tested his opponent's metal, and was supremely confident he could spot any motion—and blast first.

"I don't know what your game is, Ryan Cawdor," he said, "but it ends now. Stand up on your two feet and face me like a man."

Instead the man illuminated his own face with a small flashlight. His face was gaunt and wrinkled. His two eyes were blue, but not the winter-sky blue of Ryan Cawdor's single orb.

"Tanner?" Snake Eye said incredulously. "What are you doing here, old man?"

"Sitting in a chair facing you."

Snake Eye laughed incredulously. "Cawdor can't beat me. Surely *you* don't think you're faster than I am?"

"Nooo," Doc said, drawing the word out long. "But that bullet is."

Knowledge struck Snake Eye like a hammer made of ice.

"Shit," he said, and started to spin.

Doc was right. Something that seemed to be the size of the Earth slammed into Snake Eye's back. His vision flamed briefly red.

Then faded to black.

BY WELL-TRAINED HABIT Ryan worked the bolt action of his Steyr Scout as he rode the recoil. The empty brass bounced with a chiming note on the attic floorboards as he brought his scope back online.

A good marksman knew when he'd made a good shot. Ryan felt that now.

He saw what he knew he'd see: a body sprawled in the doorway of the abandoned shop Doc had lured the mercie into.

It hadn't been a challenging shot for Ryan. Even with a bum right shoulder that hurt like fire from the recoil of a powerful 7.62 mm cartridge in a light weapon. It had been more of a challenge making his way to this attic above the second floor of a narrow frame house without breaking his neck. But he made it, and gained an unobstructed shot across the low flat roof of a neighboring building to the doorway a street over.

Yellow light blew out the vacant doorway and empty windows in a quick flash. The supine body jerked. Doc was doing the wise thing: making sure with a shot from his LeMat.

Ryan grinned. He felt cold bleakness all the way through to his marrow.

"You might have been better than me," he said softly to his definitely chilled enemy. "But definitely not smarter than me."

It took but a matter of minutes for Doc and Ryan to find the entry to the hidden redoubt. Snake Eye had thoughtfully left the corpse of one of the greencoat sentries sprawled before the entry to the storehouse he'd been guarding.

Those few short minutes seemed endless to Ryan. He could hear the crackle of blasterfire from just outside the ville, knew that his lover and his companions were sorely pressed. Could they possibly hold out long enough?

They'd have to. Just as he had to do what remained to be done. Just like they always did.

Doc's flashlight showed an open trapdoor with another chill lying beside it. He looked at Ryan and raised a brow.

"We need to know," Ryan said.

"Indeed," Doc agreed.

Moving past him, Ryan flicked on a flashlight of his own. The beam shone on a concrete floor a story down and revealed a rectangle of darkness to one side—darkness rimmed by the glimmer of vanadium steel. They had found the redoubt, no question.

But have we found a way out, Ryan wondered, or just a well-stocked rattrap? Maybe it was only a predark stockpile and not a redoubt at all.

As he'd told Doc, they had to know.

He descended into the cold and waiting earth.

Chapter Thirty-Three

A rider aimed a sawed-off shotgun at Krysty from the back of his rearing horse. She stuck her left hand out and blasted two quick shots from her Smith & Wesson 640. It was a terrible position to shoot from, but the muzzle of the handblaster's abbreviated barrel was no more than a foot from its target.

The man bellowed in gut-shot agony. His scatter-gun emptied both barrels at the sky. He fell over as his horse bolted.

The Uplander cavalry was all over their little position in their nest of hills like soldier ants. She spotted another Uplander cavalryman leveling a revolver at one of her friends from about thirty feet away. Aiming her Peacemaker hastily with her right hand she fired at him. The heavy soft-lead .45-caliber slug smashed his bearded lower jaw.

His screams turned to gurgles as blood flooded his throat. He dropped his handblaster to clutch his face with both hands, his horse carrying him away.

A heavy thud from behind drew Krysty's attention. Looking over her shoulder as she turned, she saw another soldier looming over her, his cavalry saber upraised. She had no chance to defend against or escape the blow. The keen curved blade swept for her face.

Something whirred past the left side of Krysty's

face, then something long swung into her field of vision, meeting the saber with a clack and throwing her attacker's arm out wide. She flung out her left hand and blasted off the three shots remaining in her .38.

Two shots missed. The third bullet hit his sword shoulder as he fought to recover from having his weapon batted hard.

The object that had saved her from the sword flashed back into view. She recognized her discarded Winchester longblaster, held by the barrel, as its butt-stock shattered against the soldier's forehead.

As he fell away. Krysty waved her arm, deflecting his eye-rolling chestnut from trampling her as it fled.

Jak, his white hair dyed pink with blood, leaped on the fallen greencoat with a knife, held ice-pick-style, in one hand. With rattlesnake speed it pumped up and down four or five times as he stabbed the supine man.

She heard the roar of J.B.'s shotgun somewhere close at hand, saw Mildred go down beneath the flailing hooves of a cavalry horse. Impossibly, she rolled to the side and relative safety before the hooves came hammering down where she had fallen.

The M-4000 bellowed again. The right side of the rider's green-plaid flannel erupted into shreds and red spray. He swayed but somehow kept his seat as his horse, too, took off back toward the Uplander Army.

Krysty had her Peacemaker leveled, hammer cocked, swinging this way and that, seeking targets. Impossibly, she found none. Did we win again? she wondered wildly. Somehow?

"Aww, *shit.*"

She looked around to see Mildred on her knees,

clutching a bleeding upper left arm with a hand that still held her ZKR blaster. She was looking south.

Following her gaze, Krysty realized that all they had won was another few heartbeats of life, because a fresh group of bluecoats was just hitting the bottom of their clump of hills from the south.

A blaster cracked, its loud authority proclaiming it to be a high-powered modern longblaster.

Krysty's heart jumped into her throat. She recognized that weapon, as she did the voice of the man who had just fired it in the air for everybody's attention.

"Listen up, everybody!" Ryan shouted. "All of you—both sides."

"Ryan?" Mildred said. "Are you out of your mind?"

By the moonlight he was plainly visible, a few steps south of the dilapidated huddle of Heartbreak, waving his Steyr Scout over his head with both hands in lieu of a white flag.

"We found the redoubt," he shouted. "It's right here. The thing you're looking for."

"Ryan!" Krysty yelled. "Don't tell them!"

"Find anyway," Jak said. He stood at her side looking as if somebody had dumped a bucket of blood over his head.

"It's what you care about, right? Not us. But you can waste time trying to chill us while the other side goes for the loot! Make your choice."

"He is," Mildred said. "He is out of his mind."

"Crazy like a fox, girl," J.B. said. He had his pack on his back and a huge grin on his face as he handed Mildred her own backpack. "Get ready to move."

The bluecoat cavalry was milling around at the foot

of the hill, looking from the companions, to their own lines, and back again in confusion.

Somebody handed her her own backpack. She shouldered it without looking around.

"It's all just waiting for you," Ryan called to the rival armies. "Are you going to grab it? Or let the other side have it?"

"Kill the outlanders!" a voice roared from the Uplander camp.

Krysty looked east. The new Alliance Army commander, Colonel Turnbull, was rearing his horse out in front of his own lines and waving his sword. "I command you, take the hill!"

She saw his body jerk. He swayed, then he slumped to the grass as the sound of three quick blaster shots reached her ears.

"Seize the treasure, you fools!" a woman yelled.

In the front of the Uplander lines, Krysty saw Jessie Rae Siebert, her pertly pretty face distorted by passion. At her side stood a greencoat officer with long pale locks and a goatee, holding his own blaster muzzle-high in the air.

"For the Alliance, and you Baron!" the blond man roared. "Go!"

"Run for it!" another voice cried.

Ryan.

"We're good," Krysty heard J.B. say. "Go."

Cheering hoarsely the two armies surged toward each other as Krysty joined her companions scrambling down the hill toward Ryan. He had his longblaster held across his chest, now, ready to respond to threats, but not threatening anybody.

Shots popped as they reached the flat. Krysty's teeth

clenched, and she anticipated the slam of bullets at any second. Or the sight of one of her friends going down—especially J.B. and Mildred, laboring under the weight of double packs.

But no shots seemed to come their way. No bullets moaned past or kicked up divots of turf as they pounded toward the ruined ville, though screams and shouts had joined the deafening thunder of blasterfire.

The two armies had thoughts only for the hidden treasure, and the only thing that really stood between them and it.

Their lifelong blood enemies.

Krysty glanced back once over her shoulder as she approached Ryan, who continued to wait alertly, just in time to see the two masses of men and horses crash into each other behind her and begin to fight like packs of rabid dogs.

RYAN STOOD outside the mat-trans unit with his backpack riding his shoulders, ignoring the pain that caused him. His longblaster was still ready. He would be the last inside, wouldn't budge until all of his companions were safely ready to jump.

And miraculously, they all were, though they were dinged, gashed and battered.

J.B. flashed him a fast grin as he limped past. "We beat the Devil at his own game again, didn't we, Ryan?"

"That we did, my friend," he said. "That we did."

Ricky and Jak went in just ahead of Ryan. Holding himself upright by the sheer iron of his will, he joined his companions.

"So," Ricky Morales said, his eyes huge in a face that

was scarcely recognizable behind a mask of grime and blood, "who do you think'll win up there?"

"Who cares?" Ryan grunted, as he closed the door to the mat-trans unit and hurried to sit beside Krysty.

As the disks in the floor began to glow and a fine mist started to envelop his companions, Ryan realized that they had barely cheated death this time.

He hoped that they'd jump to somewhere peaceful, somewhere they could bide awhile.

Ryan figured it was time they caught a break.

* * * * *

James Axler
Outlanders®

SAVAGE DAWN

The Cerberus rebels confront a prehistoric nightmare.

Kane, Brigid and Grant come to the aid of a race of serpent-human mutants caught up in civil war. Hope for the mutant race lies in an alliance with the advanced people who live deep beneath the shattered islands of Japan. In a battle to the finish, Kane and the others confront a prehistoric nightmare, retooled and fortified by the deepest mysteries of the Outlands.

The battle begins on February 5, 2013, wherever books are sold.

TAKE 'EM FREE

2 action-packed novels plus a mystery bonus

NO RISK

NO OBLIGATION TO BUY

Don Pendleton
CHOKE POINT

Human trafficking funds a terrorist plot to overthrow the U.S.

A U.S. senator's murder and the kidnapping of several
children of high-profile government officials leave
the President no choice but to call in Stony Man
to investigate. But the kidnappings are only the tip
of the iceberg of a human trafficking ring. It's a race
against time as Stony Man fights to neutralize
the operation…no matter what!

STONY MAN®

Available December 2012!